Reunited in Love

~ The Maverick Billionaires ~

Book 9

Bella Andre & Jennifer Skully

REUNITED IN LOVE

The Maverick Billionaires, Book 9

Meet the Maverick Billionaires—sexy, self-made men from the wrong side of town who survived hell together and now have everything they ever wanted. But when each Maverick falls head-over-heels for an incredible woman he never saw coming, he will soon find that true love is the only thing he ever really needed...

She's the love he foolishly let go...

Ava Harrington, brilliant billionaire businesswoman, has conquered the world. And yet, scarred by a love lost fifteen years ago, she's built a wall around her heart, swearing off love forever.

Ransom Yates's culinary genius has taken him to the pinnacle of success as a magnetic celebrity chef. But that success came at a devastating price when he left behind the woman who held the key to his heart.

Their reunion is anything but sweet when Ava must swallow her pride and seek Ransom's help, though he's the last person she ever wanted to turn to in a crisis. But the sparks flying between them are hotter than ever—and their undeniable chemistry reignites their long-buried passion with steamy kisses and sultry nights.

Ransom can't help but fall for the woman he never stopped loving. But Ava's heart is still hardened with the memory of how their long-ago affair ended. Can they find a second chance at love? Or is their love forever lost in the ashes of their past?

A note from Bella & Jennifer

We have been writing about the Maverick Billionaires for almost ten years, and the honest truth is that it has been an absolutely glorious experience. Not only are we the best of friends, but our friendship grows deeper and closer with every year that passes, which is the most wonderful gift. And the cherry on top is that our Mavericks feel the exact same way about each other – and now the Harrington clan, as well.

We can never say THANK YOU enough for all the support you've given us since we first began writing about this down-to-earth family of billionaires. Nearly ten years ago, Bella woke up from a dream about a family of foster brothers who had a connection that went far deeper than blood, and she instantly knew that she wanted to write their love stories with Jennifer–who was, and remains, one of her favorite authors.

What's more, there is something extra special about this book: Ava Harrington is our first female billionaire. Hooray! As we all know, when a woman sets her mind on something that she wants, there's nothing that she can't achieve.

As always, we hope you love our new book...and we can't wait to keep writing more Maverick love stories for you in the future!

With love,
Bella Andre and Jennifer Skully

P.S. Please sign up for our New Release newsletters for more information on new books. www.BellaAndre.com/Newsletter and http://bit.ly/SkullyNews

Chapter One

They say redheads can have a temper. Ava Harrington did not. At least, not usually. But today, she was furious. When she left her San Juan Bautista care facility, she'd been near boiling. And not due to the unseasonably warm late-September weather. Now, as she entered her San Francisco headquarters after the ninety-minute drive north, her anger had turned into a raging inferno.

In the elevator, she punched the button for the top floor, almost breaking her nail. What she'd witnessed in the care home's dining room had filled her with horror. The situation was horrendous, and even now, she trembled with the aftereffects.

As she passed through the accounting department, her high heels stabbed the carpet. But despite her roiling emotions, she smiled at her assistant, Naomi Wells, as she entered the outer office of the executive suite. None of this was Naomi's fault.

And yet her blond, thirtysomething assistant seemed to be quaking behind her desk.

Ava ratcheted down her temper. She liked to think of herself as a good boss. She was firm, she was take-charge, but she secured what she wanted through diplomacy rather than haranguing. While male executives could rant all they wanted, when a female executive went off on a tear, she was labeled a ballbuster and even worse.

Though she desperately wanted to rant about what she'd witnessed this morning, she couldn't lay that on her assistant.

Naomi handed her a sheaf of pink message slips, her hand trembling slightly.

"Can you brief me on the contents?" Ava asked.

Naomi was good at synopsizing notes. Out of respect for her residents at the San Juan Bautista senior living facility, Ava had turned off her phone's ringer. And on the way back, as her driver negotiated the freeway, she'd formulated her response to what she considered a grievous incident that needed immediate action when she returned.

Though she'd asked Naomi to brief her, Ava was already thumbing through the message slips. She actually felt her gorge rise at what she read.

"It seems that in several of the Bay Area facilities," Naomi began, swallowing hard, "there are reports of nasty behavior from the catering staff. So far, the facility directors have handled such incidents on their own, but they're becoming common enough that three of our directors felt the need to report this to you."

Holding the pink message slips, Ava felt this morning's entire deplorable scene flood her senses all over again.

She'd been heading to the staff table in the back of the dining room to confer with her management team. Close to the end of the lunch hour, few diners remained, but as she'd crossed the room, waving to those she knew, she'd heard the low growl of a middle-aged server as he leaned close to Mrs. Greeley.

"Look at the mess you made," he hissed. "You eat like a pig at a trough. You should be ashamed of yourself."

Ava had been so stunned she'd stopped right there. Unable to move. So shocked she couldn't say a thing. Until Mrs. Greeley quietly began to cry.

She'd rushed to comfort the woman. And to confront the server. The nerve of the man. With a soothing hand on Mrs. Greeley's shoulder, she spoke to him in the deadliest of voices. "First of all, Mrs. Greeley has macular degeneration, and she can't see her food." She pointed to the plate. "You're supposed to put her meat at twelve o'clock, the potatoes at three, vegetables at six, and bread at nine. Otherwise, she doesn't know what's on her plate." She speared the man with a scathing look. "Secondly, she accidentally dropped her fork and *you*—" She pointed at the man's chest, her manicured nail just short of knifing him. "—didn't get her a clean one. Third—" She lasered him. "You never, *ever* speak to one of our guests that way. And *fourth*." Her nostrils flaring with anger, she smiled like a feral animal. All teeth. "You're fired."

The man spluttered for a couple of seconds before he finally said, "You can't fire me. I don't work for you. I work for the catering company."

She glared at him. "Then they're fired too." Her eyes narrowed on him, and his face turned pasty.

As the man scuttled away, she sat in the empty chair next to Mrs. Greeley. "Are you all right? Here, let me help you." She arranged Mrs. Greeley's food in the appropriate spots on her plate and retrieved a clean fork from another place setting.

Across the table, one of Ava's favorite ladies, Edith, punched her fist in the air. "You go, girl." She grinned at Ava. "I've wanted to tell him where to get off for ages."

"I'm so sorry this happened. But rest assured, you won't have to put up with that kind of behavior anymore." She'd spent a few more minutes with the two women, until Mrs. Greeley seemed calmer.

And now Ava had come back to more reports of the same kind of nastiness at other facilities.

She looked at Naomi. "Please get George Twisselman on the phone." Her voice was tight, her anger still at a boil. The new president of Consolidated Catering was about to feel the brunt of it. Then she managed a smile for her assistant. "Thank you."

Ava made personal visits to each of her retirement communities, senior living homes, and memory care facilities at least once a year. As CEO of Harrington Community Care International, with more than a hundred facilities in the US and now expanding globally, once a year was the most she could manage. But with her five Bay Area senior communities, she took one morning every other week to visit, wanting to keep in touch with the workings of each residence and getting to know the people living there.

And now, having been gone for several hours, and with Naomi's usual efficiency, reports and letters to be signed had stacked up on Ava's desk.

Her office wasn't ostentatious, but large enough for her desk and credenza with two computer monitors, a sofa and two chairs for chatting with suppliers or clients, and a corner conference table. She also had her own bathroom, complete with shower, along with a closet of clothing in case she had to make a quick change. The furnishings were tasteful, though not overly expensive, but the view of the San Francisco Bay made the space spectacular, the sun sparkling on the water, the towers of the Golden Gate Bridge brilliant in the afternoon light.

Unfortunately, Ava wasn't in the mood to appreciate the magnificent view.

Her office phone rang, and she rounded the corner of the desk to pick up the receiver. "Yes, Naomi?"

"I have George Twisselman on line two."

"Thank you." Ava switched over. "Hello, Mr. Twisselman." She didn't want to act the ballbuster and went for polite, rather than ripping him a new one the way a male executive could do with impunity. "Ava Harrington here, from Harrington Community Care International."

"What can I do for you, Ava?" George said, skipping the more formal address she'd used with him.

She'd worked with Consolidated Catering for a couple of years for her San Francisco Bay Area needs, but George, the new president, had come in a few months ago. As he'd set about cutting costs, hours, and wages, people were leaving and he was hiring new. She'd discussed her concerns with George over all the new staff. "We're transitioning," he'd told her. "But we're getting up to speed, and our menus will continue to surpass your standards."

And that was true. There'd been no complaints about the food. She'd tried it herself, and everything was tasty.

But the attitude and behavior complaints were new. She needed to jump on the problem immediately.

"George," she said sternly, "you assured me you had the new staffing situation under control. But your transition period is over, and it's not working at all. I've had various reports from different facilities regarding the way some members of your staff have been treating our residents. I won't tolerate such disrespect. What are you going to do about it?"

The ball was in his court. But he didn't run with it. "As you know," George said, his voice oily even over the phone, "our first consideration is providing adequate meals, which we do. We can't be responsible for any touchiness your residents might feel. They're older, and they get their feelings hurt over trivial things."

"Excuse me?" Every molecule of her blood was boiling now. She could have blown her stack at him. But she'd discovered that a polite response was the better way to get what she wanted. If they were rude—like a man could be—women weren't listened to. Even though she wanted to tell him to go pound sand, she said, "Telling one of my residents—or anyone for that matter—that she eats like a pig at a trough is not trivial. And I fired your man on the spot."

George Twisselman sputtered, "You can't fire anyone. They work for me."

She bared her teeth like a jungle predator and only wished he could see. "That's what your man said. But what I hear, George, is that you're unwilling to discipline your employees. You don't even seem to understand that they need training. Therefore, our association isn't working. And this contract is terminated."

He sputtered again, maybe apologies, but Ava no longer cared to listen. She ended with a polite, "Have a good day." After she'd hung up, she said aloud, "And you're fired."

It felt good. She'd kept her temper in check and was polite throughout. The way she was expected to be. But the job was done. She wasn't putting up with that kind of crap.

Her elation lasted less than thirty seconds. What the hell would she do now?

* * *

Three hours later, Ava was still groaning, this time in extreme frustration. She'd managed to find a company that would step in for two weeks at the five facilities. But that was the time limit.

Looking over the long list of caterers Naomi had drawn up for her, she'd crossed off every single company after phone calls where she'd practically begged. But it was a no-go. The staff was ill, or the owners were going out of the country, or they were leaving to see their kids get married, or they didn't do the kind of catering she needed. The reasons abounded. She'd worked with a lot of these outfits before, and she had to say that some of them just simply sucked.

Ava had found catering to be the most difficult part of running her care homes. That was why she'd been so thankful to find Consolidated Catering. She'd hoped it would be long term. They weren't perfect—no one was—but after Twisselman had taken over, things had rapidly gone downhill. She'd given him a chance. He'd failed miserably.

Picking up the phone instead of yelling out the office door, she asked Naomi, "Is this everyone?"

Her assistant had called half the people on the list. "That's it." Naomi's voice held the same defeat Ava felt. "We're completely out of catering options after the next two weeks."

But Ava refused to roll over. "There's always another option. We just need to think outside the box."

With those words, a face popped into her mind. Ransom Yates.

Why on earth would she even think about him? He was a master chef. He owned restaurants, and he catered galas and huge receptions, not ongoing dining room needs. He'd never stoop to working at this level anyway. There was no glamor in providing good, basic food for senior living homes.

Besides, she'd never work with him, not after what happened fifteen years ago. So what if he haunted her dreams and sometimes entered her thoughts in the daytime too?

There was absolutely no way she'd ever call him.

Ava glanced at the phone, its digital clock blazing at her. Time had gotten away from her, but it would be a short walk to the restaurant for the family mastermind, a name she'd coined for the gathering. In fact, she'd pushed for these meetings, wanting her own family to have the same camaraderie the Mavericks enjoyed.

With Dane finally admitting he had feelings for his personal assistant, Cammie—after twelve freaking years!—it was the right time. She adored her family, and they'd always been close, especially after their parents had died almost eighteen years ago in an avalanche while skiing in the Alps. Ava had been in her first year of university and Dane two years ahead of her. They'd both had to drop out to take care of the younger kids—Troy and Clay still in high school, Gabby in middle school. Ava and Dane had been each other's rock.

The timing for tonight's mastermind couldn't have been better, because the only choice she had now was to ask the family for help. Her brothers and sister were some of the best resources she had, and she was about to send out a distress signal to them.

As Ava stepped out of her office building, a blast of cool air hit her. It was only the third week of September, not quite autumn yet, but the San Francisco fog had rolled in, eclipsing the heat from earlier in the day and turning everything as cold and damp as if it were winter. She was glad she'd put on her overcoat.

Hustling down the busy street, she clutched her coat tight around her neck as a sudden gust of wind blew through. They were meeting at a tapas restaurant only a couple of blocks away. Ava had always been the party planner, from birthdays to Thanksgiving, Christmas, and Easter. Even as the so-called big boss at work, she'd planned all the birthday parties, bridal showers, and baby showers. She liked seeing the results and the fun everyone had. Yet somehow she was still on the outside looking in. It was probably her own fault—fear of too much fraternization with her employees. But now, she might have a bridal shower to look forward to. Although neither Dane nor Cammie had mentioned wedding bells yet. They were so cute, she thought with a smile. Dane would probably bop her on the arm if she ever said that aloud.

At the crosswalk, she waited to make sure the drivers would actually stop for her. You took your life in your hands if you stepped out just because a traffic light had changed.

Sure enough, she would have been flattened by a bus thundering by.

Yet, in the next moment, she *was* flattened, at least emotionally. There he was on the side of the bus. Ransom Yates. The famous chef. With his own cooking show, *Recipes from Ransom*.

God, the man was gorgeous, even after fifteen years. No, he was better. With light streaks of silver in his dark hair and those deep mocha eyes that could see right into you, he was to die for. At forty-six, Ransom Yates was the epitome of a silver fox. No wonder his marketing company put his face on the sides of buses. And billboards. And magazine covers. Ten years younger than he, Ava wondered if she'd held up as well. Of course, the photo was probably airbrushed to smooth out every flaw the man had.

Except that he hadn't had a single physical flaw fifteen years ago.

The bus blew by, and the cars behind it stopped for her. She stepped into the street, and damned if the man wasn't on the back of the bus, too, as if he were haunting her.

If she didn't know better, she'd say the photo actually winked at her.

Chapter Two

As Ava entered the restaurant, she was assaulted by a cacophony of voices. The ceilings were high, the floor concrete, and all the noise seemed multiplied in between. Diners shared deliciously scented plates, servers rushed back and forth, and a great flame rose up from the open kitchen, where some specialty of the house was being crisped to perfection.

They were all there, her big, beautiful family, seated at a center table. Just looking at them, her heart swelled. They'd gone through so much together, both before and after their parents died. And they'd made it out the other side, all of them doing so well for themselves, and with a closeness that other people envied. If any one of them had a problem, they all pitched in to help. She'd been known to make and receive midnight phone calls, sometimes for a shoulder to lean on, sometimes just to shoot the breeze. They were totally there for each other.

Her big brother Dane looked positively domestic, his arm draped around Cammie seated next to him. He was still her tall, dark, and handsome brother, like all her brothers were, but there was a new contentment about him. Cammie ran his life for him, and now Dane had finally realized she was the love of his life too. Ava would say he glowed, but he'd probably bop her on the arm for that as well. She was happy for him. For Cammie. They made her wonder if there was hope for the rest of the family.

Except for her. She'd pretty much proven she sucked at the love game.

As she made her way around the table kissing cheeks—Dane and Cammie, her brothers Clay and Troy, her sister Gabby—she stopped in front of Fernsby. Good old Fernsby. If she didn't know better, she'd think that was a scowl on his face. But that was just Fernsby. He'd probably worn that look as a baby. Except it was hard to imagine Fernsby had ever been a baby. And yet, over the summer, since he'd won the top prize on *Britain's Greatest Bakers*—or maybe because of Dane and Cammie—Fernsby had actually loosened up. Not much. Just a bit.

"Miss Harrington, may I say you look lovely this evening," he said in his cultured British tones.

The consummate British butler, he went everywhere with Dane. But to the family mastermind? Well, yes. Fernsby was part of the family.

"Thank you, Fernsby. Where's T. Rex?" Dane and Cammie's excessively adorable long-haired mini dachshund also went everywhere with them.

"Since this is a restaurant and they don't allow dogs, Lord Rexford," Fernsby drawled, because he always used the dog's formal name, just as she was always Miss Harrington, "is at the Nob Hill flat." While Dane's main estate was down in Pebble Beach, he kept a pied-à-terre in the city.

Ava smiled and took the seat between Clay and Gabby at the round table. Though she'd called for these meetings, she was still the last to arrive. It was always the one who came the least distance, right? While Cammie, Dane, and Gabby—who ran a vegan café in Carmel—had driven up from Monterey Bay, both Troy and Clay had probably come straight from the airport, the two of them always on the move.

Despite the Maverick holiday events and weekly barbecues, Ava had opted for instituting their own family mastermind once a month. Distance and travel made weekly an impossibility.

Ava beamed at her family. "I'm so glad you all made it."

A smile in his dark eyes, Dane said, "Cammie and I thought we'd combine the trip into the city with a show tomorrow night that we both want to see."

Below the table, Gabby nudged her, and Ava knew exactly what her sister was thinking. Neither of them had thought Dane would admit he was in love with Cammie, even though the entire family had known it right from the beginning. Well, except Troy, who'd had the temerity to ask Cammie out. Dane had tried to explain away his histrionics as Troy trying to poach one of his employees. But everyone knew he never would have gone nuts like that if Troy had tried to poach Fernsby. Not that any of them would dream of poaching Fernsby. The man was simply un-poachable.

She and Gabby shared a smile. It was so good to see their big brother finally happy.

He'd built his business from one small resort in Napa to a multinational corporation that was the leading name in luxury resorts. And Cammie had been right there, backing him all the way. Now they were embarking on their most ambitious resort yet—one for people with special needs, which would combine resort quality with therapy, team sports, and camaraderie.

After a swig, Troy set his beer bottle on the table. "Sorry to say I've only got a couple of hours. I have to fly out again tonight for a conference tomorrow."

A gold-medal Olympic diver and owner of a billion-dollar sports equipment empire, Troy was a regular keynote speaker, telling young athletes of his own journey, of his parents' deaths, and how his siblings never let him give up his Olympic dreams. He inspired young people to go for their aspirations, to strive to be their best, to never give up. Her brother's heart was as big as the number of trophies and medals he'd won.

Ava blew him a kiss. "Then it's even more sweet that you're here tonight."

He grimaced at the word *sweet*, and Clay took the heat off him by saying, "I've got a flight out tomorrow morning. Meeting a new prospect in New York." His eyes gleamed at the potential.

While both her brothers were based in the San Francisco Bay Area, they did their work all over the country. Clay, their tech wizard, had started a new internet platform for artists, from painting to woodworking to metalwork to music to writing. He searched for new talent and brought them onto his platform, a safe place for artists where no one would rip them or their work apart. Right now, it was by invitation only. Clay toured the country interviewing potential candidates, and his platform was growing exponentially. Ava secretly wondered if it would soon outpace the giant video platforms out there right now.

"And thanks to you too." Ava squeezed Gabby's knee.

Her sister had torn herself away from her vegan café and bakery. Gabby, only thirty and herself a vegan, had franchises all over the country, but she chose the Carmel bakery to test new recipes before distributing them to her franchises.

Eighteen years ago, when their parents passed away, who would have thought that they would all accomplish the amazing things they had? Ava knew in her heart it was due to their loyalty to each other, their willingness to help. And she needed their help now.

The tapas plates began to arrive—spicy roasted potatoes, bite-sized empanadas, some made with veggie ingredients and gluten-free, plant-based crusts for Gabby. But Ava adored the coconut shrimp, the spices piquant on her tongue.

She laid aside a shrimp tail and held up her hand for their attention. "After I say this, you'll think I brought you here just for my own benefit. But I have a problem that only came up today, and I need to talk it over with you guys."

Dane's eyes flashed with interest, and he leaned forward, elbows on the table. The entire family followed suit. This was what they loved to do, even when they were younger. Just as they'd kicked around the soccer ball with Gabby when she'd joined her middle school soccer team—they were still known to indulge in a cutthroat game or two even now—these days they enjoyed kicking around ideas.

"It's my catering at the five Bay Area care homes."

"But the catering was great down in San Juan Bautista," Cammie said.

The facility provided care at all levels, from independent living to assisted living to memory care, and Cammie had stayed there a few months ago while taking care of her uncle Lochlan who, sadly, had recently passed away from Alzheimer's. Cammie had been the only one who could keep her uncle calm, despite Ava's excellent staff.

"I liked to take Uncle Lochlan into the dining room as often as possible," she said. "Even if he wasn't aware of much."

Ava nodded sadly. "It's not the food. The company we were using has been under new management for the last few months. And things have taken a nosedive." She related what had happened to Mrs. Greeley and the reports of bad behavior by the catering staff at other care homes.

Cammie gasped. "That's awful. There was nothing like that when I was there."

"The management change occurred after you left. I spoke with their president today. His answer was that my residents were *too touchy*," she finished with a growl.

Fernsby harrumphed and muttered, "A disgustingly poor excuse for bad behavior."

"That's what I said when I fired him." She sighed heavily. "I've found a group who can manage the catering for a couple of weeks. But I need to find someone longer term ASAP. The problem is that I've tried every name in the book."

"Tell us who you've talked to," Dane said.

She pulled the list from her purse and laid it on the table. Every single caterer had been crossed off.

Dane shook his head gently. "What about Ransom Yates?"

Ava jumped on that immediately. "Why would you bring him up? He doesn't do retirement homes. He's a superstar chef," she said, using air quotes. "This is more like cafeteria work. He does resorts and cruise ships and big galas and five-star restaurants and TV shows."

But did she really know what he did these days? She'd been so careful never to look him up on the internet. Except for seeing his TV commercials or his face on the sides of buses and his cookbooks in bookstores, she'd avoided finding out anything more about him.

But her brothers were still friends with Ransom through various functions they attended. Dane still used him at his resorts. In fact, Ransom had catered Gideon's New Year's Eve gala at Dane's Napa resort. Ava had made sure not to run into him.

But the food had been pretty darned amazing.

Dane shrugged. "Who knows, he might do it—at least for a while, until you find someone permanent. There's no harm in asking."

She would rather cut off a limb.

She'd met Ransom Yates more than fifteen years ago, when she'd taken care of his grandmother at the convalescent home where she'd worked after leaving university. Her parents had left behind massive debts. There'd been no money to finish college, not even enough for the basic needs of her younger siblings. So she and Dane had gone to work. But that first job was exactly why she'd chosen eldercare, why she'd pursued a degree in healthcare and senior living management. Because she'd wanted to provide homes and staff that gave older adults the respect they deserved.

Ransom had come often to see his grandmother. Then he'd started coming to see Ava.

Of course the family didn't know about it. They didn't know how it had ended either.

Dane pushed. "No, for you—for family—he'll do it."

She was still shaking her head.

Clay chimed in. "Come on, you're being ridiculous." He drummed his fingers on the table. "You've got a big need. Sure, your residents aren't rich people in fancy resorts, but in fact, their needs are even more important. He'll do it. I know he will."

The only one who knew anything about her past with Ransom was Gabby. Thankfully, her sister kept quiet, and Ava shot her a look, speaking her gratitude with her eyes.

"Look," Dane said, "you have the right to ask. Just as he has the right to say no. But you at least need to talk to him."

She felt Fernsby staring her down, before he said in his usual spot-on way, "Lochlan, Cammie's uncle and one of your very special residents, would have told you that calling Mr. Yates was an absolute must."

Cammie gave a nod of agreement.

Defeat loomed over Ava like a wave.

The only way she could get out of calling Ransom for help was if she told her brothers—and Fernsby—about their relationship. And she absolutely would not do that. Ever.

Ransom Yates had completely bombarded her all day. First, he'd popped into her head when she was thinking about her catering issues. Then he'd cropped up on the bus. And now, her family was throwing him at her.

Three times in one day? Really?

And yet, she had no choice. Hadn't she told Naomi they needed to think outside the box? Well, Ransom was definitely outside the box. Pandora's box.

Finally, she had to say, "All right. Who's got his number?"

All three of her brothers whipped out their phones and started scrolling through their contacts.

She was stuck.

* * *

Fernsby felt the need to dance a jig. He'd experienced that same need quite often over the last few months. But due to his legendary restraint, he only jigged in the privacy of his own quarters.

Well, well, well. If he didn't know better, he'd think Ava Harrington had a secret. And of course, Fernsby always knew better. Ransom Yates. What was going on there? The idea intrigued him.

Handsome, fit, mature, and well established in a brilliant career as a celebrity chef, the man was eminently suited for Ava. Her success wouldn't intimidate him, as it did so many lesser men who couldn't appreciate her fine qualities, her intelligence, assurance, business acumen, and compassion. Many men simply couldn't handle a self-made *female* billionaire, as if billion-dollar corporations were the purview of only men.

Coming off the delightful project of bringing Dane and Camille together, his little matchmaking heart was anxious to sink its teeth into another mission.

Ava was it. Fernsby knew it in his deepest innards. And he was always right. Well, except for that one time long ago.

Over the next few weeks, he'd ferret out the details. Then he'd make his plans.

The family get-together, of which he heartily approved, was breaking up, and out of the corner of his eye, he detected Gabrielle Harrington hustling over to him. They were to drive home together, since Dane and Camille would be spending the night in the city and attending the show.

Gabrielle gripped his arm. She had quite a grip for a young woman on the more diminutive end of the spectrum, but then, most men often underestimated beautiful blondes. Not that he was most men. Oh no-no-no, he was Fernsby.

"Fernsby, I know you're taking me home," she said ever so sweetly. "But I really wanted to have a drink with Ava before we leave. Would you mind hanging out for a little while?"

She gave him such a beseeching look that he drawled the only answer he could. "Of course, Miss Harrington, you must absolutely have a drink with your sister." He called all the Harringtons by some sort of honorific—sir, miss—but in his own mind, he used their first names as if they were family. Though in truth, he couldn't think of her as Gabby. She was *Gabrielle*. Just as Camille could never be Cammie in his mind. Why did these Americans always want to shorten such lovely names? Or perhaps that was just *him*. Because he had to admit the Brits did it too. *Crikey.*

"But I must pick up the *dog*," he informed her in a drawn-out syllable. "I will remind you that he's at the flat."

Not that he would ever admit it to anyone, except Lord Rexford himself, but the mini dachshund was cute as the dickens.

Gabrielle beamed. "Oh good." She clapped her hands. "Rexie can sit on my lap on the way home."

Rexie? Fernsby shuddered. The dog was called anything from T. Rex to just plain Rex to Fernsby's preferred moniker, Lord Rexford. But Rexie had to be the worst.

He suspected Gabrielle used it on purpose just to irritate him.

"He absolutely cannot sit on your lap," Fernsby said in his sternest voice, applying an exaggerated eye roll. "He needs to be in his harness should we be involved in an accident."

Gabrielle gaped at him. "We've never had an accident while you're driving, Fernsby."

The little minx was laying it on a bit thick. "Of course it would never be *my* fault," he said, hand splayed against his chest. "But should a Mack truck broadside us, we wouldn't want Lord Rexford to be creamed." Not that Fernsby would ever allow himself to be creamed by anyone, let alone a Mack truck. However, there were safety protocols to follow.

"You're right. He's safer in his harness." She smiled widely, and he knew the next request would be huge. "So, can you come back to get me in… like… a couple of hours?"

"A couple of hours. Of course, miss." It meant they'd be driving until nearly midnight. But, as always, Fernsby was up to the task.

He was up to any task the Harringtons could possibly think of.

And next on his list was Ava Harrington.

He wanted to smile with glee. Or do a jig. On the way home, he could pump Gabrielle for information about Ava's secret, which he was ninety-nine percent sure was all about Ransom Yates.

Gabrielle moved as if to hug him, then thought better of it. "You're the best." She beamed at him with those cornflower-blue eyes.

He couldn't help a long-suffering sigh. "Of course. I'm Fernsby. And I did pass muster with my vegan Victoria sponge." For which, naturally, he'd won the top award on *Britain's Greatest Bakers*.

Her smile lit up her pretty face. "Your Victoria sponge was the absolute best." She was most definitely buttering him up. And he suspected that as much as he might pump her for information, she wouldn't reveal a thing.

Blond, she was a striking contrast to Ava, the redhead in the family. The Harrington men were all Heathcliff types, the tall, dark-haired, blue-eyed, and exceptionally handsome heroes typical of romance novels. The family genes were actually quite phenomenal in the appearance department.

If he couldn't wrest any information concerning Ava from her, Fernsby would content himself with pumping her for the 4-1-1 regarding her vegan tiers on the four-tier cake they would be making together for Gideon Jones and Rosita Diaz's wedding. He couldn't let the little minx beat him with a better cake.

Even if he had to admit that she was a master baker almost—but not quite—on par with himself.

Chapter Three

Gabby grabbed Ava's arm and pulled her away from the family knot near the entrance. "Fernsby's game to wait," she said. "We can have a nice yummy cocktail and a good long chat. He'll be back in a couple of hours."

The two of them exchanged hugs with their brothers and Cammie, though Ava stopped short of hugging Fernsby. He just wasn't the huggable sort. She'd seen him hug Dane and Cammie at the get-together three months ago to celebrate his big win on *Britain's Greatest Bakers*, but she was sure that had been an anomaly as rare as the win itself.

Besides, she was terrified of the look he was giving her. What did it mean? A *look* from Fernsby could be only an ill omen.

When they were outside, Gabby dragged her down the street to a hole-in-the-wall bar, its dark and dingy interior suiting Ava's emotional state. It might once, in its heyday, have been a jumping joint, with a mahogany bar, hardwood floors, and wood-paneled walls. But now there were scratches on the bar's surface, dents in the hardwood, and streaks of dried condensation—or something—on the panels.

Thank God someone had wiped down the seat of the circular booth they slid into.

"I know this must be a really difficult decision," Gabby said, her mouth drooping in a frown.

"It's the worst," Ava agreed. "Because Ransom *is* the only choice left. Dane is probably right that even if he won't do it for me because of how badly we left things, he'll do it for our family." She huffed out a breath and finally smiled. "Thank you for not spilling the beans to the brothers. You're the only one I ever told about me and Ransom."

Her sister laughed. Gabby had a beautiful smile and a beautiful laugh. She was blond like their mother, whereas Ava's red hair had come from some weird recessive gene in their father's line. And while Ava could be called statuesque, Gabby was almost but not quite petite.

"You didn't tell me," Gabby declared. "I figured it out because I'm smarter than they are." She scoffed from deep in her throat. "Like you were really going to tell your fifteen-year-old sister about your affair."

Gabby was six years younger, and when Ava had met Ransom, her sister had barely started high school. Ava would never have thought of confiding in her. She'd never intended to tell anyone. Ransom had been her delicious secret. Until the relationship had soured.

"Well, I'm glad you figured it out, because I got to cry on my baby sister's shoulder. I'll always love you for being there for me." She leaned over to hug Gabby tightly.

The waitress arrived then, and Ava was happy to know they had a server in a place like this. Especially when most of the clientele were huddled around the bar and only a very few of the tables were occupied.

"What can I get you two?" the woman asked. She looked like a college student, probably paying her way on salary and tips.

"I'd love an espresso martini." Ava usually had a champagne cocktail if it was late, but after the day she'd had, she wanted the espresso boost. "That is, if your bartender knows how to make one."

The young woman smiled. "If he doesn't, I'll look it up on the internet. We'll make sure you get what you want."

Ava smiled her appreciation. "Thank you." And vowed to leave a good tip to help the waitress on her way to that college degree.

"I'll have the same," Gabby said. "As long as there's no cream in it."

"No worries." Ava did a finger-drum on the table. "It's just a couple of liqueurs and coffee. Nothing from a cow."

The sisters laughed together, although Ava wasn't sure the waitress got the joke.

"I've tried to think of alternatives to Ransom," Gabby said as the ponytailed waitress bounced off to the bar, eager to fill the unusual order. "But none of my suppliers are equipped to do something like this."

Ava covered her hand. "You're the best for trying."

All roads led to Ransom, it seemed.

When they'd met at his grandmother's convalescent home, she'd been pleased to see that Ransom visited religiously every week. So many of the residents received no visitors at all. He'd told her he was working with Dane on the new resort her brother had been opening at the time. Had it been coincidence or serendipity? But the attraction had been instant.

She fell back into the present as her sister said, "I hate even saying this, because you know how I feel about that man." Gabby had been her only confidante when things went south. "But you'll just have to pretend nothing happened between the two of you."

Ava felt a grunt rise from her throat. "How am I supposed to do that? He almost ruined my life."

She'd thought herself in love. She and Ransom had spent every available moment together, though that hadn't been a lot, since he was always flying off to Hong Kong or Dubai or London. His career was on the rise, and the man was literally going places. Ava had to admit she'd been no less busy. She'd enrolled in night school and was studying hard on her healthcare management and senior living degree.

But when they came together, they flashed like comets in the night. They'd filled up every one of those moments, hiking, talking, cooking, loving. Oh, the loving. The way he'd touched her, kissed her, even the way he'd *looked* at her had set her on fire.

Until he'd returned from Costa Rica one morning and said he had to fly out to Paris that night. They'd made a fabulous dinner together, he doing the cooking, she chopping vegetables, acting as his sous-chef, something she'd always loved doing for him.

Then over dinner, he'd made the offer that absolutely destroyed her.

Gabby said, "He didn't get a chance to ruin anything, because you left him before he could." She punched the air. "Way to go."

Ava said a little indignantly, "I didn't leave him. He flew off to Paris and left me behind. After, mind you, he told me he'd give me a job working for him so I could always be with him. He treated me like Edward treated Vivian in *Pretty Woman*, basically saying I could come along as his mistress."

As though her dreams meant nothing. As though only his rising career was important. He'd even said she could come back and finish her degree in a few years. The nerve. She could hear him even now. *You'll gain valuable life experience.*

As what? Being a hanger-on, a woman he could introduce to

his clients, then shuffle back to bed that night? She'd told him bluntly, "That's not the kind of life experience I want."

After she left that night, he hadn't called, hadn't even texted. She hadn't either. He was the one who'd made that offer. The one who'd been in the wrong.

Gabby agreed with her. "He totally *pretty-womaned* you."

After Ransom was gone, they'd often watched the movie together over bowls of popcorn and buckets of tears. But Ava always turned it off before the ending, when Edward came back. Because Ransom never had.

Ava's heart turned over with love for her sister. "You've always been my staunchest supporter." She squeezed Gabby's hand tightly.

Her sister's eyes were limpid pools. "You can't know how I feel about that man for what he did to you."

"But I do." To escape painful reminders, Ava had avoided following Ransom's rising celebrity status as much as she could. But Gabby had gone a step further, her animosity for Ransom coloring even her career decisions. "I never meant that you should pass up huge opportunities," Ava said. "When Ransom needed a vegan chef—"

Gabby held up a hand. "I would never have worked with someone who could do that to you."

Her sister's loyalty always hit that soft spot in Ava's heart. "But you just said I was the one who walked out."

Gabby shook her head, her blond hair flying. "You had good reason to."

"But I never wanted you to put your career second to my feelings."

A growl rumbled up from Gabby's throat. "I wouldn't work for that man if hell—" She stopped herself. Because Ava might now have to work with *that man*.

The waitress arrived, two martini glasses filled with coffee liqueur on her tray. "Try these, ladies, and see what you think."

The two drinks were foamy, with a scattering of espresso beans on the top. "It looks delicious. Thank you."

The woman waited while Ava lifted the glass to her lips. And truly, it was ambrosia. "Oh my God. This is so good." She flashed a smile. "You're a wonder."

Shrugging shyly, the waitress said, "I looked it up online and told the bartender how to make it. He didn't even know we had all the ingredients."

"Above and beyond," Ava told her.

"You did great. Thank you." Gabby licked the foam mustache off her lips.

"And no cream," the woman added with a smile before she walked away.

"She deserves a big tip." Ava fortified herself with another delicious sip. "Okay, here's what I've learned over the last fifteen years. Yes, I'm still angry with him. I can't help it. I really did think I was in love with him." Gabby opened her mouth, but Ava forestalled her. "But I don't think I ever really *believed* in love. Especially after Ransom. You know what our parents were like."

Gabby answered softly, "Yeah, I know."

"They were never great examples of shining love or family loyalty."

Gabby could only agree with a nod. "I remember how it felt every time they left on another trip—"

"—and never took us along," Ava finished. She'd spent her formative years trying to gain her parents' approval. She brought home the best report cards, joined the debate team, worked on special projects, did whatever she could to get them to notice her. To spend time with her. To love her. But she was never good enough for them to stay.

She'd done the same with Ransom, always trying to do whatever he wanted, always trying be perfect for him. It hadn't worked with him any more than it had with her parents.

She could say it now, though she hadn't been able to when they died, or even long after they were gone. "They only showed us the selfish side of love. But their kind of love wasn't the real thing."

Her parents had always been more concerned with their next junket than they were with their kids. The family had gone through several nannies, none of whom ever said a thing about the parents' attitude, even though they all must have wondered how the Harringtons could leave their children behind so often. Her parents had been like playmates, always off on the next fun adventure. All they'd known how to do was pump out a passel of kids, then go on their merry way.

Maybe their parents' legacy was why none of them could deal with the subject of love. While they could talk about almost anything else with each other, love was off the table. None of them had ever broached the topic with Dane, even though all of them knew he was in love with Cammie. It could also have been why she'd kept Ransom a secret.

None of that mitigated the hurt she'd felt over Ransom's betrayal. But maybe it explained a little. "I'm not sure I ever really believed in love." Which might have been a self-fulfilling prophecy. The moment Ransom *pretty-womaned* her, she'd known the whole relationship had been an illusion. She was nothing special to him, no matter how much she'd tried to please him. It was painfully familiar territory.

She'd thought he wanted someone who worked as hard as he

did, someone with the kind of ambition he had. She'd gone back to school for herself, but she'd also wanted him to respect her. And while she'd been doing everything she could to please him, he'd made that offer as though none of it mattered. As though he hadn't even noticed.

But her little sister called her on the comment about love. "What about Dane and Cammie? You don't think their love is real?"

Ava shrugged. "They probably think it is."

Gabby's blue eyes blazed. "Of *course* they're in love. Dane has been in love with Cammie since the day she started working for him." Twelve years, to be exact. "And Cammie has stars in her eyes when she looks at him."

"Okay. I admit they're totally in love." She'd known it for years too. She just didn't want to admit that the problem was her. Despite their parents' poor example, Dane had learned how to love. But she and Ransom had failed spectacularly.

Gabby wasn't finished. "And what about all the Mavericks? The way Gideon looks at Rosie, the way he always put his hand on her pregnant belly." Rosie had recently given birth to their little girl. "And Matt—the way he so tenderly touches his new son's head, then kisses Ari."

The babies had all been introduced at one of the weekly family barbecues. Ava admitted that the look in Cal's eyes as he gazed at Lyssa, the youngest of the Spencer children, was love and nothing but love. "I know you're right. I don't think I've ever seen looks like those."

"Those men *love*," Gabby insisted, heartfelt. "So do their wives and partners. And look at their parents, Bob and Susan Spencer. A love that's lasted more than thirty-five years."

Ava held up her hands in surrender. "All right, already. I get it. They've all got fantastic relationships. And Dane loves Cammie with all his heart and vice versa." She took a gigantic breath, filling her lungs, then let it out. "So basically it's just me and Ransom who suck. *We* couldn't make love work." Before Gabby could say yea or nay or deny the obvious, she turned the conversation on her sister. "What about you? Have you ever been in love?"

Gabby gave a half smile and a half shrug. "There was a French boy when I was at cooking school in Paris." This time, it was a full shrug. "But I'd never call that love. It was just nice to have someone help with the language barrier, someone to hang out with."

Ava wondered how big a story lay behind those words.

But Gabby preempted her by asking, "So you know you have to hire the guy, right?" When Ava grimaced, Gabby finished, "He might suck at love, but he sure as hell doesn't suck at cooking or catering."

With those fateful words, Ava flopped down onto the table, laying her head on the surface.

Gabby groaned. "That's disgusting. What if they don't wash these very well?"

Ava could do no more than mumble, "I don't care. I don't want to call him."

Gabby tugged on her tightly wound chignon, and Ava opened her eyes.

"You're a different person now than you were then. You can handle him. You're strong and confident, and you'll do whatever you need to do to make sure your residents are well taken care of."

"Yeah. But I can still grumble about it." Ava had known all along that she'd have to contact Ransom, even as she'd been fighting herself. "He's the only one left to turn to. So I have to swallow my pride and act like nothing happened fifteen years ago." Because her business and her residents came first, always. "I listened to all that crap George Twisselman gave me about how they were transitioning, when really he was just cutting costs and not giving us trained personnel. I should have seen that and started looking for a replacement right then."

Gabby leaned in close, her mouth a deep frown. "Don't beat yourself up. You've got a lot of balls in the air. If one of them drops every now and again, that's just part of running a business."

Ava had done her very best never to let a ball drop.

"You gave the guy a chance," her sister went on, "instead of firing him right out of the gate. That was a reasonable decision."

But Ava couldn't erase poor Mrs. Greeley's tears from her mind. The guilt that any of her residents had to go through that kind of nastiness weighed on her. "I've obviously got to do *something*, so this is what I'm doing. Then I'll find a replacement for Ransom as soon as I can." Mrs. Greeley's tears had been her undoing. She had to fix the situation any way she could, even if it meant burying her emotional scars. She would act like the no-nonsense businesswoman she knew herself to be.

And she *was* no-nonsense in her business dealings. In her dating life too. The truth was that after Ransom, she'd been very careful that no relationship got too serious. She just wasn't good at them.

Sitting up straight, she looked at her little sister. "You know, I haven't dated in two years."

Gabby went with the flow, as if she understood how Ava's mind flitted from one thing to another. "Oh, that sucks."

"It just seems that the more successful I've become over the years, the more the men who are truly interested in being with me as a woman instead of an executive have dwindled."

Gabby nodded knowingly. "Emasculated by your success."

Ava laughed. "I never thought of it in those terms."

Her sister shrugged. "They're intimidated by you."

"They all seem to want something from me."

Gabby grinned. "Other than to let you use them ruthlessly?"

It had been a long time—a very long time.

Ava thought of all the ways she and Ransom had used each other—beautiful, pleasurable, ecstatic ways. Her breath quickened and her pulse began to race.

But there was no way she'd ever go there again. Not with Ransom.

* * *

The following morning, Ava dressed for success. Or rather, she dressed for an ambush.

She'd trolled her closet for the perfect outfit. And there it was—a buttoned-up bespoke power suit she'd had made for meetings with executives who thought they were the only high-powered people in the room. She hadn't worn it yet.

This was the perfect occasion for its debut.

Dressed and turning in front of the mirror so she could see it from every angle, she satisfied herself that the suit would make Ransom drool over what he'd given up all those years ago.

It was frowned upon for women to use their sensuality in a business setting. Yet men dominated with their size and their deep voices and their big muscles. Why shouldn't a woman dominate with her innate qualities, intelligence as well as sensuality? It was a natural part of her power. She'd never hesitated to use it the way men never hesitated to use their misplaced sense of authority.

After checking the mirror one last time, she slipped into her high heels.

There. The perfect picture of a consummate businesswoman. With an edge of sensuality.

Let him drool.

After stopping by her office to check in with Naomi, make some calls, and answer a few emails, she headed out. Ransom's office was only a couple of blocks from hers, and walking it, she marveled at how close they'd been since she'd opened her headquarters in the city.

Had they passed each other on opposite sides of the street? Been seated in the same restaurant without seeing each other?

No, she would have felt him if they'd been so close. She'd certainly never booked a table at his San Francisco restaurant.

But now she was about to face the wolf in his den.

Her blood froze with an appalling thought.

What if he refused to see her?

Chapter Four

Ransom was seated behind his desk, his office door open. Which was why he heard and saw the commotion. A beautiful woman with hair the color of garnets pushed past his two assistants.

"Ma'am, you can't—"

"Please, we need to—"

She answered imperiously, "I can and I will," with a slight curve of her lips.

He'd know that luscious voice anywhere. Still heard it in his dreams, in fact, though he hadn't spoken to her in fifteen years. He'd seen her at Gideon Jones's New Year's Eve gala in Napa, but somehow she'd eluded an actual meeting.

He'd followed her career through tidbits Dane Harrington had shared. Proud of his two sisters and two brothers, Dane often spoke of them. Ransom had also read articles in business magazines about her company's meteoric rise in the senior living and health management field.

He'd met her when she was still working at a nursing home, but he'd known even then that Ava Harrington was a determined woman. She had brought her dreams to life.

And she was still his dream woman.

There'd been times he might have thought about standing on her doorstep and asking, *What went wrong? Why did it all just end in the blink of an eye?* But he never had.

He flashed back to the first time he'd seen her. As he sat by his grandmother's chair, talking with her, laughing, Ava had walked into the room. She was twenty-one, and he was ten years older, but the age difference hadn't mattered.

His heart and every other part of him had said, *It's you.*

Feeling the same thing now as she marched into his office, he wondered how he could have buried all of this for so many years. She stole his breath, she stole his voice, she even stole his ability to think. He could only look.

She was sexy as hell in a tailored business suit that hugged her backside when she turned to close the door. Her heels were so sharp she could stab him right in the heart. Her legs were long and shapely, the suit jacket molded to her beautiful breasts, her hair pulled back in a knot that made him want to pull out every pin, one by one, and let it fall like silk over his fingers.

In that moment, he wanted her so damn bad, he ached deep inside.

She was a beautiful, intelligent, determined woman. Even more than she'd been at the tender age of twenty-one.

Back then, he couldn't get enough of her fast enough, even as he'd poured all his energy into his career. He'd made decisions at thirty-one that seemed right for him at the time, even if they were wrong for their relationship. His career was paramount, and he'd done what he had to do. That's what he'd been telling himself all this time. He hadn't wanted to squash her dreams, but he'd absolutely had to go for his.

But he'd never forgotten Ava. When she left him, it hurt like hell, even as over the years he'd acted the ultimate chef playboy, indulging in a few affairs, some with the groupies who came with fame. But none of that truly meant anything.

Not after Ava.

Work and his career had been his solace, and he'd put everything into it. He'd still had so much to prove back then. But he'd done it. He'd reached the pinnacle.

But he'd reached it alone.

Poleaxed by all the memories and feelings, by *her*, standing in his office, up close and personal, so beautiful, so desirable, so perfect, he had to ask himself: *Did I make a mistake?*

⋆ ⋆ ⋆

They didn't need to exchange pleasantries. She and Ransom weren't buddies. They weren't even enemies—though at one time she'd thought she hated him. She didn't now. She hadn't for a long time. She was just angry.

And she was even angrier at the way the sight of him affected her.

His tailored white dress shirt fit his chest snugly and showed off his perfect muscles, his toned physique. She'd thought his picture on the bus might have been airbrushed, but no. He was really that handsome, with a few more lines maybe, but they only enhanced his features. His dark hair was frosted with the slightest, sexiest bit of silver, and his eyes were such a dark mocha they were almost black.

As he sat back casually in his chair and steepled his fingers, her heart wanted to pound right out of her chest. Her body had an instant reaction to him, the way it always had in that first moment when he returned from a business trip or she came in late from a night class. They could barely get out of their clothes before they were in bed.

But that was long, long ago. She wouldn't allow herself to feel that way now.

"I'm assuming—" Even his deep, sexy voice made her want

to melt right there in front of him. "—that you need something pretty damn bad, because clearly I'm the last person you'd come to."

His voice was calm, without inflection. He didn't even sound antagonistic.

She answered the only way she could. "Right on both counts."

But there was something else going on behind his hooded gaze and in the way she'd caught him looking at her after she'd closed the door.

Her outfit had the exact effect she'd wanted. As she'd turned, she could almost sense his tongue falling out of his mouth. The suit, the high heels, her hair, her makeup—she'd wanted to make him drool; she'd wanted him to see all that he'd given up.

It had worked. She felt utterly triumphant.

And horribly conflicted.

If he really meant nothing to her, then why did she have to shove her sensuality in his face? Was it revenge? Or did she have secret hopes they could start again?

Of course she didn't. She couldn't. But she also admitted that her plan had backfired. She was the one drooling over him.

Because Ransom Yates was still the sexiest man alive. Dammit.

If his face on the side of a bus gave her heart palpitations, standing this close to him, with only his desk between them, turned her completely combustible.

But she couldn't let him know that.

"If it wasn't the best reason in the world," she drawled, "you'd better believe I would never walk in here."

He might think the slap-down was for him. But truly, it was for herself. She absolutely could not allow her emotions to get muddled over him. She'd tried to forget him, tried to numb all those latent feelings bubbling inside her. He'd *pretty-womaned* her, he'd deemed her dreams and goals unimportant compared to his, and yes, dammit, she was still angry.

But in the moment of seeing him, after scenting him—something slightly spicy and all male that was uniquely him—after being wowed by his potent sexuality, more than anger, she was wary of her own feelings resurfacing.

She absolutely could not allow herself to want a man who'd rejected her. She was beyond that.

He rose. "I'm waiting with bated breath to hear all your reasons."

I'm waiting with bated breath. He used to say that to her over the phone, when he was at the airport or driving back to her, when she was leaving class to come home to him. When he couldn't wait to get his hands on her. With a superhuman effort, she didn't allow the memory to thaw a single chip of the ice inside her.

He rounded his big desk and headed to the sideboard along the wall opposite the full-length windows. Filled with a variety of machines—microwave, coffee maker, espresso maker (was that a waffle iron?)—it was everything a celebrity chef could want.

She'd been so intent on him that she hadn't even glanced around his office. The carpet was plush beneath her shoes, her heels sinking slightly into the pile. Everything was made of rich mahogany, from the desk to the conference table to the end tables and coffee table. The buttery soft leather sofa was inviting enough to fall asleep on.

Or to make love on.

The small collection of paintings on the walls made her mouth dry up. Was that a Degas?

But it was the view from the top-floor windows that almost blinded her with its brilliance. Was it better than hers? The sun sparkled on the bay waters, and sailboats drifted across its glassy surface as if they'd been painted there. From the corner office, she could see all the way from the Golden Gate to the Bay Bridge.

Behind her, the steamer frothed in whatever brew he was preparing, then she smelled the pungent aroma of a perfect chai.

How could he remember her favorite café drink after all this time? Chai latte. He'd probably made it to throw her off balance.

He carried two mugs to the conference table, a design expertly rendered in the foam on top. For a moment, she thought it was a heart, but realized quickly it was a leaf. Thank God. She couldn't have handled a heart.

As she took a seat before that glorious view, her first thought was to ignore the latte, but that might reveal her roiling feelings. Picking up the mug, she savored the brew and, in the process, showed him she was totally over him. Setting it down, she said, "It's as good as you always made them." Smiling, she added the zinger. "I've trained my barista to make them the same way." She'd found a replacement in one area, at least.

"You were so good at training me to do it the way you liked it."

Was that a sexual innuendo? Definitely. It set her pulse racing all over again.

She'd never trained anyone to duplicate the sensual things he'd done with her. She hadn't even tried. Because his talents in bed were innate. He'd always known just how to touch her, exactly where, and for how long.

Something lit up his eyes as he sipped his own latte. Something that said he knew the thoughts running through her mind.

The sizzle of that look was like his fingers stroking her skin.

Oh yeah, she felt the sizzle. As much as she didn't want to.

The man was the devil incarnate, always knowing exactly what to say at just the right moment. Until that last night. When he'd said all the wrong things.

She thought he might go on, sending out veiled innuendos, teasing her, testing her, but he sat back in his chair and smiled. "So how's the family?"

She wanted to say something pithy. But what could possibly be pithy about that answer? "They're all doing great. But you see Dane often enough. I'm sure he's kept you up on everything Harrington." Then she raised an eyebrow as if she were a teacher telling off a student. "But I'm not here for small talk."

And she certainly wasn't here to rehash their long-ago relationship.

Or to start it all over again just because she hadn't been on a date in two years and no man had ever touched her, kissed her, pleasured her the way Ransom had.

* * *

Ransom thought he'd seen a spark there, for just a moment, a flame in her mesmerizing amber eyes that he wanted to fan into a conflagration.

But Ava Harrington turned all business right before his eyes. The CEO of an empire. The sight of her doing her thing made him even hotter.

He couldn't help wondering what life would have been like if he'd never made that fateful offer.

"I have five Bay Area facilities," she began.

She had over a hundred retirement communities, nursing homes, and senior care facilities around the country and was expanding internationally as well. Dane was extremely proud of everything his sister had accomplished. The man was proud of all his siblings, and he'd never been shy when talking about any of them. But it was talk of Ava that always pricked up Ransom's ears. He wondered if Harrington had ever suspected the affair. If he had, he'd never given a single sign during any of the events or projects they'd worked on together.

"And I need someone to take over the catering for those five facilities," she said.

She paused long enough for him to wonder why only those. But then, it made sense to split up catering between regions. He said nothing, though, letting her go on.

"I'd like you to design menus for older adults. We can't have food that's too exotic. They need meat and potatoes, but they also need nutrition. But most of all, they need to feel like food is something to be enjoyed during their later years."

There was the Ava he remembered. She'd always operated on a huge scale, not just with her job, but with her heart. Now that she'd brought her dreams to fruition, so much more was at stake for her residents.

He gave her a nod, indicating she should continue.

"We have breakfast, lunch, and dinner, and a snack bar in the afternoons where we offer things like soups, salads, and sandwich fillings. Something to tide people over until dinnertime or if they missed lunch altogether."

He sat back, propped his ankle on his knee. "That all seems like a normal schedule. Definitely doable."

Finally, she smiled, the beautiful smile he remembered playing on her lips. "They have their favorites too. We always have a hot-dog-and-beans day, a pizza day, something for them to look forward to. I can't tell you how many times I've heard them say excitedly, 'It's hot dog day.' One woman at my Los Gatos facility plans her daughter's visits around hot dog day. Mrs. Anderson told me I can never cut out hot dogs, or her daughter might stop coming to visit." She looked at him, her head tipped, a dazzling smile on her kissable lips, not the harshness she'd shown him when she walked in. "Her daughter would visit her anyway, but we like to joke about it. So you can see that it's much more than just the food. It's about the community."

No, Ava hadn't lost her huge heart. "What's wrong with your current caterers?"

He saw the hesitation in her eyes. But the only thing she gave him was, "They no longer meet my company's standards." Holding his gaze, she added, "Or my residents' needs."

He waited, but she said nothing else. He'd have time to push her about the real reason later on. If he decided he could work with her.

"I'm assuming you're not just talking about menus, but that you want procurement, preparation, and staffing for both kitchen and dining room as well."

"Yes. I've always found that's much more efficient than doing it all in-house. Our caterers also handle special events within the complexes, such as providing drinks and appetizers for recitals or lectures."

In addition to the cookbooks, restaurants, and TV show, he catered special events—anything from elite private parties to huge galas like the one for Gideon Jones at Dane's Napa resort. He also created menus for resorts, cruise ships, retreat centers, and more.

But this was an entirely new field for him. "You're asking a lot."

She picked up her latte, took a long swallow, then set it down again, the mug's *clink* on the table sounding empty. "Yes, I am. But my residents deserve it."

He understood completely. This was about her community, and that was everything to her. It was even in the name of her corporation: Harrington *Community* Care International. But he had to warn her. "This isn't exactly what I do."

Years ago, he'd done the cruise ship circuit, but then he'd been more concerned about enticing passengers, and his responsibility had been only the food.

"Maybe not, but it's something you *can* do." Maybe she was remembering his cruise days as well. "It could be a win-win for both of us—a new sector for you to move into. And it doesn't have to be forever."

Forever. What they'd never had. It had ended all too soon.

She went on, "I just need someone to fill in until I can do a more exhaustive search."

"How long?"

She shrugged. "Three months? Six months? I don't have an exact timetable. It depends on how soon I can find a suitable replacement."

He looked at her a long moment, considering, the gears in his mind already engaging with the problem. Just as she had, he took a long swallow of his latte. Finally, he said, "We just wrapped up filming for the cooking show, so okay, I'll do it. When do we start?"

He had the feeling she wanted to punch her fist in the air, but she maintained her cool façade. "I need this done in two weeks."

Oh, she'd gotten him. Hook, line, and sinker. Allowing him to say yes before she gave him the most pertinent detail. But then, he should have asked *before* he agreed.

Although it was Ava. He would have said yes anyway.

"I know you can do it."

Was she pandering to his ego? Not that it mattered. He wanted more time with her, and this was the only way he'd get it.

She stood, bringing the meeting to an end. "I'll have my assistant send you all the details."

Even though she must have known the shock he felt at the two-week deadline, she was still trying to dictate the terms.

"I'll only work with you personally." He dealt the *coup de grâce*. "Or the deal's off."

* * *

Ava should have known he'd play that card. He knew she was in a bind. But despite the shock she'd seen in his eyes when she'd said *two weeks*, he hadn't backed down.

She, however, could fight back. "I have an extensive business to run. My assistant will be much more suited for the job."

But he stood, shaking his head and smiling. "I run a vast business too. And this project will get done a lot faster if you and I work together. So that's my deal—you or no one."

Dammit. She was stuck with only one answer. She had to give it for the sake of her people. "All right. Fine. We'll do it your way."

When the words were said, she tamped down a secret little place inside her that was jumping up and down with joy.

God, when would she ever learn to crush her feelings for him? Except anger. But how could she be angry with the man who'd just agreed to bail her out of a mess?

She said the polite thing. "Thank you. I appreciate it. My situation is dire enough that we literally need to start tomorrow. I've got a company willing to handle two weeks for me, but that's it. So the catering issue can't linger."

He nodded. "I'll clear my schedule for this." Was that triumph in his eyes? Probably. But she had no other choice.

She'd gotten exactly what she'd come for. With that one little exception of working personally with him. He truly had saved her, and she appreciated it more than he could ever know. She left him with another, "Thank you," but as she turned for the door, she felt his eyes on her as she walked out.

From another man, it might have been creepy. But with Ransom, it felt more like—

She wouldn't even *think* about what it felt like.

Striding from his office, she passed his two assistants, a man and a woman, who were still agog at the way she'd barged in. And at the fact Ransom hadn't thrown her out.

In the elevator vestibule, she stabbed the button, watching the numbers flick up and taking way too long.

She felt him beside her before he said, "That's the problem with being on the top floor. The elevator takes forever to get up here. Sometimes I just take the stairs."

They both looked down at her shoes. No way could she take the stairs in her killer high heels.

He did *not* go away. "I look forward to working with you on this project."

She simply smiled. Why was he being so friendly, making chitchat, when they'd already said everything that needed to be said back in his office?

Finally, *finally*, the elevator arrived, and she stepped inside the empty car. The doors were about to close when he smiled. Just that, saying nothing.

But that sexy smile on his lips hit all her buttons.

Though she tried to maintain control of her emotions, all he had to do was smile and her legs melted like butter in the sun.

Dammit. How easy it would be to fall for him again.

But that she would never do. Not ever.

At twenty-one, loving him more than she'd ever thought possible, she'd been crushed to know that when he looked at her, he saw nothing more than his mistress.

* * *

The elevator doors closed on his view of her.

Ransom had been so close to stepping in there with her. His brain felt muddled just standing beside her. Still wanting her. It took all his willpower to stop himself from touching her, kissing her, even from saying anything at all.

After fifteen years, he'd actually grown up a little, and he was emotionally aware enough to know that he needed to process this inconceivable situation. Not just her showing up in his office wanting him to work for her, but the stunning realization that he'd never truly forgotten her. Even as he watched the floor numbers descend, he recognized that she still blew any other woman he'd ever dated clear out of the water.

Damn, did I ever screw that up.

Slowly, thoughtfully, he walked back to his office. Since he was being totally honest with himself, he had to say he'd been thinking about her not only in sexual terms and the sparks he was sure still flew between them, but also as the woman she'd become. A woman to be reckoned with. She was nothing like the groupies he occasionally slept with out of sheer loneliness. Or the few women he'd met and dated through his work. Ava Harrington was a smart, confident, indomitable woman. The woman he'd walked away from. She'd accused him of treating her like his mistress, but she'd never been that.

And yet, had he seen her as the woman she would become in just a few years?

He'd wanted her in his life, had cared about her, but he hadn't treated her as a strong-minded woman with plans and dreams. He hadn't valued her the way she should have been valued.

Maybe he'd begun recognizing that as he listened to Dane's tales about his siblings. He just hadn't wanted to consider why he'd glommed on to every detail Dane revealed. She'd grown into a powerful woman, even more beautiful than he remembered, even more dazzling and brilliant than Dane had described.

And if she thought she could palm him off on her assistant, she had another thing coming.

Chapter Five

Standing before the picture window of her penthouse flat in Pacific Heights, Ava looked out over the bay.

She loved this place, loved the view, which at night was lit up by the Golden Gate Bridge, the city lights, and the lights on Alcatraz, the bay black all around it.

She'd personally chosen every piece of furniture in the flat, all with a midcentury-modern flair—the leather sofa she could sink into, the kidney-shaped glass coffee table and matching end tables, the bookcases, the dining table and chairs. Thick, luxurious rugs partially covered the oak hardwood floors, and the rooms all had clean lines without an excess of knickknacks on every surface. Her brother Clay called it *minimalist*, but she had only the things she needed. A large primary suite, two guest bedrooms for visiting family, three bathrooms—hers with a massive soaker tub—and a home office where she spent much of her time.

She sipped her second champagne cocktail, though she usually limited herself to one. But tonight was different. From the moment she left Ransom's office, her thoughts had plagued her.

I cannot believe what I've just done.

It was time for a little speech to herself, saying the words aloud to give them maximum effect.

"You're going to compartmentalize," she told her reflection

in the living-room window. "Just pretend you're working with any other man. Pretend he's George Twisselman." The thought made her laugh out loud. Ransom was the furthest thing from George Twisselman.

They needed to start first thing in the morning. She had only thirteen days left. She must have something in place before then.

The doorbell rang, startling her out of her thoughts. Who on earth could it be? Maybe Dane and Cammie. At the family mastermind, they'd said they were staying over to catch a show.

She could stand there all night wondering. Or she could find out. She pressed the intercom by the door. "Who is it?"

The answer was swift. "It's me."

Her heart fluttered. He didn't say Ransom Yates, not even Ransom. Just *it's me*, as though she'd know exactly who he was. Which, of course, she did.

In leggings and a bulky sweater, she certainly wasn't elegant. The outfit wasn't even sexy. She'd had that extra glass of champagne, and though she wasn't tipsy, she was caught off guard.

But with those thirteen days counting down, she had to let him in.

"Come in. I'm on the top floor." She pressed the buzzer to unlock the street door.

After a soft knock on her door moments later, she opened it to find him dressed casually. His jeans hugged his body, his T-shirt beneath a bomber jacket tight across his impressive chest.

He looked like a bad boy. All she wanted to do was drag him inside and kiss him senseless before they tore off their clothes and made love right there in the foyer.

Heat rushed to her cheeks, and it took every ounce of control to act cool, to hide any evidence of her thoughts. Except the flush on her cheeks she couldn't seem to will away.

Lord. This was going to be the hardest two weeks of her life. Especially since the person she might have to fight the most was herself.

"How did you know where I live?" Closing the door behind him, she spoke mildly, not wanting to sound arrogant or bitchy, just curious.

He strolled after her into the living room, shrugging out of his jacket. "I saw the great spread they did on your place in that architectural magazine. Your flat is remarkable."

"Thank you." She shouldn't feel so pleased—it had shades of always trying to please him when she was twenty-one. After taking his jacket from him, she threw it over the back of the sofa. Not in the closet, where it might stay the night, but out here, easy to grab on the way out.

"I've got a place just around the corner, so I know Pacific Heights, and I recognized the exterior of your building." He took two more steps into the room, not crowding her, just filling the space with his presence. Turning to her, he smiled. "It's elegant and beautiful, just like you."

She willed away another flush that threatened to creep into her cheeks, but her legs felt buttery again, just the way they had in the elevator when he'd smiled at her. So she ignored the compliment. To do anything else might break her resolve.

Yet she couldn't help another telltale flutter of her unmanageable heart. To know that they lived and worked so close. Dane had never said anything to her. But why would he? He knew nothing of her history with Ransom. But it was as if their business and personal paths had paralleled, and all this time, she hadn't even known it. She could have seen him in her favorite market. She could have passed him as she walked through Lafayette Park.

He pointed to the champagne flute she'd left on the coffee table. "I see you still love your champagne."

She smiled despite herself. "Yes. But I can afford something a bit better than the Two Buck Chuck we used to drink." Just as quickly as the words were out, she wanted to slap herself for dredging up their past when this was supposed to be business only. To hide the misstep, she asked, "Would you like one?" He'd always loved champagne, too.

"That would be great," he said with a grin that might have held a note of triumph.

As she poured him a glass in the kitchen, she reflected that they'd progressed past the way she'd stomped into his office. He'd made her a latte, and now he was in her living room while she made him a cocktail. It didn't seem possible. She couldn't have imagined this even in her wildest fantasies.

As she handed him the flute, Ransom took the edge off her thoughts by asking, "There's something I don't understand about the situation. You agreed that unless it was for something pretty damned important, I was the last person you'd come to. But you didn't explain why. I'd like to know."

Was he talking about why she'd come to his office, what her desperate business need actually was? Or was he referring to the past? To the way he'd left her, that he'd simply taken a night flight and she'd never heard from him again.

She answered the first question, the most important one. Because after unloading all her feelings on Gabby, she was over the past. "I told you, the catering company totally sucked."

But he persisted. "You've got a ton of catering companies in the Bay Area. I'm not even a catering company in the same sense. So why me?" His use of the word *me* said it all. He was talking about far more than her catering issues.

But she wouldn't let him stray from the topic. "I tried everyone else. No one could do it. I got someone for the next two weeks, but that's it."

He stared her down, and she knew he wasn't going to let her get away with that answer.

"But I'm the *last* person." He stressed the word.

Ava, however, was good at deflection in a way she hadn't been fifteen years ago. "My brothers suggested you. And I realized they were right. I didn't have another choice. You were it—the only one."

* * *

There was a harshness to her tone, and he knew the reason was far more than her brothers, more than her failed caterer. He wanted her to say it out loud. "But you wouldn't have come to me otherwise. And we both know it. So tell me why it was so hard."

"Because we have history." She almost spat the word at him. "And history can get in the way of business."

For her, their history was all bad. But to him, he'd made a mistake—yeah, a big one—and then they'd simply ended. She hadn't liked what he said, and she'd stalked out. With another business trip in the way like always, he'd lost the chance to run after her. Back then, everything had been about his career. He hadn't called her while he was away, which was a jerk thing to do, but he'd told himself he was giving her time to cool off and that they'd talk it through when he got home.

But he returned to an empty apartment, all evidence of her erased as if she'd never been in his life at all.

It was clear she'd never forgiven him for that last fight. Yet they'd been so good together in every other aspect. Yes, they'd been like ships passing in the night—maybe he should say *planes*—but she'd given up after one fight. He couldn't remember them fighting before that other than in the minor disagreements every couple had. Mostly, they argued about his travel. But she had her job at the nursing home and her education. It wasn't like she had any more time than he did.

Yet he realized now that he *had* screwed up. That he *was* the one at fault. That if he'd given her dreams the value they deserved, things would have been different. It was seeing her again. The confident woman. The elegant woman. The totally sexy woman. It was the clarity that came after fifteen years of absence.

And Christ, she was sexy in tight leggings and an oversized sweater that made him ache to find out exactly what she was wearing under it. Which did he love most? The suit she'd worn earlier? Or the leggings and sweater? His heart pumped faster and harder no matter how she was dressed.

But she was still not giving him a full answer, saying instead, "I'm willing to put our history aside because my residents are more important."

He couldn't say why those words in particular cut through him. Maybe because she was bending over backward to do anything and everything she could for her people... but when he'd asked for something, she'd walked out and never looked back.

As if their *history* had been satisfactorily dealt with, at least in her mind, she sat on the sofa, pulled a pillow across her stomach, and settled in. "Let me tell you about my residents."

Even as his insides felt sliced and diced around her, he admired her empathy, her compassion. It wasn't simply catering. These people she took care of were *hers*.

She leaned over and patted the other end of the sofa, or at

least as far she could stretch, inviting him to sit. He wanted to crowd her, sit right in the middle, right next to her, his thigh pressed against hers, her scent filling his head.

Yet he took the seat she indicated. Coming on too strong right now wouldn't get him the answers he wanted. Nor would pushing for those answers succeed until she was ready to give them. "All right, tell me all about it."

Passion took over her features, glittering in her eyes. Not the same passion she'd once shown him, but passion nonetheless.

"I visited our San Juan Bautista facility and witnessed one of the servers abusing my resident, Mrs. Greeley. He told her *to her face* that she ate like a pig." Her hands came up in an angry gesture, her fingers fluttering, as if she wanted to strangle the man. "He actually said she should be ashamed of herself."

Ransom had to admit that shocked him. If he ever heard one of his servers speak that way, they'd be gone before he could snap his fingers. "That's pretty damned reprehensible. But one server isn't the whole bunch."

The glitter in her eyes could have been tears, and her voice came out with a slight tremor. "Mrs. Greeley was beside herself. She was in tears. It took me ages to calm her down. And yes, I fired him on the spot—or tried to. But honestly, if that had been the only incident, I would simply have called up the president and jumped all over him for hiring someone like that."

"I assume there were more."

She nodded, her hair shimmering in waves against her shoulders. The bun she'd worn earlier today had been brushed out. He'd always loved running his fingers through her hair, loved its shampoo scent, loved the silkiness of it falling over his skin when she kissed his chest or his stomach.

When she'd—

She went on as though she had no idea of the effect she had on him. "When I got back to the office, my assistant, Naomi, showed me reports from other facilities. They were all about the same kind of disrespect." Disgust laced her words. "The disrespect the lovely men and women who live in my homes received. I understand that the company has recently undergone a massive management change, but there was never anything like this before. And when I talked to their president—" She gritted her teeth. "—he actually implied that my people were *too touchy*." She looked at him, her eyes almost caramel in the room's low lighting. Or that might have been her emotion shining through. "My people deserve the best."

He smiled. "Are you calling me the best?"

Over a sip of champagne, he watched her face flush and her chest rise with a deep breath.

For all the months they'd been together so long ago—almost a year—he had been the best for her. And she had been the best for him. He wondered if he could make her see that he was still the best, and for far more than catering.

But he let her off the hook. For now. "I admire how much you care for your residents. And not just as CEO of a billion-dollar company."

She wasn't just beautiful, confident, and smart. Ava Harrington had a heart of gold.

Even as she said, "Thank you. I appreciate your saying that," he saw how the compliments touched her in the warmth on her cheeks, the sparkle in those caramel eyes, her quickened breath.

He told himself she was fighting their innate attraction. Something that hadn't died in fifteen years.

Oh yes, he knew her signs. The slightly dilated pupils. The way she bit her lip for just a moment. The way her fingers laced so she couldn't reach out to touch him.

She burned. The way she'd always burned for him.

The way they still burned for each other.

Or maybe that was just wishful thinking.

"Right from the beginning," he said, "that's why you went into healthcare management for seniors. You wanted to open your own facilities because you hated the apathetic, uncaring way in which older people were often treated."

She let out a long breath. "Did I ever say that?"

"Maybe you didn't. But I knew. I saw." He saw *her*. He saw her dreams. Yes, he traveled a lot, and they always came together with a bang, tearing off their clothes, sometimes never even making it to the bed. Loving each other for hours until they fell into an exhausted sleep.

But that didn't mean he didn't see *her*.

If her parents hadn't died, if she'd gone on to get her business degree, she might never have found her true path. Because her negligent parents had left their family of five in terrible debt, she'd gotten a job as an aide at the eldercare facility where his grandmother resided. Ava had loved the old people she cared for. She'd always had time to offer kind words, to listen to the same stories she'd heard over and over. She never scolded his grandmother for repeating herself. She just nodded, smiled, and if his grandmother forgot the end of the story, Ava seamlessly finished it for her. Ava was that way with all the residents, speaking gently even to the ones who couldn't understand her anymore. She bathed them with gentle kindness, smoothed lotion into their dry skin, brushed their brittle hair. He'd even seen her use a curling iron on a woman who hated the flatness of her gray hair.

Ava had climbed mountains for the people she took care of.

Her billion-dollar business was really all about her big heart.

"You know, I wouldn't do this for just anyone. But I admire everything you've done for your people. I admire how you feel about them. That's why I said yes to helping you."

* * *

His words wrapped around her as if he'd folded her into his arms.

If her parents had ever spoken like this, if Ransom had spoken like this all those years ago, what might have happened?

Oh God. She'd just hired the devil. A silver-tongued devil who knew exactly what to say.

Her devil.

Stunned by his empathy and his admiration, all she could say was, "Thank you."

Then, afraid he'd melt everything inside her just like he'd done every time he touched her, she got down to business as if that could ward off the emotions warring inside her. "So let's talk about what I really need."

His mouth curved slightly, as if he was thinking about all her physical needs he'd satisfied so perfectly when they were together. That knowing smile made her rush on. "I don't use the same caterer for all my facilities. I like to choose someone local because I feel we get better menus more specific to the local area." She huffed out a breath. "Except in this case."

"I can manage the five in the Bay Area."

"I'm hoping you can bring some of the flair to the menus that I'm sure you have on your cooking show." She couldn't help smiling. "I saw your face on the side of a bus yesterday. Advertising your show."

That handsome face affected her again. Though older, he was still stunning. The silver in his hair only added to his magnetism.

But she needed to stop thinking about how attractive he was, how his shirt outlined his muscles, how the faded jeans fit him so well. How his hands would feel on her skin.

If she wasn't careful, she'd start drooling. Just like she had in his office.

Ransom saved her. "Let's see what your menus look like now."

On safer ground, she led him along the hall to her office, where her computer was already running. She opened the first week's menu. "Pull up that chair."

He didn't just sit beside her like a normal person. No, he eased in at an angle, his legs spread around her as he leaned in to see the screen. Surrounded by him, she felt heat rise in her all over again.

Concentrate, Ava. "We rotate menus every week for four weeks. So we require four weeks' worth of meals. But I'll understand if the time limitation means we have to give up the rotation for now."

He didn't say anything. Instead, he read each menu item carefully, his breath warm across her hair. Finally, when she thought she might be going a little crazy, he said, "The food looks pretty appetizing, if the names mean anything."

She nodded. "The food wasn't the problem. It's the service that sucked."

"I see you've got a special Sunday brunch."

"Yes. People love it. They all dress up in their Sunday best."

He touched the mouse to flip to the next menu, and his scent washed over her. Something indefinably him—more than aftershave, potently male. The scent that came to her in the night when she thought of him.

It set her nerve endings jangling. She even had to push her chair back, away from him, so she could breathe.

After going through all the menus, he sat back in the chair. "I can do four weeks. We need to give your people their same routine. I'll get you some initial plans right away."

It was more than she could have expected. "The sooner the better."

The sooner he got it all done, the less she'd have to see him. Scent him. The less she'd close her eyes and envision him the way he'd been all those years ago. Naked. Ready.

If she didn't stop herself, she'd have to turn on the air conditioning. Or tear off her sweater.

* * *

Ransom walked back to his flat, his hands shoved in his bomber jacket's pockets. Late September could be lovely in the city, especially this year, but the air cooled down quickly at night.

He couldn't get the scent of her out of his head. Not now. Not then. He'd never gotten *her* out of his head. She'd haunted his dreams, though he was only now seeing that.

He would get this done for her, even if it took all freaking night. Part of it was to make up for never reaching out to her after he'd returned from that business trip to Paris. For letting her slip away. For never explaining what he'd really meant by the offer he'd made.

There was all that, but there was also the compassion she had for her residents. He needed to help her.

Maybe he even wanted to impress her. The truth was, as he strolled from streetlight to streetlight, he wanted that badly.

Chapter Six

Ransom showed up in her office at nine the next morning. Ava hadn't expected him to get through the entire meal plan overnight, and certainly not this early.

"Good morning." Then she took in the state of him.

In all the years of seeing him on TV and in the press—not that she'd been searching him out—he'd never had a hair out of place, never looked anything less than immaculate. But today, a shadow of beard covered his chin, wrinkles creased his T-shirt, and his hair stuck out at all angles.

But God, he'd never looked better.

Despite herself, her breath caught in her chest. He was so *real* right now. Looking like hell and tired as all get out, but still gorgeous.

"Did you even sleep?" He'd obviously been up all night working on her plans.

His answer was a mere grunt as he stalked to her desk, dropped a sheaf of papers in front of her, then turned and flopped down on the sofa, closing his eyes.

She suddenly regretted being such a hard-ass the day before. Because today, looking over the work he'd put in on her behalf moved her beyond measure. He'd created an incredible proposal. The menus made her mouth water, and his execution plans, right down to the staff he'd need and an incredibly reasonable budget, stunned her.

How had he accomplished this overnight?

But then, he'd always been amazing at whatever task he took on. Her catering needs were no different. She looked up, ready to give him the kudos he so deserved. "This is brilliant."

He was asleep, completely out, slumped against a sofa pillow.

She had two choices. Like they did in the movies, she could grab a glass of water and throw it in his face to wake him up. Or she could put a blanket over him and let him sleep. She'd slept here many times when work consumed her.

A crushed piece of her heart obviously still lurked inside her, because part of her actually wanted to throw that glass of water on him. But she wasn't that young woman anymore. She had to move past the pain he'd caused her, had to be bigger than throwing water in his face.

Because she was grateful for the effort he'd put into helping her. Even if he decided against working on the project, with these plans she was far better off than she'd been before. And she was mature enough to feel gratitude.

She pushed to her feet and removed a blanket from the top shelf of the closet. Spreading it carefully so she didn't wake him, she looked down at him for a long moment. With his face in repose, he looked like the younger man she'd known.

And more than taking her next breath, she wanted to touch him.

But she dragged herself away.

Going over the plans a second and third time, she made a few notes, then got down to the other pile of work while he slept.

It had been only an hour when he startled himself awake, sitting up straight, one side of his face lined with pillow marks. After lifting the corner of the blanket as though he couldn't figure out where it had come from, he stared at her groggily, blinking, then his gaze traveled the room as if it would tell him why he was there.

He hadn't spoken since he'd walked in, but she said to him, "The shower's through that door, if you'd like to freshen up." She hooked a thumb over her shoulder at the closet. "And my brothers have some clothes in there for the odd occasions they need them. I'm sure there's something that'll fit you if you want to change."

He heaved himself up from the sofa with a grunt, swaying slightly as if he was still woozy, and spoke in a raspy voice. "Thanks. I appreciate that." Then he disappeared behind the door.

When she heard the shower running, all manner of thoughts zipped through her mind and shimmied down her body. Good Lord, the man was in her shower. Only three feet away. Naked. And though her anger and lack of forgiveness for the past simmered somewhere inside her, she could barely keep herself from ripping off her clothes and joining him beneath the hot spray. The vision was so vivid she could almost feel his hands on her, almost taste his skin beneath her lips.

She actually groaned aloud. Why couldn't she have a boyfriend? It would make everything so much easier if she had a man in her life. She wouldn't be having all these thoughts.

But that near constant hum of desire inside her belied the words. A boyfriend would only make her feel guilty about the thoughts she'd inevitably have about Ransom.

Why did he have to be the best she'd ever known? Not just his cooking skills, but in every skill he possessed. And Ransom had been so very skillful with her body.

She damn near jumped from her chair, paced her office, then

stood in front of the long windows with their view of the bay.

But she could still hear the pounding water.

She suddenly realized he hadn't taken any of her brothers' clothing into the bathroom. Seized by the need to open that door, she now had an excuse. Riffling through the various articles in the closet, she found something she was sure would fit.

Knocking first, loudly, she cracked the door a couple of inches. Steam billowed out. It bathed her face in warmth, but the perspiration on her skin had everything to do with him.

She slipped her hand through the slit she'd made and dropped the clothing on the floor. "You didn't take anything in with you," she called. "These should fit."

He gave a muffled reply, and she snapped the door closed, rushing back to her desk—before she pushed it all the way open and walked in.

It seemed he stayed in there an interminable amount of time after the water shut off, though the clock told her it was only a matter of minutes. Impatiently, she drummed her fingers on the arms of her chair.

She held her breath when the door opened, then it came out in a rush when he stepped through. The scent of shampoo and body wash and masculinity drifted out with him.

Tailored slacks, fitted shirt. Every muscle defined. It was even worse than last night when he'd taken off the bomber jacket. She could make out the tight beads of his nipples through the material.

She held on to the chair for dear life. Because if she didn't, she might jump into his arms. He was a magnet for her. It hit her then that all those years ago, they'd just been kids, even if he was ten years older. Now he was all man.

And she wanted him badly.

But she was a CEO, a professional at all times. So instead of throwing herself at him, she said ever so politely, "I read through your entire proposal, and everything looks excellent."

He was more alert, his eyes brighter, his chin clean-shaven. Thankfully, she had men's razors in the bathroom for her brothers.

When he smiled, she did *not* allow herself to melt.

"Did you stay up all night working on this?"

He'd literally walked in, laid the plans on her desk, sat down, and fallen asleep. Of course he'd been up all night.

He grinned. "No big deal. I work on stuff overnight all the time."

She folded her arms beneath her breasts and raised one eyebrow. "I'm not sure I buy that. You've got a lot of people working for you to pull the all-nighters. Just like I have."

He tipped his head in acknowledgment. "You want the truth?"

Did she ever—not just about this, but about their past, and why he'd never come back after she'd found her own success. But of course she'd never ask.

She only nodded.

His eyes crinkled attractively. "I haven't pulled an all-nighter in years." He paused, then added, "Clearly, I'm too old for it."

She had no compunction about saying, "Well, you are pretty ancient." That had always been their joke. With their ten-year age difference, she'd razzed him about being an old man, and she couldn't help doing it now.

Yet it hit her like a punch to her rib cage. Not only was she working with him, now she'd made another inside joke. What the hell was she doing? Why was she letting him back in? Yes, she needed him to do the job. But exchanging cute inside jokes? It was untenable.

Things between them hadn't ended with a bang heard around the world. They'd simply ended without a single explanation. They'd never spoken again, as though she'd been nothing more than a casual fling or his temporary mistress, and since she hadn't accepted his offer, he had no further use for her. His rising star had only been climbing higher in the sky, and he'd invited her along on his journey, completely ignoring her dreams. When she'd become angry, he'd ghosted her for fifteen years.

That was the thing she couldn't forgive. Being erased from his life as if she were nothing important to him.

* * *

She was so damn beautiful in her pale blue power suit—tasteful, elegant, while the lines accentuated all her curves.

As he'd stood naked in the shower with her only a few steps away, Ransom remembered all the showers they'd taken together. All the sexy, mind-blowing things they'd done with each other beneath the hot water. And he'd wanted nothing more than to drag her in there with him, strip her down, and make love to her with his lips, his hands, his whole body.

They were dangerous thoughts in the here and now.

She might still feel the temptation of their past, but she hadn't forgiven him. He'd seen that clearly in the tense lines of her body when she'd walked into his office yesterday. There was history there. Bad history. And coming on to her would only make everything worse.

So he went back to what he'd planned to say when he walked in earlier. Before he'd collapsed on her couch. "I need to see one of your facilities. The kitchens. The equipment. The dining room. Everything. As soon as possible, since we've only got twelve days to pull this all together."

She stood abruptly, without even teetering on those sexy high heels of hers. "How about now? We'll go to San Juan Bautista."

He rubbed his hands together. Not just because she'd agreed to his suggestion, but because he'd have more time with her. "Great. I'll call my driver."

She wagged a finger. "No. I'm driving."

She probably had a sedate luxury vehicle that would be far more comfortable than his sports car. And if she was doing the driving, he could do all the watching—her, not the scenery. He didn't even know how good a driver she was, since they'd been apart far longer than they'd been together. When they'd gone anywhere, to a park for a hike or the beach for a swim, he'd done the driving.

But he knew Ava. She was good at everything she did.

Absolutely *everything*.

The car was waiting for them when they stepped into the garage, and Ransom almost let his jaw drop.

All those years ago, lying in bed with her in his arms, he'd told her every one of his dreams. About the restaurants he wanted to own, his vision of his future. And more. *As soon as I get rich, the first thing I'm buying is a Pantera.*

And there it was, the car he'd coveted. The red 1972 De Tomaso Pantera was a beauty, with its flying buttress styling in the back that made it such a classy sports car. Elegant Italian design paired with a brawny Ford engine, the car had been a joint venture between Ford and Italian sports-car maker De Tomaso. Only seven thousand of the cars had been produced, which made them rare in the current market.

Ava shot him a knowing smile as he drooled over her car as if it were a woman. As if it were her. "I haven't taken a good long drive in quite a while," she said. "I'd really like to feel her tearing down the highway again."

On her lips, the words were sexy as hell.

"Where did you find her?"

She waved a hand. "A private seller."

"I bought mine from a private seller too."

She didn't even raise an eyebrow, as if she'd known he'd make his dream come true. The way he'd made all his dreams come true.

Except one.

He marveled at their similar paths. A flat in the same neighborhood. Their headquarters in the same downtown district. The same car in the garage.

She must have been thinking about him over the years. Otherwise, why would she buy that car? What was she trying to prove?

The attendant handed her the keys, and she rounded the hood to the driver's side, while Ransom opened the passenger door. He had to bend deeply to slide into the low-slung car, and once in, his head almost touched the roof. But the nice thing about the Pantera was its legroom.

Not the easiest car to drive, though. You really had to control the clutch or it would stall, especially on the San Francisco hills.

But as she revved the engine and gunned out of the parking garage, Ransom knew Ava Harrington would never stall this car.

* * *

The thing Ransom Yates had loved second best to cooking was a sports car. When they were together, he'd driven a beat-up old Alfa Romeo that broke down as often as it ran. But he'd always said that when he had the money, he'd buy a Pantera.

Ava hadn't bought the car because of him. She'd simply fallen in love with the sleek styling when he talked about it.

Naturally, he would have bought one himself.

She'd chosen San Juan Bautista in order to check on Mrs. Greeley after the other day's horrific incident. But she also wanted Ransom stuck in the passenger seat for ninety minutes while she drove south. And maybe, too, she wanted to show him how she'd mastered the car. The first few times she'd taken it out, she'd stalled it over and over. Pounding the steering wheel, she'd been certain Ransom would never stall *his*. But she'd conquered the beauty, had become its complete and total boss.

As she negotiated the San Francisco traffic heading out to Highway 280, usually the clearest route down to San Juan Bautista, it struck her that they were like two halves of a whole. The same Pantera, living in Pacific Heights, high-rise headquarters in the city.

Dammit, she was *not* his other half. She didn't need Ransom Yates to make her feel whole.

But she did love this car, loved its power beneath her hands.

When they'd merged onto the freeway, he said, "You might just handle her better than I do."

"That's because it needs a woman's intuition, listening to it and feeling what it wants. Instead of a man trying to bend the car to his will." She pulled into the fast lane and realized she'd jumped all over him because of her own emotions. But he was actually paying her a compliment. So she said very softly, "Thank you."

Since it wasn't rush hour, there was little traffic, and it was almost a straight shot down to San Juan Bautista, with just a couple of freeway changes.

"So," Ava said, "give me the rundown on your career from thirty-one to forty-six." Without looking, she could tell he'd turned slightly in his seat. "I know you've done some TV." She sounded as if she'd never seen the show. And really, she'd seen only a couple of episodes, maybe a few more, only by accident as she was flipping channels. It wasn't a lie to act as if she didn't know, more like an omission. "And I've seen your cookbooks in the bookstore. So tell me the rest."

There were the snippets she'd heard from Dane and those couple of shows she'd watched. And maybe she'd leafed through a cookbook or two when she was breezing through a bookstore looking for something else. She'd never bought one, of course. Between the recipes, there were too many pictures of him doing what he was good at.

"You know a lot of it from when..." He let the words drift away. *From when we were together.*

She didn't want to think about those times. Didn't want his scent surrounding her in the close confines of the car. Didn't want to feel that prickle of desire his body's heat seemed to bring out in her. Maybe she should have let him call his driver. His car would have been bigger, and she could have pushed herself into the opposite corner, far from him. But Ransom seemed to take up the whole cabin of her sports car. She even rolled down her window for air. Being around him made it hard to breathe.

But she pushed on, just in case he tried to turn the conversation personal, the way he had last night. She would make absolutely sure they stayed all business. "Fifteen years is a long time. I can't know everything. Catch me up." She hoped she sounded conversational, not overly interested.

"There's not much to tell. After—" Again, he cut himself off, as though he knew she'd steer the conversation away from their history. "I did a lot of those celebrity cook-offs. And the catering for a bunch of celebrities. It's funny how it only takes one person to like what you do and then it's all word of mouth." She glanced over long enough to see him smile. "They all want the best for their big parties. And if they think you're the best, then they all want you."

She couldn't help thinking that Ransom *was* the best. Of course everyone wanted him. Many of the exquisite meals he'd made for her had almost been an aphrodisiac.

"And somehow I just slid into the cooking show after the cookbooks took off in stores."

"Do you enjoy preparing food on camera?"

"I like giving people tips and tricks to make their cooking time easier." He gave a throaty laugh that weaseled its way inside her. "Like recommending a really good package mix for béarnaise sauce. It's a pain in the ass to make, and the package mix tastes just as good. When I first did that, the producers were shocked I didn't make everything from scratch."

She gave him a sideways glance with a little smile. "Oh, so you take shortcuts."

God, he'd always had the biggest, most beautiful laugh. "If I can't make it any better than something I can buy, you're damned right I use a shortcut."

She snorted, pretending she was aghast. "Don't tell me you use precut vegetables," she drawled.

He waved a hand. "I have to draw the line somewhere. Precut can be dried out and flavorless. I'm not afraid of telling my viewers that."

"I see the cooking show and the cookbooks are doing amazingly well." He was always number one in the online bookstores. Not that she'd looked for him specifically.

"I always enjoyed when you and I sliced our vegetables together." His voice dropped to a sexy note, sending a shiver running through her.

She couldn't let that happen. "You're going off topic here," she singsonged.

"I'm still answering the question about packaged versus fresh." Humor laced his voice.

But she had to push past it. "You've done catering for the rich and famous, extravagant billionaire parties, fancy resort celebrations, cruise ship festivities." His events were so impressive they were written up in magazines. At least, that's what Dane had told her. She might have seen a few articles when she was leafing through the magazines at the dentist.

"Yeah. Like Gideon Jones's New Year's Eve fundraising gala at Dane's Napa resort."

When Dane had told her Ransom was catering the gala, Ava had almost backed out. But the whole family was there, and they'd needed to support the Mavericks. Gideon's charity, Lean on Us, for veterans as well as foster kids, was a good cause, and she'd donated. But she'd steered clear of the kitchens. And when she'd seen Ransom across the ballroom talking to Dane, she'd made sure to stay on the opposite side.

"So you know the Mavericks," she said casually, hoping her voice hadn't gone too high.

She picked up his nod in her peripheral vision. "The Mavericks are great. They invested in my restaurants and helped me open the first three in Vegas."

She raised her eyebrows as if she didn't know. It was uncanny how much she actually did know, as if she'd been following him on social media. "You opened three restaurants at once?"

"We figured it was a great marketing strategy. Different restaurant styles. A Brazilian chophouse. Something slightly lower-end that anyone can afford. Then a high-end dining experience on top of a casino."

"Obviously, the strategy worked."

He chuckled. "Big-time. The Mavericks are savvy businessmen. I wouldn't have attempted it on my own, but we keyed off the cooking competitions I'd done and some of the better-known events I'd catered. But with the lower end, we were also saying you didn't have to be a billionaire to dine at a Ransom Yates restaurant. Since I had all the contacts overseas, once the Vegas restaurants took off, things seemed to go viral. Now I've opened a restaurant in every major city." He paused, and she sensed he was looking at her. But she didn't turn. She just kept smiling. And driving.

She couldn't avoid walking by his San Francisco restaurant—it was right there downtown—but she'd never gone in, had never even felt the urge.

A voice inside whispered, *Liar, liar, pants on fire.*

Not wanting to even acknowledge that naughty voice, she said, "So you've spread out internationally. Restaurants in London, Paris, Berlin, Oslo."

"We've hit all the capitals of Europe. But they're not all high-end. I don't want only the very rich to taste my food."

Just like his mom and dad's burger and milkshake joint back in the Midwest. She knew his history. That's where he'd caught the cooking bug and the desire to be a restaurateur. He'd come out to San Francisco only because his grandmother was living in a care home. After marrying her second husband, she'd moved to the Bay Area, and Ransom had visited often.

When he'd become the huge success he was, he could have pulled up stakes and gone anywhere. But obviously, he'd loved the area and stayed.

He certainly hadn't stayed because of Ava.

Chapter Seven

"So now you have world-famous chefs working for you in your restaurants." Ava glanced at him, her eyes sparkling in the brief instant of contact. "Do you still do your own cooking at home?" Then her smile dimmed, as if she realized she'd stepped into personal territory.

Ransom knew she'd been purposely avoiding it. "I even chop vegetables." He smiled to take the bite out of the memory of all the times they'd worked together in the kitchen. It had been one of his greatest joys in their relationship. Almost as much as their lovemaking.

"When I'm not working on the cooking show—"

"—or writing a new cookbook—"

"—I like to fly out to the different restaurants and just take over the kitchen for a night, to keep my hand in."

He still supervised some of the major events himself, like the New Year's Eve gala, especially since Gideon was a Maverick and Dane was organizing. He'd jumped at the chance to cater that event because he'd thought Ava might be there. He'd spotted her glossy red hair across the ballroom, but every time he made his way over, she seemed to disappear.

"Doesn't a world-class chef get ticked off when you take over?"

He laughed. Ava had always made him laugh. When she

wasn't driving him wild with that beautiful body of hers. "Most of them say business booms in the few weeks afterward." He shrugged. "There are a few who resent it, but that type doesn't last long. I don't want prima donnas who run their kitchens like tyrants."

"It's like a test, then," she mused.

"As much as I enjoy it, yes, it's a way of testing how they treat their employees."

He was also known for hiring female chefs in a male-dominated field. As if women hadn't been doing the cooking for millennia. He didn't mention that to Ava. She would say that women didn't need to be given a chance by a man, that they could make it on their own, just the way she had—spectacularly.

"That's kind of admirable," she said, glancing at him. "You don't just walk away from all your employees when you move on to another project."

"The work environment at all my restaurants is important to me." He was gratified that she approved of what he'd done. Not because he needed approval in general, but because he wanted hers.

They chatted about his career, and with each topic, he thought, *That happened before you left me.* Or, *That came after you were gone.* The discussion made him think of how it all started for him, too, in his family's mom-and-pop restaurant back home in Milwaukee. People referred to places like theirs as a *greasy spoon*, although his mother had kept everything spotlessly clean. But his parents were always working, and they had him and his brother working there too.

In fact, his father had worked himself to death, dying of a heart attack when he was only in his fifties.

Ransom had already struck out on his own by then. He'd

worked as a caterer, been on cooking competition shows, worked cruise ships as a chef. He'd been a personal chef and created menus for resorts. He'd already been thinking about a cookbook too.

When his father died, his mom wanted him and his brother to take over the restaurant. But there was no way Ransom could go back. He'd been twenty-four, and Milwaukee just wasn't in his life plan.

His mother had stopped speaking to him, and it was only when she became ill with cancer that she finally forgave him. But even in those last few weeks he had with her, he'd still felt the pain of her rejection. He felt it even now, but at least he'd repaired his relationship with his brother, Adam, who'd taken over the family restaurant.

He sensed his maudlin thoughts bringing down the atmosphere in the car. He didn't want to waste his time with Ava ruminating about the bad parts of his past. He wanted to remember the short year they'd had together. How good it had been.

And not for the first time, he wondered what his life would have been like if she hadn't left him.

⋆ ⋆ ⋆

His story was amazing. Some of it she'd known, a lot she hadn't. But sitting in the car with him, even as she tried to concentrate on her driving, Ava felt overwhelmed—by his scent, his body heat, his masculine presence. She hadn't realized it would be like this.

She could only breathe normally again once they pulled into the parking lot of her San Juan Bautista senior living complex, and she could finally step out of the car.

The care home had different levels, each catering to the needs of her residents—independent living, assisted living, memory care, and a hospital wing with twenty beds. Residents sometimes convalesced there until they could return to their own apartments.

As they walked up the front path, Ransom gave a low whistle. "The landscaping is incredible."

A flush of pleasure washed through her. "I want each of my facilities to feel like a home. There are walking paths throughout the grounds." Along with green lawns and flowering bushes, tubs filled with annuals and big shade trees with benches. "We have two koi ponds the residents love. Last year, the raccoons were catching the fish, so I worked with our landscaper to figure out how to keep the animals away without hurting them. Now we have netting over the ponds that protect the fish, but allow people to enjoy them."

"It's like a five-star resort."

She beamed with pride. "Of course. That's what I do. Dane caters to the younger generation at his resorts, and I get them when they're entering their twilight years."

"But only rich people can afford to come here."

Was that censure in his voice? "We do a lot of fundraising so that even people who can't afford the fees can do so with the generous help of our donors. And," she added, "I learned a lot when I worked at your grandmother's convalescent home. I didn't want my care homes to be like hospitals. I wanted them to be homes. I hire people who show great respect for all my residents." She looked at him squarely. "Which is why I couldn't abide that catering company a moment longer."

"I've always wished I could have moved her somewhere better," Ransom said with a wistful note in his tone.

Ava waved off his guilt. "You did the most important thing by visiting her often." Ava had looked forward to every visit, too, always making sure she was the one attending his grandmother. "I try very hard to encourage family visits. That's one of the reasons for our amazing Sunday brunch. I'm always pleased to have so many families coming to visit. That's very important to me."

"I'll look over the brunch menus again, keeping that in mind—enticing the families," he said, as if making a mental note.

"Shall we go in?" she asked, trying to dispel the memories that talk of his grandmother brought on.

"Of course." Ransom held open one of the big double doors.

Inside, her lobby was sumptuous, if she did say so herself. Plush wall-to-wall salmon-colored carpeting in a pattern of fish and water lilies covered the floor. There were no throw rugs anywhere, since they created a trip hazard. A pretty crystal chandelier hung from the ceiling, and paintings on the walls reflected the water motif in the carpet. The chairs and couches were a soft leather, and the reception desk was made of blond oak rather than plasterboard.

Ava smiled at Judy, their receptionist. The woman waved, obviously on the phone. Through an archway, a mailroom housed the individual mail cubbies.

Ransom took it all in. "Very impressive."

"Everyone deserves to be surrounded by beauty." No sterile linoleum halls or gray walls here.

In the wide hallway beyond Reception that led to the dining room and lounge, Ava spied a woman struggling to put on her cardigan. Walking swiftly toward her, Ava touched her shoulder. "Mrs. Hansen, can I help you with that?"

"Oh my dear, I should've put it on before I left my apartment." She allowed Ava to help her slip a hand through a sleeve, one after the other, while she held on to her walker.

Ava patted down the ruffled collar. "You're all set," she said with a smile.

The lady took her hand. "Thank you so much, my dear."

Many of her residents didn't use Ava's name. She never asked whether it was because they didn't remember it, or because *dear* was simply how they addressed someone lovingly.

Ransom stood right behind Ava. "That's a lovely cardigan."

Mrs. Hansen beamed, and Ava was glad he knew how to treat an older woman. He'd always taken such good care of his grandmother.

The lunch hour was just ending, and the vestibule between the dining room and lounge was filling up with residents. She greeted several, smiled at others. She knew all their names. That was important to her, knowing who they were. She did that for the five facilities in the Bay Area, though it was much harder to do when she visited her care homes in other regions.

With Ransom in tow, she spied Mrs. Greeley.

Her heart seemed to bubble over with grief, and taking Mrs. Greeley's hand in hers, she asked, "How are you doing? I know you were upset when I was here the other day. I hope everything is better now."

Mrs. Greeley raised sparse gray eyebrows almost to her hairline. "I was upset?"

All Ava's grief for this lovely woman melted away. "Never you mind. I'm just glad to see you're doing so well."

Mrs. Greeley's smile spread across her face, wrinkled with love and laughter and years of a good life. Then the woman turned her walker. "It's so good to see you, dear. But I must run, or I'll miss armchair volleyball in the auditorium."

Ava patted her shoulder. "You mustn't miss that." When the little lady was gone, Ava said to Ransom, "I'm so glad she doesn't remember that horrible incident. She's the woman I told you about. The reason I fired the caterer."

"Then I'm doubly glad she remembers armchair volleyball."

Ava gazed fondly after the woman's retreating figure. "We provide lots of activities, yoga, and exercise classes to help everyone keep in shape. There's also bingo and bridge and other card games. Plus, we have guests come in for concerts and lectures on various topics." She couldn't help putting her hand on his arm. "We also have some marvelous musicians and knowledgeable people right here. Some of our events are put on by our very own, which everyone loves."

"It's great you provide so many things to keep people's minds active as well as their bodies."

She nodded. "We even have shopping trips into town and to the outlet mall."

When he said, "I'm impressed," she felt herself glow with his praise.

After trying so hard to please her parents—and never feeling like she had—she'd eventually taught herself not to need people to notice her accomplishments. Though her brothers and sister complimented each other as a matter of course, it was different with Ransom. It was like being that young girl again who'd suddenly made her parents notice her. Like the twenty-one-year-old woman who'd wanted always to please Ransom.

But she wasn't that young woman anymore, and she couldn't let herself get carried away by his praise. She couldn't *need* it. "Would you like to see the dining room and kitchen now, since that's what we're here for?"

Ransom gave a flourish of the hand. "Please, lead on."

The same plush salmon carpet led into the dining room. Tables for two sat along either side, one looking out over the rose garden patio that so many of the residents loved, the other overlooking the green lawn of the quad and the steps and wheelchair ramp up to the auditorium beyond it.

The rest of the tables in the room were set up in groups of four or six. Many were already being cleared and laid for dinner as lunchtime wound down.

A woman still seated at a table waved at her, and Ava waved back. "I'll just be a minute. I need to say hello to Edith. Take a look around, then we'll tour the kitchen."

But Ransom followed her, even as he seemed to catalog the setup, while Ava took one of Edith's hands in both of hers. "You look amazing, as always." But Edith's mouth drooped into a frown. "What's wrong?"

Edith pulled from Ava's grasp and held out both hands. "My nails are atrocious. Can you do them with that pretty pink polish like we did last time?"

Ava didn't hesitate. "Of course, Edith." She turned to Ransom, saying, "I hope you don't mind. It won't take long. You can get a head start checking out the kitchen. You don't need me for that."

"I'll stay with you. I'd rather have your input on the kitchen." Then he smiled at Edith. "And I'd love to get to know this beautiful lady."

Edith beamed at him like a star bright in the sky and clapped her hands. "Oh goody. I always like to have a handsome man nearby."

Ransom did a waiter's bow. "Thank you for the compliment, dear lady."

Edith giggled, completely charmed.

She wasn't the only one.

* * *

Ava waved down a passing server. "Could you get Edith's walker, please?"

The man nodded, rushing off to do her bidding. Obviously, he was part of the new group she'd hired for the next two weeks.

He returned promptly with the walker, which, Ransom realized, had been stored outside to avoid crowding the dining room. Ava took over, situating the walker in front of Edith and taking her arm to help her grab the handles.

It wasn't only the complex that impressed him. It was Ava herself. He loved watching her with her people. When they saw her, they simply lit up. She'd reached for each of their hands, smiling, saying hello, knowing all their names. That was extraordinary considering how many facilities she owned. The way she helped Mrs. Hansen with her sweater, her hands careful, her smile caring, had bathed his heart in warmth. Her concern for Mrs. Greeley, the woman who had been abused by the former caterers, was further proof of Ava's heart of gold.

They walked slowly across the vestibule and into the lounge, where Ava strode ahead to pull out a chair. Then, once again, Edith was seated.

"I'll just put your walker over here in the corner," she told the lady.

Edith said, "Oh, thank you, dear."

Two sofas flanked a fireplace in the pleasantly decorated lounge. It was empty now of residents, but several card tables waited for their return, and a grand piano sat in the corner ready for the next recital. The latest bestsellers and DVDs filled two bookcases, and another held puzzles and games. A big-screen TV hung next to the fireplace, probably for a movie night.

With a hand on Edith's shoulder, Ava said, "I'll run to my office and get my nail kit. That pretty pink polish you love is inside." Then she turned to Ransom. "Will you be okay for a few minutes?"

He wanted to laugh. It was as if she'd forgotten all the times he'd visited his grandmother. "Edith and I will be fine." After he waved her off, he sat at the table with Edith. "Your nails are beautiful as they are. But I'm sure Ava will perfect them."

Edith, her silvery curls bouncing, leaned forward to put her hand over his. "She's such a dear. I know she's a busy woman, but she never seems to mind doing my nails."

With a smile, Ransom said, "She's a gem." Edith couldn't know how much he meant it.

"She must have been a manicurist in a past life. She does the most amazing job." Holding up her fingers, bent at the joints, she surveyed her nails. "With these hands," she said, acknowledging her arthritis, "it makes me so happy when my nails are pretty."

They chatted about the weather, about how much Edith had enjoyed lunch, with a description of each dessert she'd had, until Ava returned, setting her nail kit on the table.

Taking the seat beside Edith, Ava angled the chair. "They don't look so bad, Edith. But I'll pretty them all up."

"Thank you, dear." Her eyes shone.

Ava removed the old polish, buffing and filing, while the three of them chatted. Edith enthused about her son's visit the previous Sunday, and how he'd brought all the grandchildren, as well as a couple of great-grandchildren. Ava's smiles and her attention made the woman feel special.

He would make sure those Sunday brunches were the best, now that he'd seen how important they were to Edith and all the lovely people living here.

As Ava began painting Edith's nails, another woman entered the lounge, walking toward them, a cane gripped tight in her hand.

"Oh goody. We're having a nail party." She looked at Ransom, blinking rapidly, which might have been a fluttering of her eyelashes. "Can you do my nails?" The words seemed to tumble out of her.

Before Ava could speak, he said, "I'd love to. Ava has several different polishes. Why don't you pick out your color?"

Ava stared at him, her mouth agape. Ransom smiled inwardly. Oh yeah, he still had some surprises for her. He'd been known to do his niece's nails, and his brother's little girl always loved it. He didn't see the family often enough, so it pleased him to be able to help this sweet lady.

Standing formally, he pulled out a chair. "Let me help you." He hung her cane on the side of the table and helped her to settle. Then he put a hand to his chest. "My name is Ransom."

The lady gave a craggy smile resembling Edith's and beamed at him through blue eyes slightly cloudy with cataracts. "I'm Myrtle," she said. "And I love having my nails done." She chose a bottle of coral polish and held it out to him. "Can you do this one?" The excitement in her voice seemed to shimmy down her arms, making her hand shake as she gave him the bottle.

"Of course." He held her hand in his, squeezing with the lightest pressure.

Ava watched him warily. He could almost see her mind working, probably thinking she'd have to redo his work. But he got busy removing the chipped polish from Myrtle's nails.

"You look familiar," Myrtle said, her gaze on him. "Have you been here before with…?" She waved her hand at Ava.

"No." He smiled. "I've never been here."

"You might have seen him on TV," Ava said. "Ransom has a cooking show. *Recipes from Ransom.*"

So she knew the name of his show.

Edith and Myrtle gasped at the same time. "Oh my," Edith said, her cheeks turning pink. "You're the hottie who makes all those delicious meals."

Ransom laughed. "Thank you very much. I'm glad the meals I cook look delicious."

Ava looked at him and mouthed, *Hottie?*

He raised a brow. And wondered if she still thought he was a hottie after all these years.

The ladies asked him all manner of questions, not letting him answer one before they asked another. The two dears did most of the talking, as if they were starved for conversation with someone younger than they were, someone perhaps who reminded them of their children or grandchildren.

Ava was putting on Edith's second coat of polish, and he'd just finished buffing Myrtle's nails, when Edith said, "You know, I miss Lochlan terribly. He was such a dear man. And his niece is such a lovely girl. She did my nails, too, while she was here."

He wondered who Lochlan was even as Ava said, "I miss him, too, and I'm so glad I could help him stay here." She put her palm over the back of Edith's hand. "And now, Cammie, his niece, is dating my brother." She actually seemed to beam as brightly as the two ladies.

He knew Cammie, Dane's personal assistant, and he remembered now that her uncle's name had been Lochlan. Ransom had worked with Cammie on many of the projects he and Dane had been involved in. He knew, also, that they were now a couple. Having seen it coming for years, he'd always wondered why it was taking them so long. But at last they were together.

Once again, Ava impressed him. It was as if she were saying to the old lady, "I acknowledge and understand your pain that he's gone, and I feel it myself." She was empathetic, compassionate. Ransom had recognized that in the way she treated his grandmother, but to see her in action here, with these two delightful women, brought it home to him again.

Ava Harrington could be described in one word: *impressive.*

Although there were many more he could use. *Gorgeous. Stunning. Amazing. Sexy. Perfect.*

Chapter Eight

When the manicures were done, Ransom stood to give both ladies a kiss on the cheek. "Be sure to wait ten minutes for your nails to dry completely."

They both solemnly promised, "We will."

As they waved good-bye and exited the lounge, he said to Ava, "So Cammie's uncle lived here." She nodded. And Ransom added, "I'm glad your brother and Cammie finally figured out they were meant for each other."

She leaned slightly into him as she laughed. "It took forever. We all knew they were in love."

Then curiosity made him ask, "You said you helped Lochlan stay here?"

As Ava waved a hand for him to precede her into the dining room and the kitchen beyond, she said, "As I mentioned, I have a fund, a subsidy if you will, to help people stay in my facilities when they can't always afford them. Though Lochlan had sold his home, he lived far longer than the money lasted. I wasn't about to kick him out," she added quickly. "And the fund helped make it possible for him to stay."

He noted the servers clearing tables, removing the buffet pans and returning them to the kitchen. But it was Ava who held his attention. "Then you really did mean that your care homes aren't just for the rich."

"I help wherever I can." She moved past him quickly, heading for the kitchen, almost as if she was embarrassed by his praise.

When he caught up with her, just before the swinging doors to the kitchen, she turned to him, changing the subject. "So where did you learn to do nails?"

He didn't want anything from the past dipping into the present right now. He wanted Ava to see who he was, in this moment, not who he'd been. And not the way he'd failed her.

But still he smiled as he answered, "My niece is eleven now, and she's a sweetheart. But even when she was a little girl, she wanted me to do her nails. You remember I have a younger brother? Adam?"

"I remember. Your grandmother talked about him." It seemed as if she might touch his hand, but then she stopped the movement. "I still miss her a lot."

His grandmother had passed while he and Ava were together. "I miss her too."

After Grandma died, he traveled even more. And he still harbored some resentment that his mother had never come out to see the old lady. It was just another reminder that his dad had never left the restaurant. After he'd passed, his mother had done the same thing, forcing his brother into the identical situation.

Perhaps all of those emotions roiling inside him had something to do with why he'd made that offer to Ava. He hadn't wanted to leave her behind so much. But he hadn't considered the fairness of it, thinking only that he wanted to keep her close, that he hated the time they were apart.

And now he wanted to know so much more about her life. To know the real Ava all over again. "So how did *you* get so good at doing nails?" It was incredible that she, head of the company, found the time. But that was Ava.

"I used to do the old ladies' nails at the convalescent home. They might have gnarled, arthritic fingers, but they feel so much better with pretty nails." Which was what Edith had said. Then she added, "Your grandmother always had the prettiest nails. That's actually what gave me the idea. I don't know who did them for her."

He felt a flush rise to his cheeks. "I did."

She gaped at him again, just as she had in the lounge. "You're joking."

"No. She loved that. But then you took over from me, and you could do them more often. So I let you."

His grandmother had loved the attention Ava lavished on her. Her compassion was one of the first qualities Ransom had noticed. "She always said that of all the aides at the home, you treated her the best."

A slight frown turned down her lips. "Not many of the aides even talked to the patients. They were so busy getting work done, thinking that was more important. And it *was* important, but the old people who lived there were even more in need of companionship. I guess a lot of the staff thought everyone was senile and talking to them wouldn't make any difference. But I loved hearing their stories and seeing them smile."

"And that's why you went into this line of work."

She nodded. "Absolutely."

"That's why you know all their names, why you greet each one of them, why you take the time to talk to them and do their nails."

It was her turn to blush. "Of course I can't do it for all of them, but there's a special few who really love it. It doesn't take much of my time to be kind."

It probably took a lot more time than she'd admit, but because she loved it, she had to do it.

"I'm curious. Some you call Mr. and Mrs. Others you use their first names."

She shrugged. "They're from a bygone age where formality was valued. I listen to the way they introduce themselves to me, and that's what I use. Mrs. Greeley prefers the formal address, but Edith and Myrtle never even mentioned their last names."

She was observant, and details were important to her.

He thought back to all the times he'd seen her with his grandmother, before they got together, before he fell for her, before he'd even kissed her.

And now she was the amazing, beautiful, competent woman he'd always known she was. Everything about her facilities demonstrated her compassion as well as her proficiency.

She straightened her suit jacket and pointed to the kitchen door. "I should get on with your tour since we've spent so much time already. I'll let you lead, since this will be your domain."

The kitchen wasn't the worst, but it was cramped. He was sure he could improve the flow. "It's a big help to see the space my team members will have to work with. But ideally, I need to bring the kitchens up to my standards. Is that a problem?"

She shook her head. "Do what you need to do and send me the bill."

"It won't hold up getting my people in here. We'll work with what we've got for now."

And renovations would guarantee more time with her.

* * *

Speaking of more time, a massive traffic jam snarled the route home. The car moved one length every five minutes.

Ransom checked the cause on his phone. "Looks like it's a possible hazardous materials spill. The freeway is completely closed."

Gripping the wheel a little too tightly, Ava asked, "Can you see if there's a way around it?"

He opened his maps app, but slow-moving traffic crammed every alternative. "Everyone else has the same idea. All the side roads are blocked. Even picking the best one, it's going to take us more than four hours to get back."

Rush hour wasn't that far off, when things would only get worse.

But Ransom had a brilliant idea. "Let's pull off at the next exit and get something to eat. Maybe it will clear by the time we're done."

"We were too late for lunch in the dining room." Ava dropped her hand to her stomach. "And I am getting hungry."

They crept along another fifteen minutes to the next exit, where he spied the sign for a burger joint. "How about there?"

"At least it's close."

Other than visiting one of his brother's restaurants, Ransom hadn't been to a real burger joint in years. His mouth actually watered for the taste of a juicy burger. It took another fifteen minutes to be seated, since they weren't the only ones pulling off the freeway.

Though Ransom wasn't used to waiting at a restaurant, mostly because he went to his own, he enjoyed the extra time with Ava. The traffic jam might not be such a bad thing.

The place had the feel of an old mom-and-pop restaurant like his parents', with a checkerboard floor and red vinyl booths, a long countertop with swivel chairs, and an old-fashioned soda fountain. Pictures of vintage cars crowded the walls next to autographed photos of ballplayers.

Once they were seated and had ordered burgers and fries, Ava asked, "So tell me, is this anything like your parents' restaurant?"

"A bit. But my brother has made some great improvements, as well as opening several other locations in Milwaukee. Adam is doing really well."

When their food arrived, his first taste of the burger made him want to roll his eyes in pleasure. "This is a great reminder that you don't always have to dine at five-star restaurants to really enjoy a meal. This burger is tasty."

Ava dipped a fry in ketchup, held it up. "And this is an excellent French fry."

As they ate, she said, "I'm really glad to know that you've patched things up with your brother." She looked down, swallowing a bite of burger before adding, "I never did understand what happened."

He hadn't wanted to talk about it. It hurt too much. But it was long past time to share that story the way he should have years ago. "You know Adam and I worked at the restaurant from when we were pretty young."

"Your grandmother told me how you bussed tables when you were seven years old," she said with a smile.

"And I was working the grill by the time I was fifteen."

"I knew restaurateuring was in your blood."

"Yes." After enjoying another big bite of his burger, he said, "But our parents were totally resistant to change. If I suggested a new menu item, they turned it down, saying that everyone wanted exactly what they'd been making for years. If I said we should start catering, they said they didn't have the equipment or the manpower. If I wanted to give the menu a new look, keeping all the same choices, they said people didn't like change and wouldn't be able to find their favorites. But it was really my parents who were afraid of change."

He remembered the fights, how tired he'd been of beating his head against their inertia. "So eventually I struck out on my own. But my brother, he stayed. Adam wasn't as bothered by their ways as I was."

"You mean he was less ambitious?" she asked.

He thought the question might be painful because it was his ambition that had eventually ruined his relationship with Ava. Maybe the thought was in her mind too. But he answered honestly. "He's got plenty of ambition. But maybe he's just got more patience. He waited until he could make the changes he wanted. Like I said, what he's done with the old place is amazing. He still serves milkshakes and burgers like our parents did, but everyone comes now for all the unusual stuff he's created. Like a pistachio milkshake or a Kahlua milkshake or a Cap'n Crunch milkshake with the cereal all crunched up. The kids love it. And he's got a million different burger variations."

She smiled. "That's probably a bit of an exaggeration."

Ransom smiled right back. "Probably. But Adam's got stuff like a Maui burger with pineapple and teriyaki sauce. A nachos burger. He's even got a limburger made with Limburger cheese that he advertises as the stinkiest burger on the planet. And he'll make a burger any way you want it too. He's doing great with all his restaurants."

"You sound very proud of him."

His chest seemed to swell with his pride. "I am. And I think he's proud of me too."

"Then you fell out with your parents because you wanted to make changes and they didn't?"

He shook his head, dipping a couple of fries into yellow mustard rather than ketchup. "No. I still talked to my parents even though I was doing my own thing. It was when my dad died. I was twenty-four, Adam a couple of years younger, and Mom wanted us to take over the restaurant. But I refused. When I said I didn't want to be like my dad, she thought I was saying I didn't want to be a failure. But that was just her perception. I never thought he was a failure. I just thought he was stubborn when he couldn't open up to new ideas. He wasn't going to change or expand, and I believe that really hampered him. And yeah, I couldn't see myself being a big success owning a little restaurant." He stared at his plate, his appetite for the burger gone for the moment. "He worked himself to death." After a beat of silence, he added, "That's when my mother stopped talking to me. She just cut me out." It still felt like she'd sliced his heart in two.

"I'm so sorry. I didn't realize."

He laughed, even though it hurt his throat. "You probably thought it was because I was an arrogant ass, and I walked out on them."

"Of course not." But he saw by the shadowed look in her eyes that she *had* actually believed it was his fault. He should have told her years ago. But he was telling her now.

"It was only when she got cancer that she relented. And even then, it was Adam who told me she was sick."

"That must've hurt a lot." Ava's gentle voice soothed him.

"Yeah, it did," he admitted. "But Mom and I reconciled before the end. She died knowing that I loved her, and I believe she loved me. And I never mentioned that I didn't want to be like my father, who worked himself to death."

Ransom worked hard, yes, but he worked for something big.

He wouldn't die of a heart attack in a greasy spoon that hadn't changed in fifty years. That didn't make his father a failure, but Ransom wanted to be open to new ideas, new ways of doing things.

That was why he needed to cater for Ava. Because it could be good for both of them.

* * *

Though it hurt Ava that he'd never shared the details of what had happened in his family, what he told her now helped her understand him better. She'd always viewed his attitude as meaning that success was more important than family—more important than her. But knowing it was his mother who had cut him off gave her a different perspective. He hadn't been trying to leave his family behind. He'd just wanted to pursue his own path.

She understood more about why success was so important to him. He wanted to change things, but his parents hadn't let him. He wanted to expand, and his parents had held him back. He had dreams, but they hadn't supported him—not out of malice, but out of a fear of change. How many times over the millennia had children wanted to blaze their own trail while parents wanted them to follow the path they'd chosen for them? It was a story as old as time.

A story different from hers, but maybe the emotions were the same. Always needing to be the best.

She was glad to know Ransom hadn't caused the rift, that he'd reconciled with his mother before it was too late, and that he was part of his brother's family. Because she valued family. Though he might still be following in his father's footsteps, overworking the way his father had. But then, she understood hard work.

Ransom licked French fry salt off his fingers. "This place is actually pretty damn good. I need to tell Adam about it." His eyes twinkled. "He might get some good ideas."

With a bite of burger, she felt secret sauce dripping down her fingers and grabbed a napkin to clean it off. "What do you think is in the secret sauce? Since you're the chef and you know all your flavors."

He lifted a bit of bun. "It's definitely got relish and mayo in it. And maybe some gochujang sauce. Or sriracha. It's sweet but spicy."

She furrowed her brow. "Does that stuff go together?"

He looked at her, aghast. "Of course it does. Nothing conflicts in my recipes." Then he pointed. "You missed a little bit of sauce right there."

She touched the side of her mouth. "Here?"

He shook his head. "No. Over there." He wiggled his finger, but she still couldn't tell exactly where he pointed.

She tried the other side of her mouth. "Here?"

He just laughed. "You're miles off." Then he leaned over the table to swipe away the sauce with a fingertip.

Ava gasped at the electricity suddenly pumping through her body. The first touch in fifteen years. They hadn't even shaken hands. And now her entire body sizzled. She tried shoveling a few more fries in her mouth just to bring down her temperature. But the way he watched her eat only heated her even more. She couldn't talk straight. She certainly couldn't think straight. She downed half a glass of water, trying to quench the fire inside her.

She was *not* supposed to feel this way about Ransom Yates. Not now. Not ever again.

And yet, that fire burning inside her just wouldn't be quenched.

She needed to get out of here. "How's the traffic doing?"

Ransom looked at the map on his phone. "It's still showing four hours to go on all the alternate routes."

"But it was four hours an hour ago."

He simply shrugged.

Outside, the traffic continued its excruciating car-length movements. They wouldn't even make it back onto the freeway. She looked at him. Though still handsome as ever, his gaze was a little bleary. After working all night on her plans, he was running on one hour of sofa sleep.

Obviously thinking the same thing, he asked, "Should we find a hotel?" His eyes crinkled with a smile. "Separate rooms, of course."

"I'm certainly not looking forward to pumping the clutch for another four hours." Then she added quickly, before she could think better of it, "Let's do it."

But a night with Ransom? Even if they were in separate rooms?

Her blood heated once more in her veins. It would be way too easy to knock on his door.

"Even if there's a Ritz-Carlton nearby," Ransom said, crumpling his napkin, "we'd never make it there on these roads." He looked pointedly at the Motel Y next door, with a pass-through from the burger joint so they wouldn't have to get on the road to pull into its parking lot.

Back straight, Ava said indignantly, "I don't need a Ritz. I'm perfectly fine with Motel Y." But she couldn't help adding, "As long as it's clean."

She wasn't a snob. At least, she didn't think so. If it was clean, she'd be fine.

As long as she didn't rush down the hall to Ransom's room.

Chapter Nine

"I'm down with clean," Ransom said.

Ava's eyes narrowed slightly. "First, I need a toothbrush and a change of clothes."

"I'm down with that too." He was down with anything she wanted.

With his chin, he indicated the Supermart department store right across the street, with a crosswalk straight there from Motel Y.

Since they planned on checking in, Ava moved the Pantera into the motel's parking lot, then they walked over to the store.

"Wow," Ava exclaimed as they entered the sliding doors. The amount of stuff was overwhelming—anything you could possibly want.

She grabbed his arm, and he was sure she didn't even notice what she'd done. "Oh my God, will you look at all the chocolate."

An entire aisle of it. Peppermint patties. Chocolate-covered caramels. Malted milk balls. Dark chocolate, milk chocolate, white chocolate. Truffles. Peanut butter cups.

He loved the feel of her skin against his, just as he'd loved the smoothness of her cheek in the restaurant as he'd cleaned off the little bit of secret sauce. Damn, but he'd wanted to lick it off. Yet he'd maintained control even as he burned, just the way he was going up in flames right now.

Keeping the smile off his face, he said sternly, "Keep away from the chocolate."

Ava laughed. God, her laugh. What it did to him.

He dragged her away from the chocolate aisle, moving on until they found toothbrushes and toothpaste and other sundries.

She stopped abruptly in front of shelves crammed with colored bags and bottles. "Look at all these different scents of Epsom salts." She looked at him, her beautiful eyes wide. "Do you think Motel Y has bathtubs in any of the rooms?"

"We can ask for one."

"All right then." She grabbed a bag. "I want to try these rose-scented salts."

She'd always loved her baths. He could see her there now. Naked. Bubbles up to her neck, sweet scents permeating the air.

He actually had to shake himself to dispel the seductive image.

She'd already sent him back for a cart, and now she plunked the bag of Epsom salts into it. "Okay, we need clothes."

She picked out way more than one change of clothing, making him turn his back when she chose panties.

Despite that, he couldn't help looking at the lacy confection, imagining her in it.

He delighted in how she went overboard. She probably hadn't shopped like this in years. The boutiques she'd frequent would bring out models to display whatever she was interested in. But now, she was so like the girl he'd loved all those years ago. He loved seeing that girl in the woman now.

After she'd helped him pick out clothes, they headed to the snack and drink aisle. Even there, Ava went overboard.

"This place is awesome." She beamed at him. "Let's get some

Cheetos and some gummy worms and some Oreos. We need snacks."

She was already putting them in the cart. Had she ever splurged on calories like this before in her life? Then she added cans of alcohol-laced iced tea to the overcrowded cart. This was going to be some night.

Looking at him, one eyebrow raised, she said with a huge smile, "All of this can be our dessert."

In the end, they had an embarrassing number of bags to lug back, but Ransom didn't care. He loved how enthusiastic she was.

They entered the motel lobby with their haul. "This is surprisingly nice," she said.

The reception station was empty for the moment, and Ransom let his gaze wander over the lobby. The carpet looked new, the walls freshly painted a pastel blue. The furniture—two couches and six chairs—could even have been quite comfortable, the blue plaid fabric matching the carpet.

The clerk, a tall, lanky, bespectacled young man, stepped out of the doorway behind the desk, and Ava headed that way. He was somewhere in his twenties, so this was probably his part-time job while going to university. Before she could even get a word out, he said, "Okay, a room for two. We have a few kings still available."

Ava opened her mouth to interrupt, but the guy went on, "You're really lucky. We're filling up fast with that mess out on the freeway." He waved a hand at the offending traffic jam.

"No, no, we need two—" Ava started, trying to get a word in edgewise.

The kid was already tapping keys. "Okay, a room with two beds."

Ava huffed out a breath. "No, two separate rooms." She enunciated each word distinctly, then flashed a look at Ransom that said, *Help me out here.*

It was like Abbott and Costello doing *Who's on First?* But she was perfectly capable of taking care of the problem, and Ransom said nothing. Maybe there was even a part of him that hoped there would be too many freeway refugees, leaving them only one room.

After a long, almost lingering look between them, the clerk finally said, "Oh. Two rooms." He cocked his head. "That sounds weird. I thought for sure you guys were a couple. I'm usually never wrong." He punctuated this personal remark with a firm shake of his head.

Ava was just as firm. "No, we are *not*—" She hit the word hard. "—a couple."

They gathered up everything, the lanky kid looking at the plastic bags in their hands. He called, "You need reusable bags. We have them for sale here."

Ava looked back at him, holding up her arm with two bags slung over it. "We can reuse these, thank you very much."

When they were out of earshot, Ransom asked, "Did you ask for a room with a bathtub so you can use your new Epsom salts?"

She huffed out a breath, stabbing the elevator button. "You must be joking. He would have changed everything again and given us one room because it was the only one with a tub."

And that, Ransom thought, wouldn't have been a bad idea at all. In fact, he would have very much enjoyed imagining her in the tub.

* * *

As she stepped into the elevator when it arrived, her cheeks were hot and her blood was up. "How could he think we're a couple?"

Ransom's mouth curved in what might have been a smile, as though the situation hadn't bothered him at all. Of course, he hadn't tried to help either. "Why wouldn't he think so?" he asked mildly.

Ava fumbled a bit. "Well, because..." And really, there was no answer to that.

Of course, Ransom pushed. "Because why?"

She pursed her lips, "You know why."

It was the same circular conversation she'd had downstairs with the clerk. And Ransom continued it. "No, I really don't."

She sputtered out a breath before saying, "Do I really need to refresh your memory?"

Abruptly, Ransom turned serious, all the humor draining from his face. "I don't need you to explain." He held her gaze, his eyes dark with something she was afraid to analyze. "I know you left me because I was a complete jerk."

The confession left her speechless until the elevator arrived on their floor and he stepped out. He was actually admitting he'd screwed her over? She couldn't let acknowledgment of this moment go by. "Yeah, you were."

She counted down the room numbers until they reached hers. Before he could stop her, she flashed her card key in front of the lock and opened the door. With a curt, "Good night," she closed it behind her.

Only then did she sag against the door, having left that very important conversation hanging.

She didn't want to address it. This was a business deal between them. She didn't want any other kind of relationship. She didn't want to take blame or cast blame or even accept that he was taking the blame.

Finally pushing off the door, she walked to the bed and dumped all her Supermart bags on it.

And then she turned.

Ransom stood in the doorway of the connecting room, his hands braced on the doorjamb as he leaned in slightly. The darned clerk *still* hadn't gotten it right.

Ransom said softly, in a voice that made all her nerve endings tingle, "We weren't done with our discussion."

Hand on the doorknob, she said, "Yes, we were."

Then she closed the door in his face, hoping he'd stepped back before it hit him, and locked it with a resounding *click*.

* * *

Ransom stared at the closed door. He'd stepped back just in time to avoid having his nose smashed.

"She closed the door on me again," he lamented metaphorically as well as literally. Obviously, she wasn't ready to hear what he had to say.

Stretching out on the bed, staring at the ceiling for long minutes that might have turned into an hour, he thought he heard water running next door.

Damn. She had a bathtub. She was taking a damned bath. In sweet-smelling bath salts.

He slept like crap, his mind turning everything over and over, not just what he'd admitted—that he had been a complete jerk—but that bath. And the connecting door. He didn't have to go outside to get to her room. He could just knock on that door.

Of course she wouldn't open it.

And it wasn't just the conversation he wanted to continue. He wanted to look at her. He wanted to close his eyes and breathe her in. Wanted to put his hands on her. Taste her.

It was time for a cold shower if he was to get any shut-eye at all. He needed a big bucket of cold water to tamp down all his thoughts.

He stayed under the cold spray until his teeth chattered.

Back in bed, though, he found the cold shower hadn't done its job. He was still thinking of pounding on that connecting door. And if she opened it…

⋆ ⋆ ⋆

Dammit, she hadn't gotten a wink of sleep. That connecting door kept calling to her.

Ava had taken a bath, because thank goodness there was more than a shower in the room even without asking the clerk for it. She'd popped a can of the iced tea and opened the bag of Oreos, allowing herself two. Okay, three. She'd thought a bath would help relax her, even make her sleepy. But then she remembered other baths, ones she'd taken with Ransom, and what happened.

She should have taken a cold shower instead.

Darn that clerk. She would have been so much better off if they'd had rooms on either end of the corridor, far, far away from each other. As it was, she couldn't stop thinking about Ransom, couldn't stop thinking about what he'd admitted. Couldn't stop thinking about his hard body and his too-kissable lips.

But she had to remember how badly she and Ransom had failed the last time. Just as she'd told Gabby, she and Ransom sucked at the love game. Dane and Cammie could make it. The Mavericks and their ladies could. But she and Ransom hadn't made it work before, and they wouldn't be any better at it now. He was still married to his career, and hers was of the utmost importance to her. If anything, the gulf between them was wider. And she had no intention of having a casual affair. At least not with Ransom. Because there would never, ever be anything casual about an affair with him.

She must have slept in the end, because she woke to the last vestiges of a naughty dream about him, his hands all over her, his mouth doing things, his body taking her to places she hadn't been in far too long.

Throwing aside the covers to dispel the sexy images, Ava jumped out of bed.

Her Supermart bags were strewn across the floor, and she knelt to rummage. The only clothing at Supermart was end-of-season summer wear. They weren't stocking the winter stuff yet, and Ava had bought a thin, spaghetti-strap dress. She couldn't pair it with her high heels, so she'd found cute white tennis shoes with multicolored glitter all over them and huge wedges. They might have been only fifteen dollars, but she loved them, even more than her thousand-dollar Jimmy Choos.

When she was dressed, she shoved her suit into the empty bag, not caring about the wrinkles. It would have to be dry cleaned anyway. She didn't bother to bring all the snacks and drinks they hadn't shared—and that irritated her too—then left her room, intending to knock on his door.

Ransom was already waiting for her, wearing a Hawaiian shirt, board shorts, and flip-flops. Together, they could have been mistaken for a couple heading off for a Hawaiian vacation.

Ava couldn't help laughing. "What, are we going on vacation instead of getting to work?"

His gaze seemed to heat up the hallway. A tickle of something—she hoped it wasn't desire—shimmied down her spine as he said, "We could. Right now. Just take off on the next flight to the islands."

She barely managed to stammer, "I was joking."

But God, how she wished he'd stop saying things like that, like how he understood why she'd left him because he'd been a jerk or how they could fly to Hawaii or the Bahamas or anywhere. Together.

He couldn't possibly mean any of it. But the thought that he might messed with her insides.

Especially since she hadn't slept much last night. And she'd awakened from that very explicit dream. But a casual affair with Ransom was out of the question. They had too much history, too many emotions. Even casual would spell disaster for her heart.

Turning, she tromped along the hallway to the elevators, both of them silent for the entire ride down.

The same young guy manned the desk. Ava marched right up to him, ready to take him to task for giving them connecting rooms with an open door.

But once again, he didn't let her get the words out, a grin spreading across his face. "You guys said you weren't together, but look at you now, all ready for vacation. I knew you were just jerking my chain with that separate-room thing." He shook his finger playfully at them, then he gasped. "I get it. You two were playing some kind of sex game, right? Role-playing about being two strangers meeting in a motel room?" Chortling, he slapped the counter. "And the door just happened to be open between those two rooms. I couldn't have planned it better."

The man literally stunned Ava into near speechlessness. All she could do was slide the key cards across the counter. "You've got my credit card on file. Thanks."

Still laughing, he said, "Thanks for all the dreams I had last night."

Oh my God. How totally inappropriate. She wanted to act like a little girl and stick her fingers in her ears so she wouldn't have to listen.

Outside, she looked at Ransom, and he looked at her.

"He wasn't actually talking about wet dreams, was he?" she asked.

Ransom said, "Yeah, I think he actually was."

After one more look at each other, they simultaneously burst into laughter, so hard she had to drop her bags on the ground and cover her mouth. And still she couldn't stop. Leaning over, hands on her knees, she laughed until it hurt.

When she could speak, her words came out in jerks. "I'm not sure—he should be—doing that job."

Ransom snorted out another laugh. "Are you kidding? He's perfect for it."

Ava got into the story. "People probably come back just so he can check them in."

"If you ever have to spend the night while you're visiting your San Juan Bautista facility, you have to come back here. I'm sure he'll remember you. And he'll say something totally inappropriate all over again."

She nodded, another peal of laughter breaking out of her.

Then Ransom said, "But speaking of the hotel room, you charged them both to your credit card. I owe you the money."

All the laughter seemed to die inside her, as if he'd reminded her that this was just a business trip, when she'd wanted to think of it as something else entirely. Even if she'd stomped away from him when he'd said they could take the next flight out.

Her insides were all messed up around him. One minute she was running and well aware of how bad it could all get, and the next wishing they were going on vacation. It was ridiculous. And she could not have a sexy vacation with him. Not even a sexy date. Because he wasn't just any man. He was Ransom, and she'd loved him. Anything, even a kiss, had the potential to destroy her all over again.

So she waved a hand. "It's a business expense. I'm hiring you, therefore I pay for the rooms."

He didn't argue, laughing once more. "You certainly got your money's worth with that guy's act."

They dropped their bags in the Pantera's trunk, which, with the mid-engine setup, was bigger than you'd think. And when she would have climbed into the driver's seat, Ransom took her arm, turning her as he pointed across the parking lot.

"Look," he said softly, his mouth right next to her ear.

It took her only a moment to read the sign. "It's a Pancake House."

His breath whispered across her hair. "I haven't eaten a chocolate chip ten-stack at a Pancake House since..." He stopped, and she knew deep in her belly exactly what he was thinking.

Since the last time with you.

"Me either." Oh God, he was seducing her with memories, and she stiffened her spine to the point where her neck popped. "One, I don't eat like that anymore." Okay, she wouldn't think about the burger and fries they'd had yesterday or the junk food she'd added to the Supermart cart. Thank God she'd left it all behind in the room. "And two, we really don't have time."

He was so close, she could smell the aftershave he'd bought at Supermart. It was enough to make her dizzy.

"One, haven't you heard that breakfast is the most important meal of the day? And two, you know you can't resist all those chocolate chips covered in all that scrumptious syrup. And three, this is exactly the kind of food that chefs eat after a long night at their five-star restaurants."

Before she could protest again, he grabbed her hand and pulled her across the parking lot.

As she stepped over the separating curbs in her high-wedge tennis shoes, the sparkly glitter on them caught the morning sun, making her smile. Shopping at Supermart and staying at Motel Y made her smile. Her sundress and Ransom's flip-flops made her smile. Even the thought of the Pancake House after all these years made her smile.

And most of all, for some terrible reason she couldn't allow herself to think about right now, Ransom made her smile too.

Oh, she really had gone crazy.

The restaurant was only half full, with fifties music playing at just the right level and the scent of frying bacon filling the air. Once they were seated, Ransom angled the menu so she could see and tapped the ten-stack chocolate-chip pancakes. Without a word spoken between them, when the waitress arrived, he ordered the pancakes with an extra plate to share.

Memories of all the times they'd gone to the Pancake House—every Sunday when he was in town—assaulted her. He could have made pancakes back at the apartment, but there was something about the Pancake House, about the vinyl seats and the Formica tabletops and the waitress with the gravelly voice and kind smile. They didn't even have to tell her their order. It was always the ten-stack of chocolate-chip pancakes, and they always shared.

Her mouth watered for them now—all that gooey chocolate, all that yummy syrup. And sharing it with Ransom.

When the stack arrived, they devoured it, practically licking the plate between them. God, the memories it brought back.

They had so many good rituals. Sunday pancakes. Chopping vegetables together for dinner. Curling up on the couch to watch a movie. Taking a hike in one of the nearby parks. Ransom pulling her into the trees where he could kiss her, touch her, excite her. Making love to her the moment they got home.

They'd been good together, at least most of the time. Yes, there'd been little arguments, like how much time they *didn't* have together, things that had probably been pushing them apart long before that huge fight.

But there'd been so many good things as well. And it was those things that were tearing her apart now.

Watching him lick syrup off his fork, she was hot and edgy, remembering exactly how those Sundays went down. Gorge on yummy pancakes, then gorge on hot, crazy-amazing lovemaking. They were sexy, seductive, hot-as-hell pancake Sundays.

Her thoughts made her feel hot and sexy now. Maybe it was the long night of knowing that he was in the next room. Wanting to knock on that door and beg him to touch her. Even if it was a terrible idea.

Ransom waggled a finger at her, just as he had yesterday when she'd worn secret sauce on her face. "You've got syrup and chocolate all over your mouth. Just like a kid."

She put her finger to her lips, then to the side of her mouth, wiping up the last streaks of syrup and chocolate.

Then she let herself go crazy, let all these hot, sexy feelings take over. With her eyes on him, even though she knew better, she very deliberately licked the remnants off her finger. He was getting under her skin, and she wanted to get under his. She wasn't about to go through this alone. She wanted him to feel the same sexiness she did, to have the same memories.

For an endless moment, he seemed paralyzed, his mouth

hanging open, his eyes wide.

All her thoughts and feelings ganged up on her. She was driven by his admission last night that he'd been a total jerk, by knowing he was on the other side of that thin door, by sharing the pancakes this morning. Maybe it was even the young man at the reception desk asking if they'd been playing some sort of sex game.

And Ransom was dumbstruck.

Mildly, she said, "Catching flies?"

When he closed his mouth, when he looked at her, when his dark eyes turned the color of the maple syrup, she owned her terrible mistake. Now he'd think she wanted to rekindle things. Which she didn't. It was just those memories. She'd deliberately opened Pandora's box and let them all fly out.

Even as she tried to back away from what she'd done, Ransom didn't let her. "Do you think I don't remember what our ten-stack of pancakes always led to?"

She steeled herself. "No." Then she added primly, "But it's just business between us now."

God's honest truth, however, was that she'd been thinking about sex since the moment Ransom stepped back into her life. And not just sex with anyone. Sex with *him*. She'd never wanted anyone more.

You could want something badly even though you knew how bad it would be for you.

And now, after she'd done that deliberately provocative thing, she'd be stuck in a car with him for ninety minutes. It would sit between them all the way back to San Francisco.

She had to get things back on track. Straightening her pretty Hawaiian dress—and mentally straightening her spine—she became the consummate businesswoman again. "I'll pay. Like the motel bill, it's a business expense."

Ransom sat back, arms folded over his chest, letting her grab the ticket and march up to the front counter. Even with her back to him, she felt him stewing in the knowledge that she wanted him.

Damn, the man didn't have to say or do anything to get under her skin.

In fact, the less he said, the deeper he seemed to burrow inside her.

Chapter Ten

On the way back to San Francisco, Ransom used the same fallback she had when they'd driven down here yesterday. Christ, was it only yesterday? "Now that I've seen one of your care homes," he said, "I'd like to know how you got started. I know you went to college, got your degree. That you wanted to get into healthcare management for seniors so you could make their last years better. But after that, how did you make it happen?"

Eyes on the road, she shrugged. "I did the same kind of thing as Dane. He worked at a resort, and when the owners wanted out, he bought it. I managed a nursing home after graduation. It wasn't owned by a corporation, just a single facility, but still, there was always someone who said no, I couldn't do this or that. But then they wanted to sell, so I bought the place. It was out in Tracy." Which was a bedroom community half an hour outside the East Bay. "I expanded from there."

He listened, but all he could see in his mind's eye was that staggering moment when she'd licked the syrup off her finger. He replayed it over and over as she drove and told him her story.

Was it a sign that she wanted to try again? Or was she showing him what he'd thrown away so carelessly, showing him what he would never have again?

Because damn, how he'd wanted to reach across that booth in the Pancake House, wrap her up in his arms, drag her back to the motel, get one room with a massive bed.

And make love to her all day and long into the night.

He wasn't sure what she'd do if he pushed it, if he made her admit aloud that she'd deliberately taunted him with that syrup.

That she still wanted him the way he wanted her.

But really, what would that get him? They might come out on the other side with far worse scars. And he did have scars. He hadn't forgotten her, and there had never been anyone else like her. But losing her had hurt, badly, in a way he'd tried not to think about in years.

And now he sensed this contract between them could become something bigger and last longer than he'd originally planned. If it did, then exactly how did he want her to be in his life? As just a business partner? Or something more?

It had to be something more. Far more.

But she didn't feel the same way. She hadn't forgiven him. Maybe she never would.

And he wasn't willing to make another mistake when he'd only just found her again.

* * *

"After you graduated from university, you were able to go directly into management?"

She nodded as if she were looking at him. "It was just lower-level management at first. Then I worked my way up."

She couldn't say why it annoyed her that he'd gone all business. Even though she was *supposed* to want it to be all business. And yet, between watching him sleep on her office sofa, hearing him take that shower in her en suite, visiting the care home, painting the ladies' nails, the fun Supermart shopping trip and the night in Motel Y, things just seemed different. Not to mention sharing the pancakes the way they always had. And that sexy little thing she'd done? Yeah, things had definitely changed.

She didn't want to think about how much they'd changed. Or what that meant.

God, she secretly wished they'd sprinted hand-in-hand from the Pancake House back to Motel Y, paid for another night, and spent the next twenty-four hours in bed.

But damn, she couldn't think like that, could not *allow* herself to. She was torn between wanting… and knowing how badly wanting him could turn out for her. As bad as the last time. Maybe even worse. They were still the same two people, just further along in their careers, and she hadn't seen any indications they'd be better at a relationship.

Suck it up, Ava. Keep it all business, and no more sexy finger-licking moves.

"I wanted to move up quickly." She allowed herself a laugh. "Maybe too quickly for all the higher-ups. But when my boss retired, I lobbied to take her position. And I got it."

She could barely hear his soft, "I'm sure you did."

Was it belief in her? Or was it laced with sarcasm? She decided it was the latter, because that seemed safer. She liked his praise too much, reminding her again of how much she'd wanted to impress her parents and never could. Of how badly she'd wanted to please him, only to find out he regarded her as barely more than a mistress. She shouldn't need Ransom's approval, not anymore.

"I wanted to run things my way, without all the constraints put on me by owners who weren't even on-site. I wanted all my residents to be treated kindly and with respect. It's the number one thing I've instilled in my people."

"That's what you always gave my grandmother. Respect and

caring. And you treated the other patients with equal kindness."

All the time she'd worked at that convalescent home where Ransom's grandmother had lived, she'd dreamed of the day when she could push her coworkers in the right direction, into treating everyone with the respect they deserved.

"I was able to finance buying that first care home, and I worked really hard to make it profitable so I could open another."

"And another," he added softly. "Until you opened them all over the country."

He'd obviously talked to Dane. "Yes. Dane and I have a lot in common in the way we did things." Her smile grew deeper. "Like I said, we're sort of in the same business. He pampers people at his resorts, treats them with respect, then I get them thirty or forty years later. And they still receive that same respect."

"Tell me a bit more about your subsidy program."

She didn't mind talking about it now that he knew. "I help those with less money to stay in the better places." She'd always felt good about that and had started the practice almost right away. "The less expensive facilities are subsidized by the ones that have higher profits, so I can make them all better. And I also take donations to the fund as well. It feels like a win-win for everyone."

"The empire you've created is extraordinary."

She didn't doubt the sincerity in his voice. "I wouldn't call it an empire. Because it's all about my residents."

"I know that."

They sped along the highway, the hazardous spill from yesterday cleared away, the road rolling out before them. It was a perfect time of day, the traffic sparse—at least, as sparse as it could be on Bay Area freeways.

"I've fed people my whole life," Ransom said. "Given them what I thought they wanted in addition to what they asked for. But you've gone so many steps beyond that. You actually care deeply for every single person living in one of your communities." She felt his gaze on her, though she didn't turn his way. "And I don't use that term lightly," he added. "You've made your facilities real homes for these people. You know their names. You paint their nails." His smile came out in his voice.

All she could say was, "Thank you," because her throat was closing up.

He actually respected her. Not only that, he was pretty much saying that her business was better and more worthwhile than his. That was a huge thing for a billionaire like him to admit to anyone—especially to his long-ago ex.

All those years ago, she thought he'd devalued her dreams. And maybe he had back then. But could he be seeing things differently now? She couldn't know for sure, but she felt honored that he seemed to admire her so much.

"Dane tells me you also do some mentoring."

Shocked to know Dane had talked about that, she said, "I'm on the board of a couple of nonprofits that help women get back into the workforce after they're divorced or they're single moms. We also provide help for women in recovery from drug problems or escaping domestic violence." She valued being a role model for these women. "It's hard working in a man's world, but I want them to know it can be done."

For the first time, she wondered if she and Ransom could build a future in which his company and hers were linked in more ways than a short-term contract. There was the potential to use his organization all over the country rather than just the Bay

Area. His menus were amazing, especially with the way he'd brought them together in less than twenty-four hours.

It was on the tip of her tongue to say that very thing. He seemed to be putting his all into this. But it was still early days, and though she felt herself respecting him more as she saw what he was capable of, he was still a world-famous chef. Once he got things rolling, she could see him saying, "So glad I could help you out, great catering for you, but now I need to return to my fabulous famous chef's life."

So really, there was no way she could think long term. They were strictly short term. Just as they'd been the last time he'd flown off to his fabulous famous chef's life and left her behind.

She had to remember that and not allow herself to get sucked into an illusion.

* * *

Ava had accomplished so much—far more than Ransom had ever imagined she could. Underestimating her had been his mistake.

Silence filled the car the rest of the way back, each of them in their own thoughts. He didn't mind. It gave him time to think—about her, about their arrangement, about where he wanted all this to go.

If they were to have something together again, he needed to take it slow now, and bide his time. Rushing her would only push her away.

As they drove into the city, he made a decision. "We need to work on the plans more, now that I've seen everything. Let's go to my office. Everything I need is on my computer there. I'll order some lunch if you're hungry."

She laid her hand on her stomach. "Are you kidding? After those pancakes? Thanks, but no, thanks."

"Good. We can go directly to my office."

"I'll drop you off. I need to change first."

"You look fine just the way you are." In fact, she looked more beautiful than ever in those sexy wedge tennis shoes, her shoulders bare beneath the flirty spaghetti straps of her sundress.

But he knew better than to say that.

"If it was a Saturday, maybe. And your office was completely empty. But it's Friday, and people will be working. No," she insisted. "I'll change. Do you want me to drop you at your flat or the office?"

He actually liked the idea of walking into work in a Hawaiian shirt and board shorts. And it could be extremely hot to have her all buttoned up in one of her sexy business suits while he was Mr. Casual. "The office would be great. I'll meet you there as soon as you can make it."

She drove expertly through the city and dropped him off in front of his building, then roared away in the Pantera, the mirror of his.

And he reflected how they'd mirrored each other in so many ways over the years.

* * *

A part of her had wanted to park and follow Ransom into his office building.

But people would get the wrong idea. Not just that the two of them might be sleeping together, but there were things a man in her executive position could get away with that were completely unacceptable for a woman. She had to dress the part. She was judged on what she wore. She had to be polite at all times. Never allow herself a meltdown. And while Ransom could get away with Hawaiian gear, she needed a business suit, shiny hair, and perfect makeup.

She'd lied to him. Even on a Saturday, she would never have gone into work wearing this outfit. There wasn't a day she went in when she wasn't as perfectly presented as possible. Because if anyone saw her like this, the first thing they'd think was, *We knew a woman couldn't do this job properly.*

She mentored other women and helped them get back into the workforce through the nonprofits she worked with. She was a role model. She had to make them understand how hard it was working in a man's world, while at the same time learning that it was doable.

It was like that Taylor Swift song "The Man," about a woman making her way in a man's world. You were held to a different standard, expected to act a certain way. And when you didn't, they tried to cancel you. Ava wouldn't allow that.

She knew how to handle herself, and she did it by being professional and businesslike. She never yelled. She was never rude. And she held her ground no matter what they threw at her. Just as she had with George Twisselman, that mealy-mouthed president of Consolidated Catering, when he'd tried to whittle down her resolve.

Searching her closet for the perfect outfit, she wanted something that would show her to be the confident businesswoman she was and still wow Ransom all over again. Bending down to pull out a pair of heels, she saw the wedge tennis shoes. The glitter sparkled in the closet's light. And she wanted them. Bad. Wanted the look in Ransom's eyes when he watched her walk in them. Slipping her feet into them, she loved the glittery feeling that seemed to surround her when they were on.

Maybe they actually were a power move.

* * *

Seated behind his desk, Ransom's jaw dropped when she walked in. Though her outfit wasn't one of the power suits she'd worn the last two days, it was no less powerful, no less seductive, hugging her delicious curves, showcasing her gorgeous legs.

And those damn sexy platform tennis shoes shot his temperature into the stratosphere.

He wanted her. Now.

But he maintained control. "Love the shoes with that suit. Very flashy."

She smiled. He loved her smile. He loved making her smile.

She lifted her foot. "The glitter has the same jewel tones as my blouse." Which was a royal blue, the suit a creamy wool that set off her skin.

The shoes and the suit, along with everything else about her, dazzled him, but he couldn't help saying, "You really didn't need to change."

She straightened her suit jacket. "If I'm at the office—even more so if it's yours—I dress the part."

She *so* dressed the part—elegantly, temptingly.

"Does it really matter?" he asked.

Walking to his desk, she said, "I'm an executive in a male-dominated workforce. It absolutely matters."

"You're not just any executive. You're CEO of a billion-dollar company. You've obviously earned any man's respect."

"You have to admit a woman in my position is judged differently than a man."

He opened his mouth to say he didn't judge her. But then he recognized the truth of what she said. He'd seen enough of it in his own field, and he'd tried to be different. "I've worked with many female chefs in my time."

She raised an eyebrow, perfectly arched. "And?"

"I have to admit that many of them feel they need to go above and beyond the men to keep their place in the lineup."

"And the women I mentor, they need help for that very reason."

He'd been witness to her heart of gold years ago, and it had been pounded into him all over again during the last couple of days. Ava Harrington didn't just walk the talk, she *was* the talk.

Leaning back in his desk chair, he crossed his arms. "But the shoes. They're not your usual style." He enjoyed the wedges as much as he'd loved her killer heels.

Striding around his desk, stopping right next to him, she said so softly he had to lean closer to hear, "They're my little *screw you* to the man."

He laughed from deep in his gut. The way Ava had always made him laugh. And the way she'd always made him feel deep down inside.

Rising, he flourished a hand toward the conference table. "I've set up the big-screen monitor for us."

He pulled out a chair for her and, once she was settled, dragged his own close. Her scent surrounded him, something sweet and slightly citrus. Something uniquely Ava. Perhaps a signature scent she'd found since they'd been together? Or maybe that was just her power.

As difficult as it was to concentrate, they went through the staffing requirements, the numbers he'd need to serve, the specific mealtimes.

"My residents like routine," she told him. "They're waiting right outside the dining room when the doors open."

"You don't have a lot of people at each site." Anywhere from one hundred to one-fifty.

She smiled, her lipstick glistening, beckoning. "I don't run massive facilities as if they were factories. I want my homes to feel more like a community. Which is what we need to talk about. I told you about the Sunday brunches. The main course rotates in that four-week cycle I mentioned—pork tenderloin, roast turkey, baked ham, roast beef. It reminds everyone of the Sunday roast their moms used to serve. We make each of the holiday brunches special, too, with decorations on the tables and themed desserts. Every month, we host a birthday dinner for residents with birthdays in that month, and they get a choice of filet mignon or lobster."

He was taken aback. "Whoa. That's amazing."

"My residents deserve it." That was her theme in everything she did.

"We also need to deliver meals to those who can't get to the dining room. I don't believe I mentioned that before. Either they're ill or more infirm, or just don't like to socialize. There's a separate dining room in assisted living as well as memory care and the hospital wing. The food doesn't need to be different, though. Just the delivery."

"You really know what you're doing."

She took the praise with a smile. "It's taken years."

He found himself equally concerned about giving her residents the best experience possible. He admired how she'd thought through all their needs, as well as providing variations they could enjoy, like the special dinners and brunches.

"I like to make each community feel cozy, like being at home rather than just institutional. We have events on Friday afternoons where we provide appetizers and wine just before dinner." She paused, breathed in. "I'm throwing a lot at you. I don't expect that you'll be able to accommodate all of this right away. I know it'll take time."

"This is why we're sitting down. We didn't talk about much more than the basics the other day. Now I'm glad to know the full scope. And yes, we can accommodate it all." He would give her people the best care they'd ever known.

And he'd make sure he gave it to her too.

* * *

"What do you do for holidays?" Ransom sat back in his chair, rolling a pencil between his fingers. He'd been taking notes all along.

"Like I said, we have decorations and themed desserts for brunch on Christmas, New Year's, Thanksgiving, and Easter. We serve a roast like we do for Sunday brunches."

"What about July Fourth or Memorial Day or Labor Day?"

She tipped her head. "We decorate the tables, put up flags, banners, that kind of thing."

"But what about a special menu?"

Her whole body felt as though it glittered as brightly as her shoes. "What are you thinking?"

He shrugged. "Something like bringing out a big barbecue in that quad between the auditorium and dining hall. Say we roast hot dogs and hamburgers and ribs on Memorial Day and July Fourth. Corned beef and cabbage and green beer for St. Patrick's Day."

"You think big."

"Of course. I'm a chef. That's what I do."

He thought outside the box. "I love it. Let's do it. Special menus for all the holidays. They'll love the barbecue atmosphere." She laughed. "And green beer."

"We'll set up tables outside on the lawns. You could even

have games."

"Perfect."

"How about a themed dinner once a month? Like a Caribbean night. An Oktoberfest night. Things like that."

She couldn't disguise her awe. "You're brilliant. I could even bring in a polka band for Oktoberfest. And a steel-drum band for Caribbean night."

They riffed off each other. "How about a mariachi band for a Mexican night? With lots of margaritas."

"And along with the green beer, Irish dancers for St. Patrick's Day."

Why had she never thought of things like this before?

He seemed to read her mind. "You always had so many other things on your mind. And you provide a great experience."

"But this will make it so much better. You're an absolute genius."

She meant it. He'd always been first in his field, and he was creative in ways she'd never imagined.

But he'd always been most creative in their bed.

Chapter Eleven

They spent a couple of hours going through everything. Ransom was so good at this. Ava marveled at the enticing menus he created and his fabulous ideas for holidays and special events. She liked to change up the rotating menus every quarter so her people didn't get bored. But would he be on board with doing this all over again in three months? With looking at her other facilities across the country?

That struck her in the heart—that he might do all of this, then go on his merry way, leaving her behind, ghosting her once again for his fabulous famous chef's life.

She didn't mention anything long term, telling herself that she had to think only about the next few months. By then, she would have found somebody permanent. Someone who could continue with all his ideas. Someone who didn't have another life they couldn't wait to get back to.

When her stomach suddenly rumbled, she glanced at the computer clock. Three thirty. How the time had flown, and even after that huge breakfast, she was hungry again.

"I would say we could push through on the rest of this." Ransom grinned at her. "But your stomach is sending out messages."

Her hand went reflexively to her belly. "I am a bit hungry."

He handed her one of the menus they'd printed out. "Pick something from this, and I'll make it for you."

The fact that she was dying to have him cook for her was going too far. She needed to get off the bus right now. They'd already spent too much time together. And while for the entire time in his office they'd been completely businesslike, she had teased him over the pancakes. It could all turn against her in a second.

She'd been fighting an attraction for him all day long, and yesterday as well. Quite frankly, the exertion exhausted her.

The voice inside her frightened her the most—the persistent little voice asking, *Wouldn't it just be easier to give in?*

She sat up straight. What the hell was she thinking?

"So what, you have test kitchens right here in your building?" Her words came off a little sharp and sarcastic.

But he didn't seem to notice. "I do." Of course he would. "But now that I think about it, I'd rather take you over to the restaurant. They have everything I need right there. And I'll choose the menu. Okay with you?"

Her heart, already ravaged by him years ago, screamed at her to say no. But something far bigger ran through her head. Though she'd never been in his restaurant, she'd walked by and maybe once or twice gazed through its windows. Now, here was her chance. She couldn't resist seeing what would undoubtedly be an incredible kitchen. Nor could she resist letting him cook for her after so many years.

That part of her won. "Yes, okay. You choose." But she absolutely would not chop vegetables for him. That task would hold far too many memories.

The restaurant was closed between lunch and dinner, so when they entered, they found the staff setting up for the evening. The tables were set apart, with tall planter boxes dividing the large room into smaller corners while low lighting turned the atmosphere more intimate.

Ransom led her straight to the kitchen, though he wasn't remiss in greeting his people, stopping at a newly laid table to say, "Brilliant work there," and patting the woman on the arm. He smiled and waved hello as if he actually knew these people. But how could he when he was always gallivanting around the world?

Just before entering the kitchen, he tapped a sweet-faced young busboy on the shoulder. "Could you set a table for two by the window? I'll be making a meal for myself and the lady." He looked from Ava to the boy, whose face flushed as if he were being called out by his employer.

"Y-yes, sir," he stammered and rushed off for linens and cutlery, while Ransom said, "Thank you. I appreciate it."

He was so polite to them, as if they were not just his staff, but people he respected, even down to the busboys.

He pushed through the swinging doors, holding one for Ava so it didn't slap her in the face. The kitchen was already warm; maybe it never lost its heat. Men and women in white coats dashed about or stood at the counters prepping for the night's menu. The actual meal would be cooked once a customer ordered, but all manner of things needed to be done ahead of time—preparing dill sauce, chopping scallions, slicing vegetables, peeling potatoes.

He was just as complimentary here. As he passed a woman whipping cream, he said, "Your peaks are perfect." The woman smiled her gratitude.

Ava wanted to laugh, hearing a vague innuendo in his words, though neither Ransom nor the chef seemed to take it that way. It was just her naughty mind. And watching him in his element, oh yes, *her* peaks were up and paying attention.

"Honorine," he called.

A tall, thirtysomething woman approached them, a chef's hat perched on her blond curls, her name stenciled above her jacket pocket, a speck of yellow the only thing marring the pristine white.

Ransom took Ava's arm. "Ava Harrington, I'd like you to meet Honorine Aubert," he said with a French flourish. "Honorine is head chef here."

Having talked about women in a man's world, Ava was pleased to see he had a female chef in his highly prized San Francisco restaurant. "Nice to meet you," she said, and the woman returned the greeting in slightly accented but perfect English.

Then he explained to Honorine, "I've agreed to cater Ava's Bay Area retirement homes for the next few months."

The next few months. All right, he certainly wasn't thinking long term. But she'd already known that, and she'd guarded herself.

"That's something new for us," Honorine said, the furrow above her brow showing her consternation. *Us*. Ransom made all his people part of his team.

"It won't change anything we do at any of the restaurants. But Ava was in great need, and I wanted to help out." There was that smile, the one that turned her inside out and made anyone within its beam eager to do his bidding. "I want to make her one of the recipes on the menu I've created. Do you have sand dabs? And lemons?"

Honorine puffed out a breath. "Of course. It's one of the regular dishes on our menu?" She made it a question, as if she thought Ransom might need the reminder.

Sand dabs in butter and lemon sauce. It was one of her favorites. And Ransom had made the dish a regular on his restaurant's menu. It couldn't mean anything. Lots of restaurants served sand dabs.

Ransom beamed that brilliant smile at her again, then put a finger to his lips. "Don't tell Ava that," he said, the joke in his tone. "I want her to think it was something special just for her."

Honorine zipped her lips. "Of course. I've never heard of sand dabs. Is that some kind of fish?"

They all had a chuckle.

Of course he hadn't created her new menus from scratch, but he had offered her favorite. And now that she thought about it, he'd included other favorites. Stir fries they'd made together, curry dishes, although with less spice to fit her residents' palates.

Honorine flicked her fingers and sent her helpers scurrying for the ingredients Ransom asked for.

When he stood at the long stainless-steel counter, she waved her people over. "*Venez*, watch a virtuoso at work."

As he prepared the meal, Ransom talked about his plans for the catering. When the sous-chef piped up with a suggestion, he listened and asked for more. He even listened to the woman who'd been whipping cream. No one was too lowly to provide a good suggestion.

Watching him now reminded Ava how much she'd loved being part of his cooking team.

When Ransom sprinkled a red spice into the sauce, Honorine made a noise. "We don't put cayenne in our lemon butter sauce."

Ransom laughed. "Let's see how it tastes. Maybe we should try it." He looked at Ava. "I know Ava likes it spicy." And he winked.

Okay, that was definitely a sexual innuendo. She didn't react, at least not on the outside. But a shiver ran through her as she remembered all the spice he'd added to her bed, to her life.

Honorine smiled thoughtfully as Ransom said, "Not that I'd add an overabundance of cayenne for your menus, Ava. Promise."

He'd seen her in her environment. And now she saw him in his, the sous-chef and all of Honorine's people watching with rapt attention. Even Honorine took note of everything he did. They respected him. They even expected that he would listen to them.

This was how he'd built his cooking empire, not by kowtowing to the rich, but by listening to and appreciating all the people who worked for him. The way she did.

Her estimation of the man he'd become grew a bit more.

* * *

Ransom examined the sand dabs, the egg batter in which he'd soaked them crisping lightly around the edges. "They're perfect."

He didn't need to hear the murmuring assent from his audience. Plating the sand dabs, he drenched them in the spicy lemon butter sauce, leaving just enough to pour over the asparagus spears poaching in another pan.

He'd always loved cooking for Ava, especially her favorite foods. He'd loved cooking with her as well. And now he loved having her in his restaurant.

Leading her into the dining room, he pulled out a chair for her at the window table. Though it wasn't dark yet, Jacob, the busboy, had lit two candles and added one rose in a bud vase, its perfume rising in the air between them.

Once they were seated, Honorine brought out the plated sand dabs, steam still rising off them. They would be perfection.

He wanted to give Ava that. Wanted to remind her of what

they'd once had, the way he remembered it all.

He thanked Honorine, who then returned to the task of readying the restaurant for the evening. Before he sampled the flatfish, he waited for Ava to taste them, since they'd always been a favorite of hers. With the first bite, she closed her eyes to savor it, a soft moan rising up her throat, reminding him of all the times in his bed—that same ecstasy on her face, that same seductive moan on her lips.

"Too much spice?" he asked, knowing it wasn't. He and Ava had always made just the right spice together.

She opened her eyes. "Perfect."

Then he tried his own plate, and yes, the spice was just right, mixed with the tang of the lemon and the buttery texture of the fish.

"And the asparagus?" He served it al dente, with just a slight crunch, enhanced by the sauce.

She told him what he wanted to hear. "You timed it with precision."

That's how he had to work with Ava now—timed with precision. If he moved too fast, their relationship would be half-baked. Too slow, and he could burn it all away.

"The wine?" He'd paired the meal with a white wine, not too sweet, not too dry.

She raised her glass. "You know everything is perfect," she said, her smile wry.

He wanted to lean over and kiss her, but all he did was wink.

As they ate, people glanced in the window, then checked the restaurant's hours, wondering how these two could be eating before it opened for dinner. Perhaps they made a spectacle, but he liked being a spectacle with Ava.

"My people have a lot of good suggestions." He steered the

conversation to her menus and her facilities.

She nodded and, after swallowing a bite, said, "I especially liked the idea of having an Easter egg hunt on Easter. I've done it for the children visiting, but never included the adults." She laughed, a tinkling sound that trickled down his skin. "After all, we're all just big kids, aren't we?"

"Absolutely. And the tree-decorating party at Christmas."

She shook her fork at him. "I should have thought of that. I always have the staff decorate the tree overnight so everyone can be astounded in the morning. But it's an even better idea to include them, with sugar cookies and hot cocoa like kids are supposed to serve Santa on Christmas Eve."

"Your thinking was sound. I'm sure they all loved walking into the lounge to feel the magic of a fully decorated tree. But this could be even more fun."

She agreed with a nod. "They love surprises, but they'll love the activity just as much. We can pop popcorn right there and string it for garlands."

Her eyes gleamed with ideas, and he was glad he'd brought her here. It wasn't just a reminder of how they'd cooked together, how they'd eaten together, and all the sexy, seductive things they'd done afterward. It was how she'd made suggestions while he cooked. How he'd helped her with her studies, sometimes quizzing her with index cards before a test. How they'd hiked together, shopped together, cleaned the apartment together, walked the city streets together under an umbrella on rainy nights. At least, when they actually *were* together, when she wasn't at school or working and he wasn't traveling.

It was about the here and now, too, working on the menus, sharing ideas, involving his people in the new project, painting Edith's and Myrtle's nails.

But how long would she need him? How long before she found a permanent caterer? She'd thrown out an estimate of three to six months when she'd come to him that first day. But it wasn't long enough.

After they'd finished every bite, the plates were whisked away. Across the restaurant, the swinging doors opened, and Honorine came through, proudly holding a flaming dessert, her sous-chef following her across the dining room.

"You didn't ask for dessert, but I thought this would be just the right ending," she said.

Two of her helpers moved the candles and bud vase out of the way, and she set the dessert plate between them.

"It's beautiful," Ava said, looking up at Honorine. "But what is it?"

The chef just laughed. "You have to try it to find out." When the flames died down, she pumped freshly whipped cream out of a pressurized canister. "Go ahead," Honorine urged. "Cut into it."

Ransom waved his hand. "Ladies first."

Ava picked up the pie knife and sliced into the round cake topped with cream, removing a piece dripping with melted chocolate.

"It's a lava cake," she said in delight.

But Honorine wagged a finger. "It's called hot chocolate pudding. You pour the sauce over the cake batter and as it bakes, the two are almost blended. I used a jelly mold to give it shape." She kissed her fingers. "A little brandy drizzled over it makes it sing."

They all waited with bated breath for Ava to take her first bite. She closed her eyes again, savored in exactly the same way she'd savored the sand dabs, ending with a hum in her throat. Then she looked at Honorine. "It's one of the most delicious desserts I've ever tasted." Her eyes bright, she glanced at Ransom, then Honorine. "Do you think we can add this to our menus? Probably just for a special occasion, like Christmas."

He wanted to cover her hand with his, and he might have if Honorine hadn't been hovering. "I can see your servers carrying out flaming plates to every table. Your residents will love it."

Honorine's face glowed with pride. "It would be my very great pleasure to provide the recipe."

When they were once again alone, he leaned forward to say softly, "Thank you. You honored her with that request."

After another bite, Ava said, "This deserves honor. It's not your creation?"

He shook his head. "No. Honorine is free to use my signature dishes or create anything she'd like." And indeed, the hot chocolate pudding was delicious.

She blinked. "You don't even taste-test beforehand?"

"I trust her."

For a moment, she seemed dumbfounded. "But she's a woman."

With an imperceptible movement of his head, he said, "She's a chef. Trained at Le Cordon Bleu."

Something shone brilliantly in Ava's eyes, as if he'd said just the right thing.

"She comes to me, we bounce ideas around, she uses some of my signature recipes, like the sand dabs, and creates many of her own straight from her heart."

"Do you do that with all your chefs? Let them have free rein?"

"I might own the restaurants, but they own the kitchen. It would do them a disservice to limit them to a menu only I chose."

She looked down then. As if she didn't want him to see the

expression in her eyes, she concentrated on the hot chocolate pudding.

But he thought that might have been admiration in her gaze.

* * *

The meal suddenly seemed too intimate. The best sand dabs she'd ever had, the candles, the rose, the flaming dessert, and his admiration for Honorine's talents and willingness to use them—it was all too much.

More than anything, Ava wanted to lean over the dessert plate and kiss the chocolate off his lips.

God, yes, it was all too much. She was almost dizzy with need. If she wasn't careful, she'd act on it. That meant she needed to get out of here. Before she threw herself at him.

As if she'd conjured it, her phone rang in her purse. She grabbed it like a lifeline. "Sorry, I need to take this. It could be an emergency."

The voice on the line was the bucket of cold water she badly needed. "It's Campbell from Los Gatos."

Then she heard the concern in the man's voice. "What's wrong, Campbell?"

"Mrs. Anderson had a fall."

Her stomach sank, and she was immediately assailed with guilt for even thinking she needed an emergency to save her from Ransom. "Is she all right?"

"She hit her head. We've called an ambulance, and they'll be here soon. They'll take her to Good Sam." Good Samaritan Hospital was only minutes away, thank goodness.

She felt Ransom's eyes on her, but didn't look. "You did the right thing." One could never take chances with a head injury. Her heart was beating fast. Mrs. Anderson was a sweet, generous woman. She always tried to give Ava a tip after she'd done her nails. And Mrs. Anderson's daughter was so attentive, visiting every week. "Have you called her daughter?"

"I wanted to call you first." Unspoken between them was that Campbell knew how Ava felt about the lady.

"All right. Let me call her."

"You have her number?"

"Yes. I'll call right away. Thank you for letting me know. And please keep me updated."

"I will."

She ended the call and said to Ransom, "I have to leave. An emergency call I need to make."

"Please feel free to make your call right here. I understand the importance."

"This could take a while. I don't know if you could tell, but one of my residents in Los Gatos, Mrs. Anderson, has taken a bad fall. She's hit her head."

"The hot dog lady."

Ava tipped her head. "The hot dog lady?"

"She told you never to stop serving hot dogs, or her daughter would stop coming to visit."

She puffed out a breath. "I can't believe you remember that."

"I remember everything you tell me."

Why did that shock her? Worse, why did it make her want to cry? It was her fear for Mrs. Anderson, of course.

She was already standing, shoving her phone back in her purse. "I really do need to go."

He stood too. "Please, call me later and let me know how she is."

"I will. Thank you for the delicious meal and all the great work we did this afternoon."

Then she ran, as fast as her wedge shoes would let her.

* * *

Ava was damn near running when she left.

Of course she needed to call Mrs. Anderson's daughter, and Ransom more than admired that about her. Out on the street, she had her phone in her hand, obviously searching her contacts. She was so caring, had always been that way with every patient at the convalescent home, not just his grandmother.

She wasn't required to personally call the daughter. Under normal circumstances, she would have received a report. The CEO of a billion-dollar care home conglomerate didn't call a relative about an accident. But Ava cared. She knew how worried Mrs. Anderson's daughter would be. And she was worried herself. He'd heard the tremor in her voice.

But she'd still used it as an excuse to run away from him.

And that made him want to break through all her emotional walls. Now. Not later.

In the car, he'd been thinking about his own scars, but now, after another afternoon spent with her, and yes, after seeing her concern for an old woman who lived at one of her homes, he no longer cared about the scars. He didn't want to bide his time or wait for the right moment. If it had been any reason other than the misfortune of the poor injured woman, he would have run after Ava, made her confront him, made her feel, made her tell him why she had to run.

Under the circumstances, he could do nothing but let her go.

The meal had been such a success. They'd talked like any other couple getting to know each other. Maybe doing that had pierced at least one emotional wall Ava Harrington had built around herself.

Chapter Twelve

The update from Campbell was good. Mrs. Anderson had suffered a bump on the head, but was otherwise fine, and the doctors were letting her go home tonight. Thankfully, her daughter had rushed to the hospital as soon as Ava called.

In her flat, she threw her purse on the chair in the foyer and breathed a sigh of relief that one of her favorite residents hadn't suffered a worse injury. She flopped on the couch, laid her head back, and closed her eyes. What a day—nonstop action, from that pancake breakfast to the drive home to working with Ransom to the amazing meal he'd prepared for her. Then Mrs. Anderson's fall.

She was tired down to her very bones. Yet her mind was still whirling like an old phonograph record.

She'd missed an entire day at the office, which meant she'd have to go in tomorrow. She should catch up on email right now, but exhaustion was quickly overtaking her. If there was anything truly important, Naomi would have called her.

When her phone rang in her purse all the way over on the foyer chair, she almost didn't get up. But it could be about Mrs. Anderson, either her daughter or Campbell. Ava prayed it wasn't a turn for the worse. Pushing herself off the couch, she dragged her feet across the floor.

The name on Caller ID shocked her. Gideon Jones.

"Hello? Gideon?" Why on earth would the man be calling her on the Friday before his wedding? Please, she prayed, not another emergency.

Gideon didn't even say hello. "You know how we're getting married in forty-eight hours?" His deep voice rattled her.

"Uh, yeah, I know."

"Well, guess what?"

He paused long enough for her to say, "What?"

"Our caterer just pulled out."

"Oh my God." What was up with these caterers?

"I know you've been looking for a new caterer for your Bay Area homes. What did you find out? Is there anyone I can use at the last minute?"

The first name to pop into her mind was Ransom's. This was right up his alley. Specialty catering. And he was the best at it. But he was already busting his butt over her care homes. If she gave his contact info to Gideon without checking first, she'd be putting him in a bind.

"Let me check," she said. "I'll get right back to you, promise. We'll find something that works." She managed a laugh. "Even if we all have to get out there and prepare the meal ourselves."

Finally, Gideon laughed too. "I bet you would. Thanks, Ava. You're the best. I knew I could count on you."

She hung up, hoping he could. And she meant what she'd said. Gabby and Fernsby were already making the cake. If Gideon couldn't find a replacement, the Mavericks and the Harringtons would make it work. They were family now, and family pitched in.

She opened her contacts list, where Ransom was at the top of her Favorites.

Then it hit her. If Ransom agreed to do the catering, he

would be at the wedding. She'd be surrounded by all those Mavericks so in love. And her brother, endlessly in love with Cammie.

She'd be inundated by true love, while she and Ransom had totally sucked at it.

Oh yeah, they'd proven that. She might have all these feelings about him, all these thoughts, all these fantasies, but they'd proven they couldn't make it work. They'd ended in an absolute mess.

But she couldn't let Gideon down, and right now, Ransom was the only game in town. On the bright side, maybe he wouldn't be able to fit it in, and then she'd magically find someone else.

Yeah, right. She hit the Call button.

"Miss me already?"

She couldn't help laughing. Oh God, her guard was so down around him. She needed to be strong now, more than ever. She needed to build a barricade he couldn't bulldoze his way through.

"I hope Mrs. Anderson is okay." His words came out fast, as if he really cared.

"A bump on her head, but the doctors say she'll be fine. They're not even keeping her overnight."

He let out a breath as if he'd been holding it. "Good."

"But that's not why I called." Ava rushed into it. "Here's the deal. Gideon Jones. Wedding on Sunday. Only forty-eight hours away. Caterer just pulled out." It all came out in one breath, and she gasped for air. "Is there any way you could loan us some chefs and servers? Or if you know of anyone who could do it, that would be amazing too." She made it clear he didn't need to take on the task personally.

Without even pausing, Ransom said, "I'll do it myself."

"That's an amazing offer, but considering everything I've loaded on you this week, surely someone who works for you could handle it." She'd say anything to keep him away from the wedding. After spending twenty-four hours being wowed by him, she couldn't handle both him and all that love in the air.

But Ransom said, "It's Gideon. It's a Maverick wedding. You know I'll do anything for them after everything they've done for me."

"But it's only forty-eight hours' notice. Can you actually do it?"

He laughed and teased her by saying, "I could do it in one day, blindfolded."

"God, you are cocky." And it was sexy as sin. She'd always found his confidence seductive. "But truly, you only have one full day," she pointed out. "It's already six o'clock. And it's an afternoon wedding." Then she had to laugh. "I told Gideon that if we couldn't find anyone, the whole family would pitch in and make the meal ourselves."

He chuckled with her. "Told you—one hand behind my back, blindfolded. No need to put on your chef's hat. I've got it handled." So cocky. And so sexy.

If he could do this, he truly was amazing.

But then, he always had been.

* * *

Of course he'd cater a Maverick wedding. Anything for those guys. They'd all helped him. And Gideon's generosity amazed him—starting his own charity with the millions he'd received for that painting.

While he'd been deployed in the Middle East, Gideon Jones

had received a small painting from a fallen comrade, Karmen Sanchez. He later learned the painting was by a famous eighteenth-century Mexican painter, Miguel Fernando Correa. When Gideon sold it, instead of keeping the millions for himself, he'd started the Lean on Us foundation in honor of Karmen Sanchez, benefiting veterans and foster children, two causes close to his heart, he being a veteran and his sister, Ari, having gone through the foster care system while he was overseas.

Oddly enough, it was Dane who'd bought the painting. Or maybe that wasn't so odd.

Ransom had been more than happy to donate his catering services to Gideon's New Year's gala benefiting Lean on Us. And now he pulled up his contacts like a man wielding a Santoku knife.

Gideon answered with enthusiasm. "Ransom Yates. I never expected to hear from *you*." But, after talking to Ava, was there really any other choice?

"Ava told me a dastardly caterer pulled out of the wedding at the last minute."

Gideon's sigh came through the speaker, filling up Ransom's living room. "Yeah." That word held everything—Gideon's frustration, his fear that the wedding would be ruined, his desire to make it the best for his fiancée, Rosie.

Ransom had met Rosie Diaz at the New Year's Eve gala, and he knew, through Dane, that she'd just given birth to Gideon's daughter in July. This was Gideon's first child, though of course he considered Rosie's seven-year-old son, Jorge, to be his own.

"I'll put you on speaker," Gideon said. "I've got Rosie here."

Rosie came on to say, "Ransom, can you really help us out? It's so last-minute."

Ransom spoke straight from the heart. "It's no problem at all.

I'm delighted to do it. Please email me a list of what you'd already planned with the other caterer." It was unconscionable to cancel and not at least give them an alternative. "But tell me what you'd like. Don't limit yourself to what you've already ordered. And let me know about anything special you'd really like to see."

Rosie took over. Gideon wouldn't care about the food. He cared only that Rosie got everything she wanted. "I'll email the menu. I'd really like a cocktail reception to start, with a few canapés, whatever you think would be good. We've also got a few children coming, so if you can provide kid food for them, that would be great. We'd planned a sit-down dinner rather than a buffet. But the meal itself is completely up to you."

"We trust your judgment," Gideon added. "What you did for the gala was fantastic."

Sit-down dinner. And carte blanche. Interesting. Ransom began planning all the things he could prepare.

Then Rosie said, "But we do have a budget."

A Maverick with a budget?

"Sorry, man," Gideon said, "but I don't have huge funds available, not like I did for the gala."

Gideon had been in the army, then worked as a contractor. Now he was VP of warehousing, shipping, and procurement at Daniel Spencer's Top Notch DIY conglomerate. Gideon also invested in Maverick ventures, just as Ransom sometimes did. Ransom figured the man would be a billionaire in his own right one of these days, and sooner rather than later.

But he hadn't kept any of the proceeds from the sale of the painting for himself. So for now, he had a budget.

"No worries at all," Ransom said. "I'm used to working within anyone's budget. And I owe all of you guys."

Rosie's sigh of relief was audible. "I'd reach right through the phone to hug you if I could, Ransom. We didn't know what we were going to do."

Ransom smiled, remembering what Ava had said. If they couldn't find another caterer, the family would pitch in. And it would have been a great wedding. But… "I'm glad I can help."

They talked logistics—when, where, number of guests. It was to be a close-knit family wedding, a few friends, but mostly Mavericks and Harringtons, as if they'd all been folded into one family. Still, that was quite a number these days.

"Okay. I got it. Let me get to work."

Rosie jumped in again. "You don't need to worry about the cake. Gabby Harrington and Fernsby are taking care of that."

Even over the phone, Ransom raised an eyebrow. A vegan and a baking butler who thought butter was the staff of life creating a wedding cake?

"I'll call Fernsby," Gideon added. "I'm sure he'll tell Gabby. It shouldn't be a problem."

"Of course it won't. But let me call Fernsby. I'll need to talk logistics with him anyway."

Fernsby had worked for Dane from that very first resort. He was a staple. Ransom had known the man almost as long as he'd known Dane and Ava. But Fernsby and Gabby baking the wedding cake together? Oh, that he'd have to see. And taste.

* * *

Fernsby answered the phone immediately upon seeing Ransom Yates on Caller ID. "To what do I owe this pleasure, Mr. Yates?" Fernsby asked in his most melodious tones.

Not that anyone had ever called him melodious. Except perhaps Mathilda. But that was long, long ago.

"I just got a call from Ava Harrington." Ransom seemed to add Harrington as if Fernsby wouldn't know who Ava was. "She got a call from Gideon—their caterer has dropped out."

That dragged a gasp from Fernsby. He credited himself with never gasping, never being surprised. For a man who never *burst* over anything, he burst out with, "This is a catastrophe."

"Have no fear, Fernsby. Ava asked me to step in. I've talked with Gideon, and I've agreed."

Because no one was looking—Fernsby was alone in his suite of rooms at Dane's Pebble Beach home—he allowed himself a smile. Well, well, well. Would wonders never cease. *Ava*, and even in his mind, he stressed her name, had asked *Ransom*, stressing that name in his mind also. And the man had agreed. Readily. At the last minute, no less. That spoke volumes, at least to Fernsby. Things were progressing between them.

And Fernsby hadn't yet lifted a finger to help.

Just think what could happen when he put his brilliant mind to it.

He wanted to sing like Fagin in the movie *Oliver*. The situation, upon review, was progressing very nicely indeed.

But Ransom was saying, "Let's talk about the cake and what kind of service you need." They went over the details, all of which were quite simple.

Then Fernsby said, "Miss Gabrielle Harrington has the cake topper. I will give her a call and let her know of the change."

He would delight in giving her a little lecture on the wonders of butter at the same time.

"Great. Thanks, Fernsby. I'm very interested in what you and Gabby come up with." Had the young man—because even a man in his forties was young to Fernsby—*snickered*?

Oh, he was sure Ransom Yates would love to know all his

secrets.

"You will be astounded, Mr. Yates," he drawled. "As will everyone on the big day."

Fernsby hung up, thinking, *Bollocks to the cake.* He had important things to do, like bringing Ava and Ransom into closer and closer contact. Thank goodness he'd put that little bug in Dane's ear about asking Ransom to help Ava with her catering.

Pure genius. But then, pure genius was his forte. Especially when it came to matchmaking.

* * *

Ransom's phone rang at noon the following day. His heart wanted to leap right out of his chest, just as it had done so many times over the past few days that he couldn't even count them anymore.

He picked up immediately. "I've got Gideon and Rosie covered."

"I wanted to see how you're doing," Ava said. "I put such a huge burden on you."

It depended on the meaning of *huge*. Too much? Not for him. Especially when he was doing it for Ava.

Leaning back in his office chair, he crossed his ankles on the desk. "It pays to be in the business and able to call in a few favors." He downplayed it all—he'd been on the phone late into the night and up again early to call in every favor anyone had ever owed him—but he was getting it done. "Do you want me to tell you the menu?"

"No, no, no. I can't know before the bride and groom. Besides, I'd like to be surprised too."

And oh boy, would she be surprised. He couldn't wait to see her face. If she understood what he'd done.

"I can't thank you enough for doing this, Ransom."

"You know I'd do anything for the Mavericks." And most especially for her.

"But I can still be amazed that you pulled it all together so fast."

"In my place, you'd have pulled it together too. I know you, Ava."

She was silent a moment. He heard her swallow. "Thank you." After another beat of seemingly embarrassed silence, she added, "I'll let you get back to it."

"See you tomorrow." But she was gone before he'd finished.

His heart beat against his ribs. *Pound, pound, pound.* Because now Ava would owe *him* a favor.

And oh, how he longed to call it in.

Chapter Thirteen

Ava had yet to see Ransom at the wedding. Thank God.

He'd done a fabulous job, and she was afraid her gratitude to him for saving the day might weaken her resolve.

The Sunday afternoon wedding was held in the backyard of Bob and Susan Spencer's Portola Valley home. Attendance wasn't a massive spectacle, just family and a few friends—some of the foster kids Gideon mentored; Zach, one of his buddies from the army, and his family; Ernestina Sanchez, mother of Karmen, the woman who'd given Gideon that amazing Miguel Fernando Correa painting. They were all friends who were important to both Gideon and Rosie.

When the Mavericks had moved the Spencers into the house less than a year ago—transplanting their parents from Chicago—they'd added a large deck and a flagstone patio around the pool. Now, for the wedding, they'd cleared more of the lot; built a gazebo with a raised floor large enough to accommodate the ceremony and the dinner's head table; planted shrubs, flowers, and a lawn for the chairs and tables; and laid down a temporary dance floor.

The sky was a cloudless blue and the weather gorgeous, but then, late September often was in the Bay Area. Ransom had set up a pre-ceremony cocktail hour with a mobile bar cart serving champagne, punch, and fruit-infused water along with canapés, blackened-fish lettuce wraps, shrimp cocktails, and tiny quiches. Ava couldn't resist trying one of each. After all, they were only a bite.

And they were to die for.

She'd then snagged a glass of champagne, and now she stood with two of her brothers, Troy and Dane, and, of course, Cammie. Dane was never without Cammie.

Nor was he without Fernsby, who'd made the wedding cake with Gabby. Amazingly, they were both still alive. At least at this point.

It was a terrible *faux pas*, but they were all talking about Clay's date.

Fernsby said the unthinkable. "Well." He cleared his throat. "She is rather..." He paused dramatically. "Well endowed." His lips stretched around the word.

Clay was deep in conversation with Sebastian Montgomery, probably about some media platform, since media was what they had in common. His date seemed to be not-so-patiently waiting, her foot tapping, her gaze roaming as if she'd been expecting to meet some huge celebrities. The Mavericks were certainly celebrated and huge, but they weren't famous actors or sports stars.

Cammie frowned. "You can't talk about a woman's personal assets like that, Fernsby."

Fernsby, tall and lean—one might even say *spare*—merely raised an eyebrow. "But they aren't something you can ignore, Camille. I don't believe she wants them to be ignored. Which is why I am giving them their due."

Ava couldn't help chuckling. He was probably right about that.

"I don't suppose he's terribly serious about her." After a

pause, Fernsby added, "Is he?"

No one answered.

Her brother Clay was a flavor-of-the-month type. He never dated anyone for long. Ava wasn't sure he'd ever had a long-term relationship. Since relationships were a taboo subject in the family—the *only* taboo subject, in fact, and what a wonderful legacy from their parents it was—Ava had no idea.

Except that Clay seemed to have friends, not girlfriends.

"I wonder if she has some artistic ability we don't know about," Fernsby mused.

Troy guffawed. "Like what? Pole dancing?"

Cammie shushed him. "Just because she's—"

"Well endowed?" Fernsby furnished with a raised brow when Cammie seemed unable to find another word.

"That doesn't mean she's an exotic dancer," Cammie insisted. "She could be a dentist."

Even Dane had to laugh then. "Drilling, filling, and billing?"

Cammie frowned at them. "You're all so bad."

A smile lurked even on Fernsby's thin lips. Ava swore she'd seen that barely there smile more than once over the past few months, especially after Dane and Cammie finally got together.

It was time to take the spotlight off Clay. Ava said to Troy, "So, tell us where *your* flavor of the month is."

Troy just smiled. Enigmatically. As if he wanted to keep them guessing. "I prefer stag for weddings. That way, no one gets any ideas."

Fernsby drawled, "This speculation is beneath all of us. I must attend to the cake."

When he was gone, Ava asked, "Didn't he *start* the speculation?"

Watching Fernsby's long-limbed figure retreat, they smiled in his wake. The man was unfathomable.

Susan Spencer left the house, crossing the deck and giving Fernsby's arm a squeeze as she passed.

"There's Susan," Ava said. "I want a quick word with her." She excused herself from the group.

Reaching Susan's side, Ava put her hand on her arm. "I just have to say that it's a wonderful way for all the kids to enjoy the wedding as well." With a tip of her chin, Ava indicated the kids' tent off to the side.

The young ones were being entertained with movies and games. Ransom had prepared several different sandwiches, including grilled cheese, as well as chicken fingers, macaroni and cheese, and personal pizzas. All the favorite kid foods.

Next to that, the moms' tent catered to those who were breast-feeding and had infants who needed changing. In this gathering, that included quite a few.

The Mavericks had thought of everything, creating the most amazing kid and mommy zone, including sitters to care for the children so the moms could enjoy the festivities.

But then, they were Mavericks. Of course they thought of everything.

"It's worked out perfectly," Susan said. "Children can get bored at weddings, with all the pomp and ceremony." She wore a beautiful peach-colored cocktail dress appropriate for an outdoor afternoon wedding, her short silver hair feathered back from her face. She was a lovely woman, and she adored her children.

From the corner of her eye, Ava saw Ransom step out of the house. Even if her back had been to the kitchen doorway, she would have known it was him. And Lord, he looked amazing in a fitted black tux, his salt-and-pepper hair shimmering in the sunlight.

She hoped he wasn't about to ask Susan's opinion on something for the wedding dinner.

Just in case, Ava steered Susan away. "You've been to a lot of weddings recently, haven't you?"

Susan Spencer was the Maverick matriarch. Even if they'd all come from different parents—except Susan and Bob's two biological children, Daniel and Lyssa—each Maverick called Susan *Mom*.

Susan clasped her hands over her heart. "It's a dream come true for my boys. They've all found the most wonderful women. And all the new babies too. I'm the happiest grandmother in the world." Her eyes sparkled with tears of joy. Three babies had swelled the Maverick ranks over the summer. Matt's wife, Ari, had given Noah a little sister, Penelope. Lyssa and Cal had welcomed a baby boy, Owen, and of course, there was Gideon and Rosie's daughter, Isabella.

Touching Ava's arm, Susan said, "And it's been so lovely watching Dane and Cammie's love story grow right before our eyes."

That was just like Susan. Romantic stars glittered in her eyes. She smiled and leaned closer to say, "Only mothers can get away with asking something like this, but is there anyone special in your life?"

Ava automatically glanced at Ransom talking with his bartender at the mobile bar cart. He looked so good in that tux, she could have drooled.

Realizing too late what she'd done, she snapped her gaze back to Susan. "No." Despite herself, the single word came out breathlessly.

"Oh, okay." Susan paused, just for a second, and Ava sensed she'd seen something in that brief glance. Then the sweet woman said brightly, "It's truly wonderful that Ransom stepped in to save the wedding feast. And on such short notice too. I know Rosie and Gideon are so grateful to you, as we all are, for putting them in touch with him. He's such a delightful, thoughtful, exceptional man."

Then, after a quick kiss on Ava's cheek, away she went.

Susan Spencer had eyes like a hawk, and with just that one look, she'd definitely picked up on something between Ava and Ransom.

Ava would have to be far more careful around her brothers.

Fernsby stepped out of the house and clapped his hands loudly enough to stop conversations across the entire yard. He cleared his throat. "The wedding is about to begin," he intoned. "Please take your seats." He seemed to have developed a new talent as a wedding planner.

Marching down the stairs, directing as he went, he told this couple to sit *there* and pointed that couple into *those two seats*. Reaching Ava, he latched on to her arm and steered her not to the row where her brothers sat, but several rows back, directing her into a chair one seat over from the aisle.

When she said, eyebrows raised, "There's room up there next to Cammie," Fernsby answered, "That seat is already taken." Then, as if he thought she didn't believe him, he tapped his temple. "I have all the seating arrangements right up here."

Ava shook her head and stayed where she was. You couldn't argue with Fernsby.

* * *

Fernsby tucked Susan Spencer's hand into the crook of his elbow. "My dear lady, since your husband will be walking the bride down the aisle, may I escort you to your seat?"

She smiled at him. "Why, Fernsby, I'd be delighted. It seems as if my boys have forgotten me."

Fernsby allowed himself a twinkle in his eye. "Never, dear lady. I orchestrated that, as I wished to have the honor."

"Fernsby," she said in the same formal tones, "you are a sly one."

"I appreciate the compliment, madam."

In only a few short months, Susan Spencer had the enviable position of making herself one of his favorite people. Her admirable spirit spoke to him. The woman had known terrible hardship, but she'd never lost her sense of duty or her ability to love with all her big heart. It couldn't have been easy raising five boys and a baby girl with so little money in an impoverished Chicago neighborhood. But she had created a strong, loving family. A miracle, when one considered that four of those boys were not even of her own union with her beloved husband, Robert.

He felt a kinship with her, as he had taken charge of the Harringtons long ago. Even if they didn't know it.

With most of the other guests seated, he slowly walked Susan down the grassy aisle. She was the closest thing the bride had to a mother, and she would take that exalted position as the last to be seated, Fernsby had determined, though he was sure the Mavericks had reserved it for her anyway.

Susan said in a voice too low for anyone else to hear, "I see you left the seat empty next to Ava. It seems to me that you, Fernsby, a man always with plans, have a plan for that seat too."

He allowed an evil smile to slide across his lips. "Indeed I do, dear lady."

There was never any artifice in Susan Spencer's smiles. And this one was knowing. "May I assume you're matchmaking?"

Again, she added a formal cadence to her words that Fernsby appreciated.

He tapped his temple and said smoothly, "As you said, dear lady, Fernsby always has a plan."

"You are a truly inestimable man," she said, laughter in her voice.

Fernsby helped her into the front-row seat, the chair next to her empty for her husband to return to after giving away the bride. Leaning close, he murmured, "Enjoy the wedding, dear lady."

Then he walked back down the aisle, heading straight for Ransom Yates.

Because Fernsby had a few fireworks to light under someone's backside.

* * *

An instrumental version of Taylor Swift's "Lover" had just begun when Fernsby guided Ransom into the empty seat beside her.

"What are you doing here?" Ava asked, trying not to sound sharp. "Aren't you supposed to be doing your chef thing?"

Ransom just smiled, a sparkle in his eye. "Everything is under control. Just as you said, I have a lot of great people working with me. They can take the lead while I enjoy the wedding with you."

With me? When did I turn into your date?

Yet there was that secret part of her heart that thrilled to have him next to her.

Ari came down the aisle first as Rosie's bridesmaid. They had been best friends since childhood, when they were in foster care together. After that came Jorge and Noah as ring bearers, Jorge carrying his mother's ring and Noah bearing Gideon's.

At the front, Gideon stood tall in a tuxedo perfectly tailored to his body. He was a big man—all the Mavericks were—a handsome blond guy whose look of love for Rosie softened his features. Matt Tremont, Ari's husband and Gideon's brother-in-law, was his best man. Matt looked down the aisle, watching Ari approach as if they were getting married all over again.

As the wedding march began, Bob Spencer walked Rosie down the aisle. She wore the traditional white wedding dress, a beautiful two-foot train trailing behind her. Pearls delicately covered the gown's bodice, her shoulders bare above it, while a filmy veil draped over her face.

Most of the children were in the kids' tent, but a nanny had brought Rosie's two-month-old to Susan only moments before the wedding began. The baby girl, even if she would have no recollection or understanding, needed to be part of her parents' wedding.

As Rosie passed, the child reached out chubby fingers, grabbing her mother's veil and tugging it off. Then, unbelievably, baby Isabella somehow pulled it crookedly over her own head.

For one long second, the entire assembly held its breath. Until Rosie began to laugh as the baby, batting at the veil, managed to make it drift down over her face just like a bride. Leaning over, Rosie rubbed noses with her sweet child and said loudly enough for everyone to hear, "That's yours, sweet pea, to wear when you're all grown up."

Sighs of awe and joy rose up all around. The photographer snapped what would be a marvelous photo of Rosie and the baby, Susan looking down at the little girl with such love it almost brought tears to Ava's eyes.

Ransom leaned in to whisper, "That's the cutest damn thing ever."

The minister began the ceremony. Ava hadn't been to a lot of weddings—in fact, she generally avoided them. But she couldn't avoid the heat of Ransom's body beside her, nor the memory of all the plans she'd had when she was too young to realize that plans never worked out. At least not where she and Ransom were concerned.

The minister said, "The bride and groom will recite the vows they've written to each other."

Gideon took the ring off the small pillow that Jorge held and, taking Rosie's hand in his, slipped it over the tip of her finger.

In a deep voice that trembled with emotion, he said, "I had so much to thank you for even before I knew you. For how you found my sister in foster care and took care of her and loved her." He glanced at Ari, exchanging a smile as a single tear trickled down her cheek. "I recognized how special you were from the moment I saw you, but I told myself I had to think of you as a sister, because you and Ari are sisters of the heart. Trying to hold back the way I felt about you was like trying to hold back an ocean wave. My love for you simply crashed over me, and all I could do was hold on and ride that wave with you. And I'm so glad I stopped fighting it. You've given me an amazing son." He ruffled Jorge's hair. Gideon wasn't his biological father, and they looked nothing alike, but his love for the boy glowed in his face.

He turned back to Rosie, the love of his life. "And now we have a beautiful daughter." Emotion wobbled in his voice, and he stopped a moment to gather himself. "I love all of you with all my heart. I will protect you with all my love from anyone who might try to harm you."

The words might seem unusual for marriage vows, but Ava knew the story. Rosie's ex had been a terrible man, and Gideon had protected her and Jorge with everything in him.

Then his voice dropped, his vow for Rosie alone, barely carrying out to their guests. "I will always love you. I will always be here for you. For our children. For our family. In accepting me as your husband, you've made me complete in a way I've never been before."

He slid the gold ring fully onto Rosie's finger, and without her veil, Ava could see tears streaming down her face.

Noah stepped up then, after a little prod from Ari, and Rosie took the ring from his pillow. Then both boys left the gazebo, taking seats next to Bob and Susan.

With Gideon's hand in hers, Rosie held the ring just short of putting it on his finger. She spoke in a musical voice that was all Rosie. "I loved you from the moment Ari told us all her stories about her special big brother. I always knew in my heart that you would find her again and, when you did, that you would find me too. You are my support, my warrior, the father of my beautiful children, and my true love. I loved you from the beginning, but I fell in love with you when I watched you with our son, when I saw the way you looked at him, as if he belonged to you as a son belongs to a father. I love the way you look at our children, the way you talk to them, the tears in your eyes as you gaze at them. You are the best man I've ever known. In making you my husband, I am now complete in a way I've never been before. And I will love you for the rest of my life and beyond."

There wasn't a dry eye in that garden. Even Ava dabbed at her lashes, and when she looked at Ransom, she swore she saw a glimmer of moisture in his gaze too.

Then the minister declared them husband and wife. "You may kiss the bride."

There were all sorts of kisses—she'd seen enough chick flicks to know—but Gideon and Rosie's kiss was one of the most beautiful. Cupping Rosie's face in his big hands, Gideon tipped her face up to his, tasting her lips as if she were a precious elixir. As if he would never let her go.

And Ava knew he wouldn't.

Everyone rose to their feet then, and the smiling couple, hands joined, walked together down the aisle to hoots and hollers and cheers and laughter and love. Ari and Matt followed, hands clasped, eyes only for each other. Grinning, rolling their eyes at all the mushy stuff, the boys followed.

When Ava turned to see the two couples reach the end of the aisle, she found Ransom right there. Instead of watching the bride and groom, he was looking at her, and something in his gaze dragged her in.

The urge to go up on tiptoe and press her lips to his was almost too powerful to resist. But resist she must, because that way lay epic disaster.

She pushed him into the aisle. "You'd better go. You're on now."

Before the crowd pulled him away toward the bride and groom, he mouthed, *I'll catch you later.*

His words seemed dangerously prophetic.

Chapter Fourteen

Ransom watched Ava flit from group to group, saying hello to anyone she'd missed during the pre-ceremony cocktail hour. The eye-popping burgundy gown she wore clung to every mouth-watering curve, the color complementing her dark-cherry hair.

He wanted to trail after her like a panting puppy. But of course that wouldn't do with all the Mavericks and Harringtons looking on.

The rolling bar cart was out again, along with another offering of canapés, though nothing in excess. He wanted his guests to enjoy the meal without being overly full. A mistake many caterers made when preparing for a sit-down meal was to provide too many appetizers, which took away from the pleasure of the meal creations.

Clay Harrington waved him over. He'd never known the man to have a full-time girlfriend, and his dates never seemed to say much, but Clay's choice for this event was certainly eye candy.

Sebastian Montgomery, who'd been speaking with Clay, stuck out his hand as soon as Ransom joined the small group. "We heard you'd stepped in at the last minute to take over the catering. Fantastic job, Ransom. Thanks so much for saving the family's butt."

That was Maverick thinking—that he'd saved the family unit.

They were so close-knit that if you did a favor for one, you did it for them all. "It was my pleasure. Anything to help out a Maverick. And Gideon and Rosie deserve the best." The couple were off now for the obligatory photos.

"Speaking of the best," Charlie, Sebastian's gorgeous redheaded fiancée, raised a champagne flute. "This champagne is the most delicious I've ever tasted."

"Yeah," Sebastian agreed. "It's excellent. I was never a champagne fan until I tasted the good stuff." And the man had plenty of opportunities to taste the very best.

Charlie said with a cheeky smile, "Talk about champagne problems. I used to drink champagne that wasn't even from Champagne."

Sebastian laughed, lifting her hand to his lips. "I'll always give you the real thing." Then he, too, raised his glass. "This is better than just about anything I've had."

Ransom simply said, "I'm glad you like it."

Gideon and Rosie had been on a budget, but when he saw the bubbly they'd chosen, he knew it wouldn't cut it. He'd thought about Dom Perignon, but he'd come across a champagne on his last trip to France that he thought would be perfect, though he'd never tell Gideon or Rosie it was four hundred dollars a bottle. It just wasn't in him to cut corners for this special wedding. He needed the libations to complement the flavors of the creations he'd designed.

"A perfect choice," Sebastian said.

Ransom wondered if the man knew that it couldn't possibly be within budget. Gideon was a good man, and he was going places, but he wasn't yet at the level where he could afford the best of everything. Ransom was well aware that the Mavericks would never force their help on him, not wanting to one-up him on his special day with Rosie.

But Ransom could still provide the bride and groom with the best champagne without their even being aware of it.

Clay introduced his date, then added, "Charlie, I haven't had a chance to say that your work is absolutely amazing."

Charlie Ballard was a metal artist, having made the sculpture that adorned Sebastian's headquarters up in the city.

"Thank you so much," Charlie said, her face aglow.

"The chariot race you did for Sebastian is phenomenal." Clay's dark eyes had the glow of fervor. He wasn't just flattering her. He meant every word. "And the dragon in Chinatown. The detail." He waved his hands in the air as if he couldn't find words to describe it. "It's unbelievable."

Charlie blushed. Clay wasn't even overdoing it. Then he laughed. "I even enjoyed the Zanti Misfits you made for Dane."

She smiled, her red-gold hair shining in the sun. "I didn't actually make them for him. They're just things I create to burn off energy while I'm thinking about a new project."

Ransom had no idea what a Zanti Misfit was, and he supposed it didn't matter since obviously both Clay and Sebastian did.

Sebastian, in what seemed to be a proprietary move, kissed Charlie soundly. "I first fell in love with Charlie when I saw her Zanti Misfits."

Laughing, Charlie clung to his arm. "I thought it was my Tyrannosaurus Rex you fell in love with."

Sebastian, his gaze full of adoration, said, "I simply fell in love with you."

The look that passed between them made Ransom search for Ava, who was talking with Harper Franconi. The first time he'd seen Ava, she'd been laughing with his grandmother. And yes, that was the moment he'd fallen in love with her, when she was doing what she did best—making an elderly person smile, giving them the gifts of love and laughter.

As if that loving look hadn't even registered, Clay said, "I've made a tour of the city to see all your pieces."

Charlie gaped at him.

"I've got a property that needs a large piece of art out front," Clay said, "so I'd like to commission something. I know you're working with Dane on sculptures for his resorts, but I was hoping you could fit me in whenever you have a spare moment. Can I call you next week to discuss it?"

Charlie's blush rose to her hairline, as if she still wasn't used to her notoriety or to the fact that she was one of the most sought-after sculpture artists in the Bay Area, and fast becoming so in the entire United States.

"Yes," she said breathlessly. "Please give me a call. Dane has given me plenty of latitude on the timing for the pieces he's commissioned."

Then Clay added, "I apologize for missing most of the family barbecues. I've had a hectic schedule these past few months, but I hope to be joining you more often now."

Family barbecues. Interesting. Ransom should have known the Mavericks and Harringtons were hooking up. It was obvious now, since the wedding guests were mostly family, as well as some of the foster kids Gideon mentored.

Speaking of the man, Gideon joined their group, the photo session obviously over, with congratulations, manly hugs, and back slaps all around.

Charlie asked, "Where's Rosie?" Then she beamed. "And the baby?"

Gideon smiled with love shining in his eyes. "She's getting

Isabella settled in the moms' tent. My little girl," he said proudly, "is ready for a nap after all the activity during the wedding."

"She was so adorable wearing her mother's veil." They all shared Charlie's smile over little Isabella's antics.

"I'd really like to join her over there," Charlie said, touching Sebastian's arm. "Just to give Isabella, and all the babies, a kiss."

"Of course." The man nodded.

Turning to Clay, she said, "I'll call you during the week." And she dragged Sebastian off.

Grabbing Ransom's shoulder, Gideon shook his hand heartily. "There aren't any words for what you did for us. Even *thank you* isn't enough."

Ransom waved him off. "I keep telling you it was my pleasure. And no problem at all."

Gideon snorted. "Yeah, right. You're minimizing your effort, but thank you." Then he turned to Clay. "I was hoping to get a chance to talk to you today. I thought you might help me with one of my foster kids."

Though Ransom could have slipped away then, he was interested enough to stay and listen. Especially since he had a perfect view of Ava, in that drop-dead gorgeous dress, talking with Susan Spencer.

Clay asked, eyebrows raised, "How the hell can *I* help?" As if he had no idea what he could ever do for a kid.

"His name is Dylan, and I've been mentoring him for a few months." With his chin, Gideon indicated a kid by the canapé tray, stuffing one appetizer after another into his mouth as if he'd never get a chance to eat again. He was somewhere around seventeen, and he pulled at the collar of his shirt as if the monkey suit were strangling him. His hair hung past his collar, and his angular, too-lean frame was apparent in the cut of a tux obviously rented at the last minute.

"He's a graffiti artist," Gideon explained, and Clay listened with interest. "He's been caught tagging in illegal places. I keep bailing him out. But he won't stop."

"I don't think he can stop," Clay said. "With some people, the art is just in them, dying to get out."

Gideon punched his shoulder lightly. "That's exactly why I came to you. I'd like your help in mentoring him. We need to find other outlets for him so he doesn't keep getting in trouble."

Clay tipped his head thoughtfully, while next to him Ransom noted his date yawning, barely covering it with her hand.

"San Francisco's Mission District is a well-known place for street art," Clay said. "It's not tagging. It's not graffiti. It's art," he clarified, as though he appreciated the work. "You may be surprised to know that street art can be quite a lucrative business. It's not graffiti tossed up anywhere. It can beautify a district. You should see some of the amazing street art in cities like New York and Paris and London. Even Reno has revamped MidTown with some incredible murals. Sometimes the work is only there for a few days or weeks until it's painted over with new street art. But that's the beauty of it—that it's always changing."

Gideon's eyes gleamed. "This is exactly what I'm looking for." He pointed a finger at Clay. "I just need help getting Dylan on the right track. Can we do it together, man?"

Clay was in his element, his blue Harrington eyes almost lit from within. "Why do you think I started my new media platform? It's for kids like Dylan, for people who need to find direction and a safe place to practice their art. Hell yes, Gideon, I'll help."

As if he felt their scrutiny, the kid looked over at their small group. Whatever he saw on their faces seemed to terrify him, and he melted into the crowd around the bar cart, hiding himself.

These two men had their work cut out for them, Ransom was sure.

As Clay and Gideon talked logistics on their new mission, Ransom melted into the crowd much as Dylan had.

He'd never met such a big, wonderful family, complimenting each other, helping each other. Susan and Bob Spencer seemed to have more than enough love to go around. They'd created a close-knit group, and then they'd welcomed the Harringtons to join them.

He saw her now—Ava, beautiful and sexy in the formfitting dress, engrossed in a conversation with Cammie. Had she even looked his way since the vows had been said?

For as long as he'd known the Harringtons, they'd been a unit that had seemed damn near impenetrable. Ava had never told her family she was seeing him, even though she was practically living with him, since they spent every hour together when he was home.

But that was fifteen years ago, and how things had changed. Watching these two families merge made him think of his brother. While their relationship had definitely improved, Ransom realized he needed to see more of Adam. They'd bonded over their mother's death, their mutual grief, and Ransom got out to Milwaukee as often as possible. But as he'd learned with Ava, *as often as possible* wasn't often enough. He needed to make more of an effort.

He imagined taking Ava to meet the family. He imagined big family holiday dinners that he and Adam cooked together, with Ava by his side. The daydream made him ache for the kind of huge, loving family the Mavericks had. Family who were there for each other in all the best ways.

He didn't want to be like his father, where everything was about work. And wasn't that really what had broken up his relationship with Ava? Because he hadn't put her or the relationship first? The truth was, he'd overworked like his dad, and he'd lost Ava because of it. He hadn't seen it all back then, but he saw it clearly now.

He came out of the fog of his thoughts to find Matt Tremont stalking straight toward him, his wife's hand in his. Matt jabbed a finger at his shoulder. "Hey, what's up with catering a wedding? We were early investors in your company, but you never catered *our* weddings." The twinkle in Matt's eyes belied his mock anger.

Will Franconi, seeming to appear out of nowhere, joined in. "Yeah, buddy, what the hell is up with that?"

These Mavericks never missed an opportunity to razz a guy. Ransom didn't knuckle under. "Why didn't any of you ever ask me? Like I'm not good enough for you?"

Will shut his mouth.

But Ransom didn't let them off the hook. "Then I had to jump in and save Gideon and Rosie's wedding. Where were you two?"

The two men frowned, glum looks pulling down their faces. But Ari laughed. "Oh boy, Ransom has got you there." She leaned in to kiss Ransom's cheek. "You did a wonderful thing."

"I helped." He winked at Will and Matt. "But you all would have cooked the meal yourselves if you had to."

"You're damn right," Will said, Matt nodding forceful agreement.

He would never tell them he'd done it because Ava had asked him. Truly, he would have done it for any of the Mavericks. But for Ava, he'd have walked through fire.

He couldn't help looking for her. Where the hell was she

now?

Rosie joined them then, the train of her beautiful wedding dress pinned up, giving the gown a bustle at the back. "I finally got Isabella down. She wanted to sleep with my veil. How she grabbed it at her age, I'll never know." Her eyes flashed, and they all laughed. "She should be fine for a few hours."

"Penelope is sleeping like an angel," Ari said of her daughter, only two weeks younger than Isabella, then she held up crossed fingers. "I hope she sleeps for a few." Plucking a champagne flute off the tray of a passing waiter, she handed it to the bride, and they all raised their glasses. "To happily ever after. Rosie, you were always the sister of my heart, but now you're my true sister. Family forever."

Ransom felt the truth in those words. When the Mavericks loved, they loved big and wholeheartedly.

Rosie held up her glass. "This ranks right up there with one of the best days of my life." Sipping rather than gulping, sadness suddenly clouded Rosie's eyes. "The only thing that could have made it better was if Chi could be here."

Ari echoed her sentiment. "Yeah. If only." Then she explained, mostly for Ransom's benefit, because everyone else probably knew, "She's our best friend from foster care. We were the three musketeers." Ari and Rosie bumped fists. "She's nannying while she's working on her degree, and right now she's traveling with the family, taking care of the kids, so she really couldn't come home, even for the wedding. They're on an African safari, and it was impossible for her to get away."

Rosie grabbed Ari's hand. "Come on, bestie, let's go make a video for Chi and send it off right now." The two women dashed to get their phones.

"Well," Matt drawled. "I guess we're chopped liver next to

making videos for the best friend."

The three men laughed. Until Ransom's attention was drawn away by a tap on his shoulder. Honorine had graciously agreed to help them out, especially after she'd met Ava.

He stepped away with her. "We've got a problem with the béarnaise," she said in the softest of voices, as if she couldn't bear for anyone to overhear this calamity. "There just isn't time to redo it." Then she groaned. "*Désolée.* I shouldn't have trusted Bertrand with it. He still has a lot to learn. But there was so much to do."

Ransom smiled, wanting to ease her frantic look. "I saw some packages of béarnaise sauce in Susan Spencer's pantry. I'm sure she won't mind if we use them."

Honorine's face turned red, and she gasped as if he'd suggested committing the foulest of crimes. "*A packaged mix?*"

"I've used it before. It tastes as good as the homemade stuff, and it's a lot easier to make." An arm around her shoulders, he turned Honorine in the direction of the kitchen and whispered in her ear, "No one will ever know. Chef's secret. Sometimes store-bought is just as good as homemade."

Honorine practically ran for the kitchen as if she couldn't bear to listen to this blasphemy.

When he turned, Gideon and Rosie both stood before him. Obviously, the video was already winging its way to Africa.

Rosie raised her champagne flute to him. "Thank you so, so much for stepping in, Ransom." She was a petite woman next to her new husband, with luscious curls of long dark hair falling over her shoulders. "I don't know what we would have done without you."

He smiled at her. "Like I said to Gideon, it was my pleasure."

Peering through the champagne in her flute, her cocoa eyes

grew troubled. "This champagne is the best I've ever tasted." She licked her lips. "But I think it's probably the whole budget."

Gideon slung an arm over Ransom's shoulders. "Honestly, I don't think we can afford it."

Ransom couldn't let them go on. "This is what you need to know about chefs. We are among the most temperamental people in the world. I needed the perfect pairing for the food." He smiled. "Unfortunately, the champagne you had on your list was not the perfect pairing. I had to change it."

Gideon said softly, "But the budget."

Ransom put a hand on each of their shoulders. "This champagne is my wedding gift to you. You don't need to worry about the budget. I'm more than happy to do it, because really, it's all about me." He tapped a fist to his chest and grinned. "Now, off with you both to enjoy your guests."

Rosie beckoned him to bend down, then she threw her arms around him, kissed his cheek, and whispered in watery words, "Thank you."

Gideon gave him a hearty hand clasp.

And finally, when they were once again mingling, Ransom could look for Ava.

Chapter Fifteen

When Ransom turned, his gaze met Ava's across the pool deck, and his eyes widened, almost as if he was shocked to see her. Then a lady-killer smile curved his lips, and his eyes—God, his eyes seemed to touch every part of her, lighting a fire in her.

Just when she thought he'd approach, he saluted her and headed toward the kitchen, where Fernsby was most likely taking over the preparations as if he were the master chef, and Gabby would be adding last-minute touches to the wedding cake. Her sister would fiddle and fiddle until she achieved perfection, even if it took hours.

Only as she exhaled did Ava realize she'd been holding her breath during the entire wordless exchange that felt as if it said so much.

Clustered with Kelsey Collins, Tasha Summerfield, Charlie, Will's wife, Harper, and Cammie, Ava was suddenly brought back to the moment as Kelsey said, "Well, that was the sweetest thing—champagne as a wedding gift." The news had swiftly made the rounds of the guests.

Ava liked Kelsey, Evan Collins's sister, her blond hair curled expertly for the wedding, when normally she wore it straight.

But it was Cammie who said, "I've always liked Ransom. He's just so easy and accommodating to work with."

Why did they have to be talking about Ransom? Ava's heart

still felt as if it were fluttering away after him.

Then Cammie asked, "How's it going with your catering problem?"

It was almost a relief to spend a few minutes explaining to the other ladies about firing her catering company. "Ransom has jumped in with both feet. It's really taken a load off my mind. The menus he's created are really good."

Kelsey nudged Tasha. "Of course he creates fabulous menus. Just like he has for the wedding." Then she smiled with a knowing look, as if she sensed something was going on between Ava and Ransom. Kelsey could sniff out even the tiniest hint of romance in the air.

But they were right. What Ransom had done for Rosie and Gideon was so sweet. She felt as though he was taking a pickax to the wall she was trying to keep high between them, and another chunk was falling away.

"He really is a great guy," Tasha said, flipping her long, silky black hair over her shoulder. Ava expected Tasha and Daniel Spencer to announce an engagement any day now. After all, love was in the air.

She didn't allow herself to blush. "He's been very accommodating." It was the best word Ava could think of without actually gushing. And without telling them about the amazing day she and Ransom had spent together—the traffic jam, Supermart, Motel Y, pancakes the next morning, and dinner at his restaurant. The details were too new to share, too sensitive, her feelings too perplexing.

Harper added in her sweet voice, "The two of you look so good together."

Against her will, Ava's cheeks heated, even as she was shaking her head. Before she could get out the word *no*, the other ladies were chiming in. "I mean," Charlie said, "we know how intimidated most men are by you because you're so brilliant and successful. But you wouldn't have that problem with Ransom."

"Of course it wouldn't be an issue," Kelsey agreed. "He's like the most famous chef in the whole country." She winked. "Even the whole world."

A nervous heat wave washed through her body, and Ava grabbed a glass of champagne from a passing waiter, downing half of it in one gulp.

All the women were eyeing her now.

"Wait." Kelsey's eyes glittered with interest. "Is there a story here?"

She didn't want to lie to them. And really, nothing was going on. Yet, even as another wave of heat suffused her body, it felt altogether different. It warmed her insides with a beautiful thought.

Maybe I have some new friends here.

They actually understood. She was a female executive who intimidated men. It was much like the discussion she'd had with Ransom the other day. She always had to be on guard, always had to look for ulterior motives, always had to fight for her right to be who she was instead of whatever "the man" wanted her to be.

But she didn't have to be guarded with these women, and she was so happy to be included in their group, included in their lives. She didn't have many female friends. She'd always had Gabby, but even though Gabby was her best friend, it was somehow different from having a friend you hadn't grown up with.

She wanted this kind of friendship for Gabby too—friendship with women who respected you, even admired you.

She and Gabby were so often surrounded by men in their chosen careers. Even when socializing, which Ava did often as part of her job, many of her associations were with men. And their wives seemed to view her differently because she was part of the business world, a world that was open to them only on the periphery. She'd felt that sometimes they even looked down on her, like there was something wrong with her that she was married to her career and wasn't a mother.

But all the Mavericks were career women as well as mothers and lovers, and they still included her. Maybe she was past throwing baby showers and birthday parties for the people at work as her only outlet for friendship.

This was totally different for her. And it actually felt wonderful.

But still, talking about Ransom? She wasn't ready for that. "You all know my story," she said with a smile, not wanting to lie to Kelsey or any of the women. "My brothers say I'm all work and no play." She was sure at least one of them had said that at some point.

She was saved from saying more when Fernsby stepped from the kitchen, clapped his hands, and called out in that delightful drone of his, "Dinner is ready to be served. Please take your seats." His tone of voice added, *immediately*.

While the guests mingled on the pool patio and the deck, the head table had been set up in the gazebo where Rosie and Gideon had said their vows. The servers had transformed the grassy area, unfolding round tables and dressing them with damask tablecloths, silverware, and crystal.

Each of the women was whisked away by her amazing man. Kelsey's older brother Evan insisted she join him at the Collins family table. And Cammie linked arms with Ava, the two of them sitting down with her brothers.

Clay leaned forward past Dane to ask, "Where's Gabby?"

"She's inside, putting the finishing touches on the wedding cake," Ava told him.

Troy snorted a laugh. "She can't leave that thing alone. Have you seen it?"

Dane answered for all of them, "I'd rather have a surprise when she and Fernsby bring it out."

Clay's date pulled out a chair, obviously having spent the last fifteen minutes freshening her makeup—or hiding out.

At each place setting sat a card saying, *If you have any allergies or foods you cannot eat, please keep this card in front of you and you will be accommodated.*

Of course, Ransom wouldn't have had time to learn who could eat what. He wouldn't even have had time to figure out how many to make of each entrée.

Across the table, Clay's date slapped the little card on the table in front of her after reading it.

But Clay turned his over. Then he laughed. "Do you see what it says on the back?"

They all picked up their cards while Clay read aloud. *"If you tear up this card, your meal will be a surprise. And you take what you get."* He tore it up. So did the rest of the family. Everyone except his date.

Laughter rang out around the garden as everyone else obviously read the back. At the head table, Rosie and Gideon leaned close, reading together and wiping away tears of laughter.

That was Ransom. He'd found a way to infuse humor into a difficult situation.

The servers hustled out carrying huge trays, and the soup placed in front of her was lobster bisque. Cammie was served asparagus soup, and Dane received carrot soup, which were both wonderful, especially made by Ransom. But lobster bisque was one of Ava's favorites, and she was ecstatic at the surprise set in front of her.

As a server bent to say something softly to Clay's date, she shook her head almost violently and waved away anything he might have given her.

When everyone had gobbled down the delicious soups, the army of servers carried away the dishes, and trays of salad came out next.

Once again, after Clay's date had turned everything down, her server asked politely, "Is there anything else I can bring instead? Whatever you'd like can be accommodated."

The young woman looked up at him gratefully. "Just kale, with only oil and vinegar."

Clay simply smiled at her as the man rushed away.

Ava glanced down at her salad, dressed up with candied pecans and blue cheese. Ransom had always made the best dressing, sweet yet tangy.

She finished faster than anyone, right down to the last bite of greens, every element once again one of her favorites. Was the salad on the menus Ransom prepared? She'd have to ask him. Her residents would love it.

As the salad plates disappeared, the servers returned once again with entrées.

Ava felt herself drooling over the scallops in a white wine sauce. Sitting on a bed of herbed black rice, they were accompanied by crispy brussels sprouts in a spicy-sweet glaze of maple syrup and sriracha.

The two other offerings were chicken tenders prepared coq au vin style, and bacon-wrapped beef tournedos in béarnaise sauce. Dane leaned over Cammie's beef and whispered loudly, "Wouldn't you rather have the coq au vin, darling?"

She pushed his hand away. "Don't you dare touch my beef." They spent the meal trying to steal bites off each other's plates.

The reality hit Ava with her first scallop and half a brussels sprout spitted on her fork.

Good God.

Everything on Ransom's menu was a favorite of hers. Like the sand dabs he'd prepared for her on Friday. He'd remembered every favorite, from the variety of soups to the salad with candied pecans and blue cheese to the scallops and brussels sprouts, the coq au vin, and the beef béarnaise.

None of which she'd had in ages—at least, not the way Ransom prepared them. And maybe not even since she'd been with him.

Yet he'd remembered every single thing she loved.

She thought about the appetizers too—the blackened fish, the quiche, the shrimp in a tangy cocktail sauce. Everything she loved.

This entire feast was a culinary love letter… to her.

* * *

The meal went off without a hitch. Ransom was pleased. For Clay's date, who couldn't seem to eat anything, he'd prepared marinated tofu over a bed of brown rice with peas, carrots, and beans. He'd wondered if she'd turn up her nose at the marinade, but the woman had smiled and said it was delicious.

After making sure Gideon and Rosie were pleased, he'd strolled among the tables to confirm that everyone was satisfied.

Between conversations, he'd watched Ava. She'd loved every bite. She'd even gazed with envious eyes at Cammie's beef and

Dane's coq au vin. But he'd known the scallops would work best for her, and the brussels sprouts in maple and sriracha would blow her mind.

He'd made sure all the champagne glasses were filled for the speeches and toasts, then the DJ had called out the first dances. Now everyone was rocking on the dance floor, Gideon and Rosie in the center wrapped in each other's arms.

Ava was still seated, laughing with Troy and Gabby, while Dane had lured Cammie onto the floor. Just before dinner, Ransom had shot Ava that smoldering look, damn near undressing her with his gaze. Then he'd let her stew in that all through his special meal.

But now it was his turn. One dance with Ava, the luscious feel of her in his arms. Oh yeah.

He never made it. Will Franconi slugged him playfully on the arm. "This champagne is delicious." He held up a bottle he'd snagged. "La Chapelle." He narrowed his eyes at Ransom. "How did I not know about this? I mean, I'm the importer here. But I missed it. Where'd you find it?"

"On my last scouting trip for wines in the Loire Valley. I couldn't resist a jaunt to the Champagne region. You like it?" He truly wanted to know. Will's superpower was finding the next big thing that people would go nuts over.

Will let his mouth drop open. "Are you kidding? My clients will love this. How expensive is it? The higher the price, the better."

Ransom glanced at Gideon and Rosie on the dance floor. "Let's discuss the price later."

Will slapped his shoulder. "Good idea. Let's get together. You and I can make this champagne bigger than any other. What do you think?"

"I'll make sure they can keep up with the demand."

His gaze drifted to Ava, her hair shining in the late afternoon sun, her skin glowing against the burgundy of her sexy dress. His gaze had drifted to her often. She was like a magnet for him.

Will eyed him. "Now you've got me wondering exactly who you did all this for. The bride and groom? Or…" His gaze rested on Ava.

Just as Ransom's had done for the past ten minutes. Honestly, for the entire wedding.

Ransom gave Will a smile. He wasn't about to reveal anything.

But Will winked. "No need to answer. I already figured it out. All those longing glances." He waggled his eyebrows and put a hand on Ransom's shoulder, almost in solidarity. "Good luck. If it helps you to know this at all, it took me a hell of a long time to convince Harper. In fact, all of us guys had a hard time with our special women. But you know, it's like they say—the harder you have to work for something, the greater it is when you finally get what you've been waiting for your whole life."

Then he sauntered off to find Harper, the woman for whom he'd searched his whole life.

It was as if the man had laid down the gauntlet for Ransom, commiserating and at the same time making him question whether he could actually pull this off.

Or if he'd screw things up again and let Ava get away.

* * *

Ransom had missed his chance to dance with Ava. She was out on the floor dancing with several of the women, her gorgeous hair flying, her smile one of the happiest he'd seen in recent days. She seemed at home with the Mavericks—the whole Harrington family did. And he relished watching her cut loose, enjoying herself.

Will had found Harper, and after making the rounds of the reception, talking with Susan and Bob, the Mavericks, Cammie and Dane, and more, they'd joined in the dancing too. A slow, close dance in each other's arms even though the music was fast.

Ransom was pleased with another business deal in the making. He and Will had often collaborated on interesting imports, joining in lucrative ventures.

He checked his watch. Almost time for the cake reveal. But before he turned toward the kitchen, he saw Clay Harrington bearing down on him, his girlfriend or date or whatever she was nowhere to be seen. Such a glower tensed Clay's face that Ransom said, "Everything okay, buddy?"

Clay seemed so worked up that the only words he could get out were, "Yeah. Sure. Great." Then he pointed a finger, almost stabbed it at Ransom's chest. "I need to talk to you."

"Okay. I'm right here."

A thunderstorm passed over Clay's face as they moved away from the main body of wedding revelers. Ransom had never worked with Clay. Most of his business dealings were with Dane and the resorts. But he knew the family, he knew that look on Clay's face, and he suspected what was coming before Clay even got the words out.

The man scowled. "What's going on between you and Ava?" Just as the Mavericks were protective of their younger sister, Lyssa, the Harrington brothers were protective of their sisters too. Which was why Ava had never wanted to reveal their relationship.

So maybe Will wasn't the only one who'd noticed all those longing glances. Ransom did it even now, his gaze involuntarily shooting to Ava on the dance floor. Before he could say a word, Clay read his expression and stepped into his personal space, his pointed finger hovering right before Ransom's nose. "You hurt her, and you don't just answer to me, you answer to my whole family, and that includes the Mavericks."

Then he turned abruptly on his heel, without even letting Ransom reply, and stalked off toward Dane.

Ransom once again glanced toward the dance floor in search of Ava. Always looking for her. And he was met by Will's wink, before the man saluted him with his champagne glass.

All that talking Will had done with this Maverick and that Maverick? Well, damn. The man had a big mouth, and he'd probably whispered his suspicions about Ransom and Ava to anyone who'd listen. Sebastian was looking at him too. Assessing.

After grabbing a glass of champagne off the tray of a passing waiter, he stalked to Will and Harper. "You've been talking, haven't you?" The Mavericks were a bunch of gossips. And the rumor had obviously spread fast. Straight to Clay.

Will widened his eyes in mock affront. "Me? Talking? About what?"

"You don't fool me, Franconi." He shook his head sadly, as if he couldn't believe it.

A smile broadened across Will's face. "The truth is—" He paused a beat. "—the butler did it." Beside him, Harper giggled.

Ransom wanted to laugh. He wanted to clap.

He wanted to rush to Ava, catch her up in his arms, and carry her off like a Neanderthal.

But the Mavericks would have a field day with that.

And Clay would probably punch him.

Chapter Sixteen

Parched after all the dancing, Ava took a glass of water off the rolling bar cart. When she'd gulped it down, she couldn't resist an espresso martini.

She couldn't see Ransom. And really, she shouldn't be looking for him. She'd actually been terrified he might sit down with her during the meal, but thank God he hadn't. The worst was over—sitting next to him during the wedding and all those sweet vows.

Refreshed by the water and martini in hand, she rejoined her compadres from the dance floor, which now consisted of Kelsey, Tasha, and Cammie. Then Charlie bounced back after her dance, while Sebastian whirled Susan, aglow with delight and laughter, around the floor.

It was only as she sipped her espresso martini that Ava noticed her friends looking at her. Kelsey's eyes were full of mirth. That woman always seemed to be laughing.

Tapping her bottom lip with a polished finger, she smiled at Ava. "You know," she drawled, "if I were single, I wouldn't kick the chef out of bed for eating crackers."

Something slithered down Ava's spine. Kelsey couldn't know. She could only be guessing.

But that gleam in Kelsey's eyes said, oh yes, she knew something. Maybe they all did. "I wouldn't kick him out for potato chips either." She fluttered her eyelashes. "Not even for tacos."

Tasha giggled. "You've eaten tacos in bed? I've so gotta try that with Daniel."

All the women laughed. Ava forced herself to laugh too. "Ransom is in the kitchen. If you want to give him some… *crackers*." She raised one eyebrow.

But Kelsey wagged her finger in Ava's face. "Oh, no. I think that chef is taken."

Good Lord. They *did* know. They *all* knew. She felt as if a bucket of water had fallen on her head. But she kept smiling.

Then Kelsey hugged her and whispered in her ear, "Go for it."

"Stop that," Charlie chided them all. "You're embarrassing her."

When Ava's eyes met Cammie's, her friend said, "Ava doesn't embarrass easily." Then she added, "Everyone's making something out of nothing." She held Ava's gaze. "After all, what's in a look?"

Good God. They'd seen her looking at Ransom. Probably way too many times.

But it couldn't be just that. Someone must have said something. Not Gabby. First of all, Gabby would never say anything to anyone. Second of all, her sister was consumed with perfecting her cake. She hadn't spent more than half an hour outside the kitchen, and that was just to witness the wedding vows and to gulp down Ransom's special marinated tofu and vegetables at her assigned table.

And it wasn't Ava's secretive looks.

That left only one person. Ransom.

"Hold that thought," Ava said. "I need to powder my nose."

She would have made it to the kitchen if Clay hadn't stepped into her path. She did not like the look on his face. She liked even less the first words out of his mouth. "Is there something between you—"

She held up her hand a millisecond before he could say Ransom's name. Leaning in close, her voice deadly, she said, "If I were you, I wouldn't go where I think you're going." She paused a beat to let that sink in. "As you well know, my personal life is my own."

Clay shut his mouth as if Ava had suddenly become an alien. She took the opportunity to add, "Not that you deserve an answer. But if I were to give you one, the answer would be no." She marched around him, turning at the last minute to say, "I'm on my way to the ladies' room to powder my nose. Don't even think about following me and adding one more word to what you've already said." Not that she'd let him say much at all.

She opened the kitchen door, stepped inside, and found such a flurry of activity that she almost walked right back out.

But there was Ransom, wearing an apron. An actual damned apron.

She crooked a finger at him. He slowly, deliberately, pulled the apron over his head and laid it on the counter, never taking his eyes off her. The racket in the kitchen seemed to go quiet, too quiet. She couldn't bear to see who else was there. Instead, she headed out the front door, closing it when Ransom stepped out with her.

She did not need witnesses for this conversation.

"Did you say anything to anyone about that night at the Motel Y? Because Clay just asked me if there was something going on between us." She was trying to remain calm, even though she could feel her blood rushing through her ears.

He said smugly—yes, with actual smugness in his tone, "But

nothing happened at the Motel Y."

Nothing happened? She wanted to say that *something* had happened. Everything had started to change.

"But," he said, "I don't think it's been that hard for anyone to figure out."

"Why on earth would you say that?" But she was afraid she knew the answer. Even the ladies were making wisecracks.

One eyebrow raised, he said simply, "Longing glances are hard to ignore."

She wanted to shake a finger at him, but she was still holding the espresso martini, and it was too good to spill. Dammit, she should have dropped it off in the kitchen before she started this. But she said with the same force she used on Clay, "I wasn't giving you any longing glances."

She wanted to slap that smile right off his face. "Maybe you weren't," he said. "But I sure have been sending them to you."

She took a step away, her back against the door. Her throat was dry, and she gulped a quarter of the espresso martini. "But it's just business between us."

He took back the extra step she'd tried to put between them and said, so softly it was like a caress, "You know damned well this isn't just business anymore."

She tried to say something, but her throat clogged up. And she had to gulp the martini. Next to a champagne cocktail, it was one of her favorite drinks. Her damn favorite cocktail—of course it had been on the bar menu. It was so good, she felt a little wobbly after all the champagne and now this.

She threw it all back at him, at least figuratively. "What's up with you making all my favorite foods for dinner?"

He arched an eyebrow. And there was that smile again. "Do you really need me to explain that to you?"

She'd seen it for what it was, then. A foodie's love letter. She'd been afraid when she called him, but she couldn't have done anything else. Gideon needed help. But *this*—all her favorite appetizers, her favorite drinks, her favorite entrées, soups, even the damned salad.

She felt as if she might topple off her high heels.

Her feet wanted to run away. But she'd run away on Friday after that dinner at his restaurant. She was better than that. Tougher than that. She had to stand her ground.

Changing tack, she ignored his question, ignored his love letter, ignored her roiling emotions. Instead, she complimented him. "You did a fabulous job. Everything was scrumptious. And the drinks." She held up the nearly empty martini glass. "They're divine. The way you stepped in to help Gideon and Rosie, that was above and beyond. Thank you. But I also want to thank myself, because I was the one who asked you."

Her sudden change had him stepping back. Then she added the *coup de grâce*, the statement that would show him she wasn't flustered at all. "Tell me what I can do to help you now."

⋆ ⋆ ⋆

The woman left him dumbfounded. First, because she didn't run. Second, because this sudden change felt like a step forward in their new relationship. In the past few days, whenever it felt like they were getting close, she'd run. But this time she didn't. Instead, she'd offered to help.

Could he trust the change?

At least she'd noticed that everything he'd prepared today had been just for her. Right down to the espresso martini in her hand.

"Thanks," he said. "I'm pretty much done with dinner now.

Honorine did most of it." But he wasn't about to let Ava go. How the hell could she help?

Of course. The cake.

"Gabby and Fernsby are making the final touches on the cake. My servers will take care of handing it out. But I need to get all the plates and cutlery out there. Can you help me?"

He had people to do it, but now that she'd offered, he couldn't let the opportunity pass, even if it was make-work.

"I'd be happy to," she said with a smile. God, how he'd longed to see her smile for him alone all day long.

She drained the last of her martini like a statement, either a *thank you* or a *screw you*, then handed him the glass. "All right, I'm ready."

He was so damn ready. He just wasn't sure they were ready for the same thing.

Guiding her back to the kitchen, he set the empty glass on the counter and turned to his two master bakers. "Ava and I will take out the dessert plates and cutlery. Are you almost ready?"

Gabby didn't even turn. "Almost." She'd been fretting over the cake the entire afternoon. Perhaps it was the collaboration with Fernsby. Or because this was for Rosie and Gideon.

Fernsby simply raised an eyebrow that could mean anything. "That's good of you, sir. Miss Harrington is the perfect help-mate." Was that a gleam in the man's eye? "At least under these circumstances."

As they piled plates and cutlery on a trolley, Ava whispered to him, "What was that supposed to mean?"

He shook his head. "It's just Fernsby. If you look up the word *enigmatic* in the dictionary, you'll find a picture of him."

Then he let Fernsby drift right out of his mind and concentrated only on Ava. As they worked, he thought of all the times they'd stood side by side in his kitchen. She did all the things that needed a careful touch, cutting precisely, chopping exactly. She was his sous-chef. And so much more.

Together, they rolled the trolley out onto the deck and down the ramp the Mavericks had laid out to make serving easier.

"Stop looking at me that way," she said so softly no one could overhear.

He raised an eyebrow just like Fernsby. "What way?"

She narrowed her eyes at him. "You know what way."

Oh yes, he knew. He looked at her with such longing that he felt his breath stop in his chest. It was impossible not to.

* * *

Fernsby watched with beady eyes as two beefy servers rolled out the four-tiered cake. Because of course the baker didn't carry his own creation. He walked behind, so that everyone could congratulate him on the magnificence of the masterpiece.

Once they were out the door, he allowed Gabrielle to walk beside him, since she was half creator of their *objet d'art*.

He dipped his head to hide his smile. Half creator. That would put Miss Gabrielle Harrington in her place. But he gave kudos where kudos were deserved. In fact, he'd grown to admire her over the years.

And the cake was splendid, with minute decorations piped in icing. No simple rosettes for Gabrielle. Icing dots banded the bottom of each tier like a double-stranded pearl necklace. She'd piped a delicate design of leaves, flowers, and baby's breath all around the sides and tops. She ended with tiny silver sugar balls in and around the piped design. Once the cake topper had been placed, she piped delicate cream flowers around it, securing its base to the top tier.

Of course, then she'd had to fiddle. And fiddle. Until Fernsby thought he might have to carry her bodily away from the cake.

But there was no doubt about it, the young woman had oodles of talent. If only she would use butter. But now was not the time to dwell on that. They had a cake to show off.

The table had been set up in the gazebo where Ava and Ransom had laid out the cutlery, plates, and serving knife.

And wasn't *that* extremely interesting.

Ransom hadn't needed to carry anything out to the table. *He* was the master chef. Minions did *his* bidding. And yet, he'd enlisted Ava's help, and they'd done it together.

Fernsby knew for a fact that it was his thoughts pervading the atmosphere to the point where Ransom and Ava were finally getting the right idea. All he'd had to do was leave an empty spot next to Ava during the wedding and guide Ransom right to it.

They still needed a nudge there, a nod here, and a wink there, but truly, it was as if they were doing the job for him.

There'd be a hot time in the old town tonight. Oh yes.

Finally, the cake was displayed on the table, the silverware gleaming as brightly as if he'd polished it himself.

He'd been afraid the cake topper might be a travesty, but once the bride and groom figurines were piped into place, he acknowledged the delightful appropriateness of it. The Dia de los Muertos bride and groom, holding hands, gazing into each other's eyes as they leaned close to kiss, their skeletal teeth not quite touching, were perfection.

Yes. The cake was a triumph. Even if he did say so himself.

As Gideon and Rosie stepped up, Fernsby allowed Gabrielle to ceremoniously hand them the cake knife, informing them softly, "The lower and the third tiers are Fernsby's. The second and the top tier are mine."

"Yes, butter and eggs on the bottom to support everything else." Fernsby sighed. "Then vegan." Even in his own mind, he heard the drawl of that word.

"I absolutely must have a piece of both," Rosita Diaz, now Rosita Jones, was a dear child. An amazing mother to Jorge, she was now also an enviable mother to Isabella. Good Lord, he hoped they didn't start calling the poor child Izzie or some such nonsense. Rosita's veil was gone, the adorable miscreant having pulled it off the bride's head during the ceremony, and Rosita had never replaced it.

Fernsby didn't chuckle. Although he wanted to. He thought of all the new babies in the Maverick realm. He wondered if Susan would allow him to babysit; Susan, being the matriarch of the family, would have to make that decision.

Wouldn't it be nice, just for an hour or so, to bounce a little tyke on his knee? And when they needed changing, they could be returned to their mothers forthwith.

God forbid he should wait for the Harringtons to get down to the baby business. While he'd maneuvered Cammie and Dane into each other's arms, he couldn't very well maneuver them into having a baby.

Or could he?

He raised an eyebrow in contemplation.

Together, Rosita and Gideon cut four narrow slices of cake, two from the all-important first tier, and two from the second *vegan* tier. Even the word was a guttural sound in his mind.

Thank God they didn't play that disgusting charade of shoving cake in each other's faces. Especially not *his* cake. It deserved to be treated with respect.

Gideon fed his bride a forkful. And Rosita glowed. Then she fed Gideon. And if a man could actually glow, Gideon Jones did.

The look of love on his face was like Mr. Darcy finally telling Elizabeth Bennet that he loved her. *Pride and Prejudice*, the greatest love story ever told. But then, these Mavericks seemed so adept at creating their own greatest love stories that they didn't need Jane Austen.

When they'd eaten from the two tiers, Rosita and Gideon turned to their bakers.

"They're both so delicious," Rosita said. Then she smiled like Elizabeth Bennet finally accepting Mr. Darcy's proposal. "I can't even tell them apart."

Fernsby muttered, "Nonsense," under his breath, just like Lady Catherine de Bourgh.

He was sure only Gabrielle heard him.

Rosita hugged him, then Gabrielle. "Thank you so much for doing this for us."

Foregoing a man hug, Gideon shook Fernsby's hand, then hugged Gabrielle. "Thank you both. You've made our wedding so special."

Fernsby waved away their thanks. "We could do no less for two such as yourselves."

Then Gideon asked, "Have you tasted both cakes?"

Fernsby harrumphed. "Of course. A baker must always make a test cake for occasions as important as a wedding."

Beside him, he could feel Gabrielle Harrington's smile. "I'm sure Fernsby's is delicious," she said mildly. "But unfortunately, I couldn't taste-test since it isn't vegan."

Fernsby, nose in the air, said, "I found Miss Harrington's cake to be... tolerable." It was actually more than luscious on the palate, but one simply couldn't say that aloud. *Tolerable* was compliment enough. Anything more might go to the young woman's head.

But Gideon and Rosita laughed.

Fernsby took Gabrielle's hand and moved aside, allowing the bride and groom to step down from the dais as the servers began cutting the cake for the rest.

When he tried to release Gabrielle's hand, she held on. "See? You don't always need butter and eggs to make a fabulous cake."

"My dear young woman, please do not delude yourself. While your cake is moist and delicious—" He leaned close for Gabrielle's ears only. "—butter and eggs are food for the soul."

"You mean they harden the arteries."

She was definitely quick-witted. Fernsby looked down at her. Then he bared his teeth in what might have been a smile. "As long as they don't harden the heart."

* * *

Ava hugged her sister, whispering into her ear, "Your cake is a freaking masterpiece." She looked around for Fernsby, but he was talking to Susan Spencer. "It was better than Fernsby's," she added. "But do not under pain of torture ever tell him I said that."

Gabby hugged her back. "Don't you tell him I actually tried his cake, even though it's not vegan. And it was totally yummy. In fact, I ate a whole piece," she ended on a whisper. "Then I got sick from all that butter."

They put their heads together and laughed, drawing a glare from Fernsby over Susan's shoulder.

Of course Gabby would have tried Fernsby's cake, since their tiers were so closely tied. Though she was generally vegan, she sometimes splurged when no one was looking. And sometimes even when someone *was* looking.

"I'll never tell." Ava zipped her lips. "Your secret is mine."

They laughed together at Fernsby's expense and hugged again.

"You," Gabby said, tapping Ava's shoulder, "were so amazing, getting Ransom to jump in at the last minute to handle all the food."

"He owed me big-time." She wanted to turn around and look for him, but she was afraid people would notice. Not that she'd made any *longing glances*. All she'd done was look.

"He totally owed you after what he did to you." Gabby was silent a moment. "But he's jumped in with catering for your care homes. And stepping in for the wedding at the last moment couldn't have been easy."

"He has amazing contacts."

Gabby was thoughtful. "Still, it must have been stressful and demanding to do it all with no notice. If Rosie and Gideon had asked me on a Friday night to make a wedding cake for Sunday?" She left the question without an answer, just widened her eyes in horror.

Ava was sure Ransom's feat hadn't been easy at all. Not only had he taken on the job with less than two full days to accomplish it, he'd managed to make all her favorite foods. And he'd brought in that fabulous champagne.

Then Gabby added, "I judged him pretty harshly for what he did to you. But maybe the guy has actually changed."

Had he? Or was he trying to win her over? Ava couldn't allow herself to be fooled by all the kind gestures, by the foodie love letter or the way he'd painted Myrtle's nails, by the Supermart shopping trip or the chocolate-chip pancakes they'd shared.

Before her thoughts could overwhelm her, she shoved her sister lightly. "Now, off you go to collect your accolades."

Gabby fluttered her fingers in her wake.

Even as something inside her wanted to soften toward Ransom, Ava forced herself to remember the last time. Doing everything she could to please him, just as she had with her parents. Trying everything she could to get them to notice her and love her—the best student, the best at sports, the best at everything. They'd never noticed.

Part of her wondered if she was still trying to please them even after their deaths, to get them to love her, to accept her. Maybe that was why she'd worked so hard to build her business.

Ransom knew just the right buttons to push by telling her what an amazing job she'd done over the years. He'd known how to do that even then, offering the praise she'd most craved from her parents, telling her how smart she was, how hardworking.

Then he'd made his offer as if none of that mattered at all. And when she hadn't jumped at it, he'd ghosted her.

What would stop him from ghosting her again once he'd set up her catering? Three months, six months from now, he'd be back to his fabulous famous chef's life. And she'd be just the ghost he left behind.

But God, it was so hard to remember their massive screw-up in the past or even to consider his future leave-taking with all the love blossoming around her—Gideon and Rosie lost in each other's gazes, Cammie and Dane returning to the dance floor, wrapped around each other. All the Mavericks, all the love. Susan and Bob Spencer dancing in each other's arms, their lips so close they could be kissing, even after all the years they'd been together.

She was wrung out by the time the reception wound down. The only thing she could be grateful for was that Ransom hadn't cornered her while she felt vulnerable.

They'd screwed up so badly before. How could she trust that they'd be any better at it now?

Chapter Seventeen

Monday morning. First thing. Ransom slammed down the phone. Luckily, Ava's poor assistant had already hung up, or he might have broken her eardrum.

Ava was sending Naomi Wells to deal with him on the catering issues.

He'd thought things had changed after yesterday, after she helped him set up the cake, after they'd talked so pleasantly. He'd thought she was softening when she thanked him for the wedding menu he'd made just for her.

Obviously, he'd thought wrong. And now his blood boiled. He'd told Ava right from the start that he would deal only with her. Yet she had the gall to have her assistant call and say she'd be coming over instead of Ava.

If anyone was going to check out his progress and ask him questions, it would be Ava herself.

He had to tackle her now—not tomorrow, not later, now. Grabbing his jacket off the hook, he flung open the door and marched past his assistants, growling, "I'll be back," without further explanation.

While his feet ate up the distance between their offices, he seethed—a thing Ransom didn't normally do. Ever. He was not letting her run away, which she was obviously trying to do. He would work with Ava, or the work would stop. That was their deal.

Once in the building, he stabbed the elevator button so hard his finger actually ached. In her office, he stalked past her assistant, who held up her hand, shock raising her eyebrows, calling, "Mr. Yates—wait—"

Ava's door was open, she was seated at her desk, and he closed the door behind him.

"Why did you close the door?" She stood, her voice halfway between indignant and terrified.

"Because I don't want anyone interrupting us when they hear a lot of shouting." He marched to her desk, facing her over the expanse of wood. "I said I'd only work with *you*." He jabbed his finger—still smarting from the elevator—at her. "But you tried to send your assistant."

"I thought you'd need a break from me after working so hard on Gideon and Rosie's wedding."

"That's a load of crap, and you know it. If I needed a break, then *you'd* be the one working with *my* assistant."

Dammit, it had all been going so well yesterday. At least, after she'd dragged him out the front door to accuse him of spilling the beans about their history. It had been obvious to everyone—except her—how he felt about her. After that minor tiff, though, she'd seemed mollified. No, more than mollified. They'd talked, laughed. It was like the San Juan Bautista trip.

And now this. He didn't get it.

"What happened yesterday?" he asked, softening his voice, taking the edge off his angry tone. "We worked so well setting up for the cake. You liked everything on the menu. And you were the one who asked me to help Gideon and Rosie. Why would you do that if we weren't getting along?"

She didn't soften. Instead, she gritted her teeth. "That was a wedding, and I was grateful you did it. But *this* is business, and I've got a lot to do today. All I wanted was for Naomi to check on your progress."

"You're lying."

Her face reddened, either because he was right or because he'd pissed her off.

"Let's not pussyfoot around," she snapped. "We both know that when you're done with this catering project, you'll say, 'So glad I could help out.'" She waved her hands while she mimicked him. "'And now I'm returning to my fabulously famous chef's life. See ya later, bye.' We both knew this was only temporary. We never talked long term."

"I never even *thought* about saying anything like that."

"Right." She lasered him with amber eyes so hot they turned gold in the sunlight streaming through the windows. "But how do I know that's not what you're thinking? 'Time's up, gotta go.'"

"I never gave you a time limit."

Frustrated, or maybe because she didn't want to answer, she threw her pen down on the desk. "Of course there was a time limit. You never thought this was long term."

He asked very softly, "Did you think it was?"

"I—well—" she stammered, as if he'd knocked the wind out of her. But then Ava straightened her shoulders. "I just thought that since you're the master of leaving..." She left it at that.

If he'd knocked the wind out of her with his question, she blew away all his righteous indignation with those words.

He'd planned to come back, to finish the conversation, to have it out with her, and yes, to bring her around to his way of thinking. But the truth was, fifteen years ago he'd left at the height of the biggest fight of their relationship, the only real fight.

When she hadn't texted him, he hadn't texted her, as if they were playing some sort of teenage game. Then he'd come back, and she was gone. Technically she'd left him; he'd been telling himself that for years. Justifying himself.

Yet, from her point of view, he'd walked out, and he hadn't communicated. How the hell was she supposed to know he was coming back? Had he actually told her so? He couldn't remember. And it didn't matter. Being older, he should have been the more mature.

There was nothing left to say but the absolute truth. "I was an idiot back then who couldn't see the forest for the trees. I thought chasing fame and fortune would make me happy. But nothing has ever made me as happy as I was when you and I were together."

He'd never stopped loving her. Not then and not now. He felt it all so clearly. He'd known the day she walked into his office that he'd never forgotten her, that no woman had ever measured up to Ava. That he had screwed up royally.

His leaving, their lack of communication, the texting blackout, had all lost her to him. Because he'd never been able to explain what he was thinking.

It was too late to say all that. They had to deal with each other in the now, with this moment's issues, not the ones from their past.

Taking a step closer, so she could scent him, feel the heat of his body, he said, "Now you're the one shunting me off to an assistant because you don't want to deal with what never ended between us." Another step. He wanted to round the desk and haul her into his arms. But he lowered his voice to a gentler note. "You're not just hiding from me now. You're hiding from fifteen years of our unrequited feelings for each other."

She opened her mouth to argue, but he held up a hand. "Don't tell me that you haven't felt something for me all these years."

He'd been furious when he came in. And as she stalked around her desk to meet him toe to toe, she was beyond furious now. "What I remember is how you treated me. How the entire world revolved around you and *your* needs and *your* wants, never what I wanted."

They were getting down to the nitty-gritty. And he didn't let up. "How did I do that? I was going to give you the world." Yet he had discounted her dreams. He had taken her acquiescence to his plans for granted.

But she couldn't read the thought bubble that was surely hanging over his head. "Seriously?" Blood dripped off the point of the word. "Give me the world? You were going to make up some random position in your company as you hauled me from city to city while you made your name. *That* was giving me the world?"

He'd subjugated her dreams to his. Or at least he'd tried to. Her words chastened him. She'd read his thought bubble and said exactly what he'd been thinking more succinctly... and less in his favor.

But he wasn't the complete ass she made him out to be. After all, she'd walked out without letting him explain. She could have stayed and talked it out. She could have said yes, they'd have had an amazing adventure, and she could have returned to her studies in a year, or two years. Would that have really been so terrible?

"Any other twenty-one-year-old woman would have jumped at the offer," he said.

She reared back like a rattler ready to strike. "One—" She stabbed her index finger close to his face. "I completely disagree."

She raised her middle finger, luckily without lowering the first. "And two, that's how you saw me? Like *any other woman*?"

He'd known his mistake the moment he'd said it. But she'd heard it even worse. "That isn't what I meant."

She laughed, a sound so lacking in humor it was as brittle as glass. "Funny, your words used to come out wrong a lot." So close to him now she could spear him with her gaze, her voice was deadly. "Do I have to remind you how you *pretty-womaned* me? Do I have to remind you how you ghosted me, just erased me from your life? And do I have to go through it all again like I did fifteen years ago?"

He was shaking his head. "*Pretty-womaned* you? I don't even know what that means."

That seemed to make her even angrier. "You just flew away for your big important meeting and left me behind." She waved at the sky outside, where a jet was passing overhead. "That's the problem. You don't know what I'm talking about because you couldn't even bother to watch one little movie." She stabbed his chest with each of the last three words.

He was losing her. He'd come here completely justified in his indignation, and she'd turned it around on him. Because she was right. He remembered it all now—her reference to that movie. And he'd blown it off. Watching it had never even been a consideration. It was just a chick flick.

But not watching *Pretty Woman* had been the biggest of all the mistakes of his life.

He backed up then, until the backs of his knees hit the sofa, and he slumped onto it, holding his head in his hands, muttering, "Dammit, dammit, I'm screwing this up again."

He let out a long sigh so heavy it seemed to crush his chest. He was supposed to tell the truth. But instead, they were battling with words again. Looking up, his voice holding all the feeling he could muster, he said, "Ava, what we had, it never died for me. And I don't think it died for you either."

She glared, what he'd said meaning nothing to her. "Don't tell me what I felt then or what I feel now."

He nodded, rising from the sofa, approaching slowly, no longer wanting to crowd her or push her. "I know I can't tell you what you feel."

Her lips were so soft, her scent so sweet. And he made what could be the next biggest mistake of his life, whispering, "I'm pretty sure that also means I can't..." He took yet another step closer, then another, until their lips were only a hairbreadth apart.

Something glittered in her eyes. He hoped it was desire, prayed it was. They breathed the same breath, and her nostrils flared slightly, as if she were scenting him the way he scented her.

He waited for that little nod, a small but clear sign that she wanted what he wanted.

When he thought he saw it in the burn of her eyes, he kissed the breath out of her, kissed a low, sexy moan out of her, kissed her until her lips parted, until she was kissing him back with the same fervor he felt beating in his chest.

Kissing him with a passion he needed to go on forever.

* * *

The kiss was so passionate, so breathtaking, so overpowering. Ava melted into him, savoring his taste as his tongue mimicked making love to her. God, she'd dreamed of this, wanted it, needed it. Even if it was the worst thing she could ever do. But she was beyond caring.

Until Ransom stepped back.

Not much, just a couple of inches, but enough to sluice cold water down her spine—even as her heart cried out for him not to stop, cried out, *Please don't leave me again*.

"Go ahead," he said softly. "Deny the sparks we just felt."

She'd never been a liar. And she couldn't lie now. "Dammit."

She shoved her hands through her hair, all the pins of her careful chignon flying. She was furious with herself, felt it pump through her veins, furious because she was actually done fighting. Because that kiss, quite possibly the most perfect kiss of all time, had drained every ounce of fight out of her. All she wanted now was to throw herself into his arms.

So she did.

Literally threw herself at him, arms around his neck, pulling his head down, taking his lips, opening hers, dragging him inside, and kissing him until she couldn't think. Because *this* had nothing to do with thinking. He hauled her up against him, letting her feel every hard muscle, letting her feel how badly he wanted her. She was drowning in his taste, his scent, his heat.

Drowning...

With only one brain cell still firing, she pulled herself out of his arms. When he looked at her as if she'd crushed his world, she could only whisper one word. "Door."

On trembling legs, she crossed her office to lock it. She didn't care that Naomi might hear that soft *snick*.

Ransom stood right behind her, so close she could smell his pheromones without even turning.

In the next moment, she turned, grabbed him by the lapels, and pushed him up against the door. He dropped his hands to her bottom, pulling her against the hard ridge of him, and went for her neck like a vampire, kissing, licking, sucking, biting.

She didn't let him restrain her for long, breaking free and stripping off his tie. She couldn't wait a moment longer—yanking off his jacket, grabbing his shirt, tearing the buttons as she shoved it down his arms.

Before she lost all coherent thought, even as she was jerking open his belt and pulling down his zipper, she said, "Condom."

"In my wallet. Back pocket."

She pulled back a moment to look at him, her heart ramming her chest. "Do you always carry a condom in case you get lucky?"

He shook his head. "Only since yesterday, after the wedding."

Blinking, she stared him down.

"Only because I was praying for the moment you finally let me in." He reached for his wallet.

It was so sexy, so beguiling. That he'd actually rushed to a drugstore right after the wedding. Just for her.

Even as she wanted to strip off her clothes and take him, a voice in her head shouted, *Don't do this. You'll regret it,* while a warring voice answered, *Shut up. Don't tell me to stop now. Not when it's so damn good.*

The devil and thc angel perched on her shoulders.

The devil won. And she threw herself at him again.

He was so beautiful—even more beautiful than before. His muscles were hard, his skin taut. Even as she tore off her suit jacket, she put her mouth to his. Because, oh God, his taste. She'd never forgotten the erotic taste of him. Sweet like fruit, rich like coffee.

Someone moaned, and she realized it was herself. She needed him so bad.

Then their clothes were flying, and he hoisted her up. Or

maybe she climbed him. And, oh God, the feel of his skin against hers. The curly hair of his legs against her calves set off tingles throughout her body. She wasn't wearing pantyhose today, all the better to feel him everywhere.

With her legs wrapped around him, he carried her to the desk and set her down, her bottom on the smooth wood. She sent the papers and pens flying out of the way. He tugged on her panties, and she yanked at her bra clasp, needing it off, needing his skin against hers, his lips on her, his mouth everywhere.

When all she wore were her high heels, she tore at his boxer briefs, and with a whisper of awe, she reached out. "You're so beautiful."

The moment before his lips captured hers, he murmured, "And you dazzle me. More now than ever before."

Everything was *more* than before. His lips on hers were like a fever, burning her up from the inside. His fingers branded her with his heat. He spread her legs, and there were no preliminaries except donning the condom. She didn't need anything else.

She pulled her mouth from his, needing to breathe, needing to whisper, "Please."

She needed this, she needed *him*, inside her, now.

His hands on her hips, he gave her exactly what she wanted, plunging deep. She bit her lip to keep the scream inside. So good. So perfect. Thick and hard, he touched every part of her, inside and out. She clung to him, breasts against his hard muscles, the soft hair of his chest a gentle stroke against her skin—his mouth, his lips, his tongue taking her the way his body did.

He'd brought her to climax so many times, and yet, it had never been like this. His harsh breath caressed her ear. His erotic male scent filled her head. Then he took her hard and fast, the way her body craved.

It had been so long since anyone had touched her this way. Touched her deep inside, touched her soul, touched her heart in a way no one but Ransom ever had. Pleasure coiled inside her, and ecstasy wrapped around her as tightly as his arms. She hovered on the edge, desperately wanting to fall over and yet needing this to go on forever.

A chant rose up from her, "Oh God oh God oh God. Please, please, please."

The coil inside her sprang loose. She clung to him, riding it through, her body pulsing, her mouth on his so she couldn't cry out. As he throbbed deep inside her, she drank in his groan of ecstasy. *Her* ecstasy. Then she gave in to it completely, gave in to him. Gave him everything.

She'd never known this level of bliss. Not even back then, with him.

Chapter Eighteen

He shattered deep inside her, his release an explosion of need and yet a whisper of love. Of coming home.

They were one, his body, her body, his heart, and—God, if only—her heart.

Her skin was like velvet against his, her taste like the finest wine. While they'd always been perfect together, in sync, knowing exactly what the other needed, this was simply more. Though *simple* was a mild word for what he felt with her.

Simple, like the ocean pounding on the shore. Simple, like the softness of a kiss against his skin, like the sweetness of cherries on his lips, like the perfume of wisteria on a spring morning. He indulged his senses in her, holding her for long minutes after the wave of passion had subsided.

"Shower," he murmured. He wasn't thinking about washing off their lovemaking. He was thinking about the hot water, her skin, her taste, and more, always more.

He couldn't get enough of her.

"We should—"

With a kiss, he cut off what they should or shouldn't do. A deep, luscious tasting. Then he picked her up, still inside her, her legs wrapped around him, and carried her to the bathroom. The room smelled sweet, like her lotion. Or maybe it was just Ava, who had never smelled anything but sweet.

He had to set her down to get rid of the condom, and he said with a grin, "You're still wearing your high heels."

Even with them, she had to rise up on her toes to kiss his lips.

He relished that even though she was a tall woman, he could still make her feel petite.

Reaching around her, he turned on the shower tap, while she closed the door as if someone might hear the water running.

"I don't want to get my hair wet," she said.

"Your hair is not where I want to make you wet."

Then he pulled the last few pins out of her chignon, waves the color of garnets falling over her shoulders.

"You're so bad," she whispered as she stepped out of her shoes.

He pulled her into the shower and didn't get her hair wet. Not yet. "If you won't let me wash your hair, I'll have to soap you everywhere else." He pumped body wash onto his palm.

"But I already took a shower today."

He smiled wickedly. "This has nothing to do with anything that happened before that first kiss." Soaping her breasts, he ran his fingers around the peaks, watching them tighten all over again. "Your skin is so soft, so smooth."

He pulled, tweaked, and she gasped, holding on to his shoulders as if her knees were weak without him.

Plastering her against him, he slid his hands around to her spine, his fingers trailing down her back to her bottom, soaping her, molding her to him until she had to feel how hard he was for her already.

She groaned. "But I have a meeting."

"Screw your meeting," he said, burying his face against her neck, nibbling her sweet skin, biting her lightly until she arched into him.

He followed the curve of her hips and slid his hand between them to find her center. With his mouth to hers, he whispered, "I told you there were other ways I wanted to get you wet."

"Ransom." His name was a moan on her lips.

He stroked her until she whimpered with need. With all the soap washed away, he slid his hands down her thighs and went to his knees before her. Pushing her back against the wall, he tasted her. Christ. She was ambrosia on his tongue. He didn't care that the water plastered his hair against his head. He simply wanted her moans, her sighs, her pleasure. He wanted *her*.

"Ransom. Ransom." She fisted her hands in his hair. "Oh God." Then twisted her fingers as he brought her closer to the edge.

But he needed to go deeper, so much deeper, and he pulled her leg up, her thigh over his shoulder, and filled her with his fingers while he played her with his tongue.

"Ransom, please, oh my God, *please*, Ransom."

His name hadn't been on her lips in the throes of ecstasy in fifteen years. And the words stroked him like her fingers on his skin.

He gave himself up to the sensual taste of her, the feel of her, the scent of her as her shuddering climax rippled through him. Her cries melted away with the steam.

Finally, she pulled him up to tower over her, then down to take his lips with hers.

They parted just enough for her to say, "I want you inside me. I need you."

Her need caressed his soul, but all he could say was, "I don't have another condom."

"Then I want this." She wrapped her hand around him, and if he was hard before, he was like steel now.

She went to her knees.

"Your hair's getting wet."

Before she took him between her lips, she murmured, "Screw my hair."

* * *

His taste was the nectar she'd dreamed of for years, even if she'd never wanted to admit it. His skin was smooth beneath her fingertips, his muscles taut against her palm. Groans of pleasure rained down on her, and he was a hard jewel in her mouth. Fingers in her hair, he gave her the sweetest massage as he guided her. A sound rose from her throat, came out as a moan around him. And his legs trembled.

His taste, his feel, his musky male scent—it was all like waking from a dream. While all they'd done had been dazzling when she was twenty-one, it was as if they'd only been practicing for this.

She didn't care about the water raining down on her, didn't care about the meeting she'd be late for, didn't care that Naomi would have heard the lock turn or the water running.

There was only this—his granite hardness in her mouth, his muscles bunched beneath the hand she steadied him with, and those delicious sounds that fell from his lips.

She felt him throb and wrapped her hand around him, stroking him while her mouth took him. His legs quivered beneath her touch.

He growled, "Goddammit. I'm so ready. I can't stop."

She heard the warning but didn't stop, loving him between her lips. When he climaxed, she took all of him, needing it, wanting it, glorying in his salty-sweet taste.

He was delicious beyond her memories, beyond her imaginings, beyond anything she'd ever tasted. Beyond her wildest desires.

When she'd taken his essence, every last drop, he pulled her up to wrap his arms around her, capturing her lips in a kiss that tasted of them both. He took her mouth ravenously, kissed her with a passion she hadn't known since the last time with him. Kissed her with the promise that it would only get better.

His hands roved her body as he bent to lick water from her throat, going lower still to take the tip of her breast in his mouth. Her pleasure spiked all over again as he made love to her with his lips, his tongue, then his fingers between her legs. He stayed there only a moment, as if he were teasing her, but then his hands were everywhere, kneading her back, sliding down her spine, cupping her bottom, pressing their bodies together as he once again plundered her lips.

She rubbed against him, wanting him again, the taste of him still filling her mouth. Then he slipped a hand between them and went straight to her core. He surrounded her, filled her, his fingers inside her, then sliding back out to find the hard nub of her desire. She fell apart in his arms, waves of erotic pleasure swamping her body, her mind.

Her heart.

She gave herself up to the sensations, reveled in them, savored them. Gloried in him.

Her release was so wild she would have fallen if he hadn't been holding her.

It was how she'd felt at twenty-one, as if she couldn't stand on her own without him.

She clung to him, kissed him with the passion she'd banked all these years. With the crazy need she'd held at bay, telling herself she didn't feel it anymore.

But, oh God, how she felt it all now.

He pulled back, cupping her face for one last beautiful kiss, then running his hands through her hair. "I've so missed feeling you come apart in my arms."

The words made her knees buckle.

Yet she couldn't say them back, couldn't tell him how much she'd missed all the emotions he brought up, all the sensations his touch elicited, the roar of release, the languor of satisfaction.

Still trapped in the thrill of his arms, she managed to say, "I really do have a meeting. I've got to dry my hair and redo my makeup."

He smiled with a fondness that only people who have been together for years could feel. But they'd had only a few months together back then. And only a few days now. And as badly as she wanted to stay right where she was, to send Naomi out for a packet of condoms, to do this all day long on the sofa, on the conference table, on her desk, and back to the shower again, she couldn't.

Finally, he let her step out and grab a towel. She handed him one too. As she dried off, she watched him towel his hair. He was so beautiful, so strong, so perfect. His body was like something a master had sculpted.

She covered her head with the towel, blotting out the sight of him as she squished the moisture from her hair. Her robe hung on the back of the door, and she pulled it on, began brushing her hair.

When he was dry, he stepped out of the shower, and his body heat filled the too-small room, turning it hotter even than the steam.

"I'll get our clothes." His voice was thick with emotion about what they'd done.

She let him go, and only then realized she'd barely taken a breath. Gulping in air, she looked at herself in the mirror. Her hair was a tousled wet mess, her makeup gone except for mascara smudges beneath her eyes.

What had she done?

He was like a lightning strike.

With him outside the bathroom and her inside it, all the potential pain she'd opened herself up to washed over her. It could be even worse than the hurt she'd suffered before. Because kissing him, tasting him, taking him—it was all like poking a wound that had never healed completely. Even as she'd told herself that she was fine, that she'd moved on, that she had her life in order, had attained her dreams, she could feel it all draining away with the possibility that her heart would break all over again.

It had been half an hour of glory. After he'd ghosted her for fifteen years. She'd discovered nothing during all that time that made her believe love between her and Ransom could actually work.

Not Dane's love for Cammie. Not all the love she saw between the Mavericks. Love wasn't the problem. She and Ransom were. And what did thirty minutes of the most amazing lovemaking that was even better than she remembered, better than her body had ever felt—what did those thirty minutes mean stacked against fifteen years?

The last few days had been great. He'd listened to all her needs and come up with a fabulous plan. He'd done an amazing job on the wedding.

But truly, how was anything different now? All this time, he hadn't even understood that he'd *pretty-womaned* her, that he'd ignored her dreams, that he'd made her *less than*. How could she know for sure that he understood now?

She didn't want a few stolen minutes in her office. She didn't want a casual relationship where he drifted into her bed and right back out again when he had another flight to catch or a TV show to shoot.

She wanted nothing less than a love like Dane and Cammie's, like the Mavericks.

Letting this go on would break her heart. And her heart absolutely could not survive another break. Like Humpty Dumpty, she could never be completely put back together. If Ransom broke her again, she'd never be the same.

He was dressed when he returned, setting her neatly folded clothes on the vanity beside her as she pulled her hair dryer out of the drawer.

"I'll wait for you."

Something welled up inside her. More than fear. Maybe even terror. She turned to face him. "No. Please don't wait. I'll be a while." Her voice was soft, but she hoped it wasn't broken.

"I don't mind," he said with a tenderness that was like nails on a chalkboard.

"No. I really need you to go now." The words were so low that he leaned forward to hear, his scent washing over her.

"Why?" His brow creased with utter bewilderment.

She didn't want to sound like she was throwing him out. Or as though what they'd done hadn't been what she'd wanted in that moment. All she could say was, "I really need some time to think."

And even though she didn't want to beg, she added, "Please."

⋆ ⋆ ⋆

What they'd just shared had been far more than amazing. There wasn't a word in the English language that could describe it. And yet, the crumpled look on her face and her downcast eyes spoke to her conflict. It was clear their lovemaking had meant something to her, but it was equally clear that she wasn't ready to handle it.

He'd walked into her office and realized how badly he wanted her, how much he still loved her, that he'd never fallen out of love with her.

But she wasn't there yet.

He could only pray she'd get there the way he had.

He tipped up her chin, held her gaze for a long moment of eye contact as he searched for more clues to what she was thinking.

But she was shuttered now.

They still had so much to talk about, and maybe he'd been an idiot for letting his desire take over. Not that he would change a moment of the last half hour. But as he looked into her beautiful eyes, as his gaze roved over her gorgeous features, his gut told him that anything he said to her in this moment would be wrong.

She drew a shuddering breath, clearly on the edge—emotional, even frightened.

If he pushed her now, she might never let him in again.

This wasn't like the last time. He wasn't walking away. He couldn't let her be the one to do it either.

But he could give her time. "I understand. I'll leave you now, and I'll work with Naomi." Taking her hand, he squeezed her fingers lightly. "But call me soon. We really need to talk this through. We can't let it be like last time, where neither of us said anything."

He leaned in to kiss her cheek, tasting the salt of a tear. Then he released her, backing out of the door and finally turning to go.

He was leaving. But he wasn't walking away.

Chapter Nineteen

Ava's meeting went by in a blur. Thank God Naomi took notes, as Ava, for the first time ever, couldn't remember a thing that was said.

Had Naomi been shooting her sly glances?

But she couldn't worry about Naomi or meetings or anything else right now. Those thirty minutes with Ransom had been an out-of-body experience. They'd been as in tune as if years hadn't gone by. Like tactile memories on her skin, all she could think of was his touch, his kiss, his taste, and the feel of him filling up every single minute of those empty years.

His caresses had touched so much more than just her body. They'd touched her soul and her heart. God, her heart. If her heart was involved, it could be broken all over again.

When they broke up, he'd had his career to build and consume him. While he might have missed her at first, at least for a little while, he'd made his choice. And it wasn't her. The end of their affair had blindsided her. She thought she'd been doing everything possible to make him happy, only to have him show her how he really felt before he hopped on a plane like her parents always had.

She didn't want to be blindsided again at thirty-six. She didn't want a repeat of all that angst and heartache. And maybe she'd channeled all her heartache into anger to ease it a little.

Yet she didn't feel the anger anymore. These past few days with him, seeing him perform so many sweet acts—painting nails, making Myrtle laugh, stepping in to make Gideon and Rosie's wedding the best it could be—all the old anger had drained away.

Leaving behind only the memory of her broken heart.

If the love she and Ransom had once shared wasn't real, then why had it hurt so badly to lose it? And why did it hurt her heart now? In answer to that, she'd tried to tell herself it was just she and Ransom that couldn't work, that they both sucked at love, that they could never make it right, make it good.

But standing in her office, she couldn't help closing her eyes and remembering the look in his gaze, as if he adored her. The touch of his fingertips, as if he revered her. The kiss of his lips on hers, as if he relished her. The climaxes he gave her, as if he savored every shudder and shiver of her body.

The way she'd savored his.

Could they work?

Her heart leaped at the thought.

It was that very leap that terrified her. He could be playing a game. It could be just for now. He could go on his merry way just as he had before. He could ghost her all over again. She knew, deep in her bones and like a fist wrapped around her heart, that this time she wouldn't be able to pick up its broken pieces.

But the way he'd left her office, with such tenderness in his voice, in his words. *We need to talk.*

As if this time he wouldn't ghost her.

But then she remembered the other thing he'd said. Before he'd kissed her. Before he'd made love to her.

Any other twenty-one-year-old woman would have jumped at the offer.

He'd tried to backpedal, tried to say he hadn't meant it the way it sounded. But still, those words said it all. *Any other woman.* As though she'd been just one among many. Nothing special. Easily replaceable.

Her emotions were so mixed up. She was floundering in a way she hadn't since he'd left her the first time. The one thing she could do was pick up the phone and call her sister. Gabby was the only one who would understand.

As her sister said, "Hell—" Ava cut her off. "I really need to talk to you." Then she heard the echo of that one syllable: *hell.* That's where Ava was right now. In hell.

"It's about Ransom, right?"

Ava could only mutter, "Yeah."

"I'm still in the Bay Area. I stayed in Woodside at Canyon Ranch because I needed time beforehand to make a masterpiece of the cake. Then I treated myself to a spa day." Ava could hear the languor in Gabby's voice. "I just checked out. You still in the city?"

"Yeah." That was the only word she was capable of.

"Let's meet at that steak and chophouse out by the water, the one near all the fancy airport hotels."

Naomi had brought Ava a sandwich after the meeting, but she'd taken only a bite. "I need a drink. Even more than food."

"You've got it, sis." Gabby paused a couple of seconds, as though she was looking at the time on her phone. "I can be there in half an hour. Will that be good for you?"

Sighing, Ava said, "I'll be there. Thank you." The words wobbled, but she didn't allow herself to cry.

After they hung up, Ava stood a moment longer. She couldn't even think about driving herself. She'd probably have an accident. Naomi called her driver, and the Town Car was already waiting at the curb as she left the building. Ava slumped in the backseat as they made their way out of the city.

Beneath the portico of the chophouse, she stepped from the car just a little over thirty minutes later, delayed by traffic. Since it was between the lunch and dinner hours, thank goodness the restaurant was still open. She hadn't even thought to check, she'd been so determined to get to her sister.

To the maître d', she said, "My sister is probably already at a table. Gabby Harrington."

After a slight bow, the man led her to a table by the windows overlooking the ocean.

And Ava stumbled, catching herself before the maître d' could reach out.

Seated at the table with Gabby was none other than the inimitable Fernsby.

No. Oh no, no, no. She couldn't do this in front of Fernsby. She couldn't lay her heart bare with him looking on and judging her.

She remembered the look Fernsby had given her in Dane's home theater, after they'd viewed him winning the top prize on *Britain's Greatest Bakers*.

A look that said he had matchmaking plans for her.

Oh God, please don't let him be here to matchmake for me and Ransom.

She almost turned around, but she needed to talk to someone. Now. Not later. Not over the phone either. If it couldn't be Gabby alone, it would have to be Fernsby too.

Which didn't stop her from death-glaring her sister as she approached the table.

Fernsby stood, holding out the chair by the window for her to slip into before he seated himself beside her. She was trapped now, Fernsby on one side, Gabby across from her.

Instead of jumping right into her problem, she gave herself a moment. "What have you done with T. Rex?"

Fernsby didn't smile. Although that might have been a slight smirk on his lips. "Please, Miss Harrington, don't trouble yourself about Lord Rexford." She didn't believe Fernsby had ever called the mini dachshund T. Rex. "He is safely ensconced in the car with perfect temperature control, water, and a bit of food. Not too much." He wagged a finger. "His owners," he said with a hint of admonition for Cammie and Dane, "insist on feeding him too many treats." She suspected—but couldn't be sure—that Fernsby snuck the dog treats when no one was looking.

He pointed to the champagne flute in front of Ava. "We took the liberty of ordering your favorite libation. I understand you need it."

Ava took a drink before she could say anything, and the sweetness of the champagne wet her parched throat, the bubbles threatening to go to her head. Though maybe that was a good thing.

Obviously having read Ava's thoughts written on her face, Gabby said, "I know you weren't expecting Fernsby. But trust me on this one. He is a wise man. Dane and Cammie might never have seen the light and gotten together if it hadn't been for him."

Fernsby added in the drollest of voices, "Having dealt admirably—" He preened as he said the word. "—with Mr. Harrington's lackadaisical approach to romance—and look how well that turned out—I believe I'm well equipped to provide any necessary advice here. You may not believe this, but I know a thing or two about love."

Love? Fernsby? She couldn't believe the man had ever been in love in his entire life, not even as a hormone-ridden teenager.

In fact, he might actually have been hatched just as he was. Dane had always speculated that Fernsby was anywhere between the ages of forty and sixty. Ava secretly thought he was far more ancient.

But she put all that aside. "I'm desperate. I need advice."

She would even take it from Fernsby.

* * *

Fernsby felt himself going a little misty-eyed at the memory of his lost love. But no, it wasn't appropriate here.

Oh, the woes of young love and all the mistakes we make, he thought. It was obviously up to him to fix Ava's troubles—he, the inestimable Fernsby. This was yet another job he had been made for.

"One more sip of your champagne, my dear. You need the fortification." If it was up to him, he'd have ordered bourbon. The shock of it would have brought forth every detail trapped inside her.

Perhaps it was his own failed romance that gave him the ability to fix everything—and he did mean *everything*—for everyone else. Of course, it had taken him twelve years—twelve *years*, for God's sake—to get Dane to realize he was madly in love with Camille. But the timing had to be perfect. They had to be best friends. One couldn't rush these things. And Ava, by the beleaguered look on her face and those longing glances he'd seen with his eagle eye at yesterday's wedding, was ripe for his help.

He put his hand on her shoulder, like a comforting uncle. Fernsby prided himself on playing whatever role his charges needed.

"Start from the beginning, my dear," he said. "And leave nothing out."

* * *

Ava put her elbows on the table and her hands over her face. There was just something about Fernsby that had her blurting it all out. Fast, almost without a breath. "We had a bad breakup fifteen years ago. I never talked about it back when it all happened. And now I just had sex with Ransom in my office." She splayed her fingers so she could see Gabby's reaction. "Twice."

Her sister's jaw dropped. Fernsby leaned over, tapped her chin, and Gabby closed her mouth. Giving her head a shake, Gabby said, "You actually had sex in your office?" With two fingers to each temple, she puffed out a long breath. "I'm not sure my brain can even compute that."

Ava hardly recognized herself either, as though the time she'd spent with Ransom had opened up a new emotional chasm inside that she'd forgotten was there after all the years of keeping it tightly closed. Before this afternoon, she would never have said anything like this to anyone, not even Gabby. And never in a million, trillion years would she have said it to Fernsby. Yet that's where she was now—in a place where she'd say whatever had to be said because she needed answers. Badly.

She'd asked herself why it hurt so much. And out of the chasm came the answer—that maybe she'd closed herself off to love when she was much younger, even before Ransom, when her parents were alive and she'd never been able to get them to notice her. To love her.

Was that why she'd been so quick to leave Ransom all those years ago? While she'd been doing everything she could to please him, deep down, had she been waiting for him to prove he'd never really loved her?

And he had. He'd *pretty-womaned* her. He'd ignored her dreams. And then he'd ghosted her.

Ava closed the gap between her fingers, shutting off her view of Gabby's face. "What makes you think I've never had sex in my office before?"

Gabby rolled her eyes. "Duh."

Of course. Ava had always been the consummate businesswoman. Then again, maybe there'd never been anyone with whom she *wanted* to have sex in her office.

Until Ransom came back into her life.

She felt Fernsby's fingers on her hands then, prying them away from her eyes. And really, she couldn't do anything but meet his gaze.

"How do you feel about him now?" he asked gently.

Fernsby? Gentle? But there it was.

Before Ava could even formulate an answer, Gabby chimed in. "You were so angry with him back then." She cocked her head. "But I wonder if he's still that same man. Do you think he is? I mean, he totally squashed your heart. I just want to make sure he doesn't do it again." She reached across the table, touched Ava's hand. "I never want to see you as miserable and hurt as you were then. If you think he's going to do that, then that's what we need to talk about."

Fernsby let out a low *hmmm*, then said, "The man has hidden depths that perhaps fifteen years ago he had not yet plumbed."

"That's the problem," Ava said. "I don't know if he's changed." That wound, just as Gabby said, ran deep. "There were times, as I built my business, when things got so hard that I wanted to quit. And part of the reason I didn't was because I wanted him to know that I'd made my own dreams come true."

Good grief. Even the success of her business might be tied to him. She'd never truly admitted that to herself until this moment. "After he erased me from his life, I never wanted him to think I'd simply collapsed into misery without him."

Gabby smiled softly. "You might have been miserable, but you would never have collapsed. You've never let anything stop you."

Ava's voice trembled. "I just don't know how to get over what happened. He offered me a job following him around the globe, like a temporary mistress. But while he was on his way up, so busy working to become this megastar, I was just getting started. When I said no to his offer, he was like, okay, things aren't going to work. And boom. He was gone. He completely ghosted me for fifteen years."

Fernsby—was that a hint of emotion in his gaze?—said, "I realize that he has a lot to make up for. And you have a lot to forgive."

She nodded, picked up her champagne flute, took a sip, and finally said, "That was the worst. The total erasure."

She'd always said it was the *Pretty Woman* thing that got to her. But even more, it was the ghosting. It was being erased. As if they'd never been together at all.

Fernsby touched her hand. "You told us the two of you broke up. But you were a bit scant on details." His mouth stretched in a grimace as he said the word. "Not *those* details."

He didn't want to know how fantastic the sex had been. He didn't want to know how utterly amazing the lovemaking had been in her office today. He wanted to know how it had all gone down.

Ava's stomach clenched even before she started. "He was supposed to fly out that night to Paris. We wanted to enjoy a marvelous dinner before he left, so we cooked together. I was always his sous-chef, helping him."

Fernsby nodded knowingly. "You were his helpmate. I'd be

willing to wager that many of the recipes he later came up with were from those nights you cooked together."

"I suppose they were." Recipes made out of love, at least on her side.

While she'd tried never to stalk Ransom, there'd been times in a bookstore when she couldn't resist opening a cookbook and had discovered many of the recipes were ones she'd loved making with him. The memories had hurt her even then.

Feeling herself going under with the pain of all the good memories, she plunged into the story again. "We were on dessert. Rice pudding with raspberry sauce."

Every detail came to her, even the sweet taste of the raspberry sauce on her tongue mixed with the creamy flavor of the pudding. She felt Fernsby's and Gabby's gazes on her, both well aware that the memories had never been erased.

She pushed ahead. "And lattes."

God, the delicious coffees he'd made for her. Just like he had that day in his office when she'd barged in and asked him to help her with the catering emergency. It had never been the sex that made her fall for him. It was all the other things—the cooking, the food he prepared for her, even the coffee beans he bought with her in mind. The trails they hiked in the hills, the ferries they took to Sausalito, Tiburon, Treasure Island. The times they'd walked across the Golden Gate Bridge, hand in hand, through packs of tourists. The late-night strolls through quiet neighborhood streets, the sound of voices and laughter rising up from Union Square or Chinatown or Fisherman's Wharf or Ghirardelli Square. It was watching him with his grandmother and holding him while they'd grieved together after she passed.

Stop it stop it stop it, she wanted to scream. *Concentrate on the story of that last night.*

The anger she'd harbored for years was now only grief.

"Then he asked me if I'd come along with him on his trips, that he'd find me a job, make one up if he had to. That we had so little time together between our work and my classes, but that he wanted me with him."

"But he never seemed to consider your dreams," Fernsby said wisely.

"That's what I told him. I was going to night school, and I wanted to get my degree." She'd needed that degree even after her parents died, as if somehow they would know she'd done it. But there was so much more. There were people she wanted to help. "I wanted to manage nursing homes and make life better for the residents. Even then, I wanted to own those nursing homes. I wanted to make them places that people would choose over anywhere else." And she'd done it. Despite him. "He told me I could do all that later, after he'd established his career, when he would be home more. And he would help me do it. But for now—" She thought of his words, of how they'd hurt. "He said I'd get so much more life experience seeing the world, that I could step back into my education later." She turned her champagne stem on the white tablecloth, stared at the tiny bubbles still fizzing to the top. "But I'd already given up my education once before, when our parents died."

"You gave it up to take care of us," Gabby said, her voice tremulous. "Then he wanted you to give it up to take care of *him*."

Ava looked at her sister, awed at her insight. "He wanted me to give up my dream to help him attain his. He wanted me to trail after him like a groupie. Even worse, like a mistress who had a job title, but what she really did was crawl into bed with him every night. And everyone would know what I was. I told him he was treating me like Vivian, where everyone knew she wasn't Edward's niece or his ward or whatever the hell he called her. That she was just a kept woman he took to his bed every night."

Fernsby, with his usual stern countenance, said, "He *pretty-womaned* you."

Ava gaped. Gabby did too. And Fernsby, nose in the air, said, "It's a butler's job to keep up on all the latest movies, Broadway plays, and TV shows. In case their employer should need a recommendation."

Good God. Fernsby had actually watched *Pretty Woman*.

Chapter Twenty

Ava cut off a gasp. She'd already gaped once. "But you weren't even with Dane when that movie came out."

"I didn't simply spring from God's green earth," he drawled, "the day I began my employment with your brother." His lips worked in either a smirk or a smile. "Nor was I *hatched*." He said the word with emphasis, as if he'd heard them all pondering his origins over the years.

Ava had the good grace to blush, as did Gabby, all the way to the roots of her blond hair.

Fernsby breezed right past that. "May I surmise that you told him to stick it where the sun does not shine?" He blinked, maybe even smiled. "If you'll excuse the crass phrase, it is quite apt."

Totally apt. "I told him there was no way I'd give up my education or my dreams."

"And may I presume also that he did not relate to your *Pretty Woman* reference?"

Ava, still reeling from thirty glorious, mind-blowing minutes in her office, and now Fernsby's revelations, said, "He didn't get it at all. He actually said something like, what the hell did a movie matter?" Or maybe that's what she'd heard rather than what he'd said.

"After which, when the *young*—" Fernsby stressed the word. "—man didn't get what he wanted, he walked out."

"Uhh," was all Ava managed at first. "It wasn't exactly like that."

Fernsby seesawed his head. "We must know exactly what happened if we are to advise you, my dear."

"I left first. It was his apartment," she said, adding a shrug. "He couldn't walk out. So I did."

Fernsby let out a long, "Ahhh," as if it were a sigh. As if suddenly he had a complete understanding of the entire situation.

She added quickly, "Then he never called me, never texted, nothing. I didn't hear from him at all."

"May I glean from this information that you didn't call him either?"

He made her feel churlish. He made her feel... What was the right word? Sort of responsible? "I just figured that if he wanted to apologize and rescind the offer, he would call me. He never did. And I assumed that meant he was done with me."

Fernsby once again drawled, "You know what they say about the word *assume*."

"Yes. I know." Her cheeks felt hot.

Finally, Fernsby patted her hand. "You were young."

She hadn't felt young after the break with Ransom. She'd felt as old and haggard as the ages.

"The young often see things in black and white. No gradations. But perhaps our *young* man—" Again, Fernsby stressed that word. "—should have known better."

Gabby jumped in. "Yeah. He should've known better. I remember how you were back then. Totally devastated."

Fernsby added, "And you buried yourself in your studies. You graduated with honors, I know. Then you grew your business into what it is today."

Her deep breath actually hurt. "I'm starting to wonder if I

worked so hard all those years just to prove something to Ransom." As well as her parents.

Gabby shook her head, her hair flying before drifting back down over her shoulders. "Maybe that was part of what drove you, but from where I was sitting, it looked to me like this was always something you wanted to build. You didn't do it for him. You did it because you had a dream. You hated that dreary place, and you wanted to make the lives of older adults better."

Ava looked at her sister with new eyes. Gabby had been so young then, but perhaps she'd also been the wiser one.

"Maybe I'm still trying to show him." She thought for a moment. "For this catering issue, I took him down to the San Juan Bautista home. He asked to see the facilities his people would be working in, but… okay, I wanted him to see what I'd built." She put her hand over her mouth, emotions roiling inside her. "I drove him down there in the Pantera because I wanted him to see how well I handled the car. The car he'd always dreamed of owning. I see now that I was trying to show him how far I'd come."

"Oh my dear," Fernsby said with more feeling than she was aware he had. "You don't need to show anyone what you've done. The miracles you've brought about are self-evident."

Her eyes misted. The man had never been free with his praise. And what he said made her feel almost as good as Ransom's admiration had.

"I wanted to show him. But over the last few days, as we've worked on menus and logistics, he's revealed a lot about himself too." She pressed the corner of her eye before a tear could trickle out. "He feels that what I've created is brilliant. He made it very clear he was impressed with how I've made my dreams a reality."

She had to take a sip of her champagne before her throat

closed up.

"But it's not just what he thinks I've accomplished. It's what he gave my residents. He actually painted Myrtle's nails while I painted Edith's. He *knew* how to paint a woman's nails. I didn't even know he used to do it for his grandmother. And he does it for his niece too." The words seemed to rush out of her then. "You should've heard how he talked about his brother. He really loves the guy. And he loves his brother's family. In fact, he adores them. Then there was the way he jumped into the wedding, producing that meal at a moment's notice." She raised her eyebrows. "He didn't scrimp on one thing. He gave Rosie and Gideon that fabulous champagne for a wedding present. He made something spectacular out of nothing, and he did it for Gideon and Rosie."

Fernsby added, "And perhaps just a little for you too."

"He might have," she acknowledged. "He pulled an all-nighter to get the catering plans for the residences back to me the very next day because I told him I had only two weeks to put everything in place."

Her mind raced with all the generous, warmhearted things Ransom had done this week—the times he'd just been himself, not a billionaire celebrity chef.

"On the way back from San Juan Bautista, we were caught in a terrible traffic snarl and had to spend the night down there." At the look in Gabby's eyes, she added quickly, "In separate rooms. But we didn't have any clean clothes for the next day, so he took me over to Supermart." She smiled at the memory, at the feelings that swamped her now, feelings that had swamped her that day and, if she was honest, had swamped her since the moment she'd walked into his office to ask for his help. "I've never had so much fun. I bought a pair of glittery platform tennis shoes." She looked at Gabby. "You would love them."

Suddenly, she heard herself gushing about a man. About *Ransom.*

"The next morning, we went for pancakes. I've haven't had pancakes like that in years." She almost said she hadn't eaten them since she was with Ransom. "We shared them. A ten-stack of chocolate-chip pancakes, and we finished them all."

Gabby's blue eyes rounded. "I never thought I'd say it, but he actually sounds like a keeper."

All Ava could do was stare. She felt how wide her own eyes were, how fast her heart was beating.

"And since that seems true," Gabby added dryly, "then I want to know why you still look like a deer caught in the headlights."

Ava wanted to think it was the sex in her office. But it was also the things Ransom had done. And it was Gabby, her staunchest supporter, who'd called Ransom every name in the book. Gabby, who'd refused any opportunity that would have allowed her to work with him and advance her career. How could it be that now Gabby thought Ransom was a keeper?

It left her wide open, like a deer jumping into the road, blinded by the lights.

Fernsby, who seemed to know everything, said quietly, "Even when someone has shown that they can change, the pain of the past still lingers."

The man was wise. Maybe he actually was a hundred years old. How else could he know exactly how to explain what she felt to Gabby?

Ava had wanted to skewer Gabby the moment she'd seen Fernsby seated at the table. But now she wanted to take her sister in her arms and hug her tightly.

Because Fernsby was a godsend.

Then the wise man gave her the softest, saddest smile. This from a man whose number of smiles she could count on one hand. Just when she thought she'd controlled her tears, her eyes misted all over again.

"You must take as long as you need to get to a point with Mr. Yates where you are even willing to think about love again. Love isn't something you rush." He wagged a finger. "Love is something you must earn, especially after you've wronged somebody. It takes time to earn that trust again."

A soliloquy on love. From Fernsby. A man who never dated. A man she thought had never been in love.

"I know this might be hard to hear." He patted her hand. "But I believe you need to regain his trust as well. Because love is a two-way street."

With anyone else, her hackles would have risen, and she'd have gone in fighting. But this was Fernsby, and the man knew things. "I truly am starting to see that. But I still don't see exactly why I need to regain *his* trust." She needed Fernsby's insight now more than ever.

He blinked, the corners of his mouth lifting in what might actually be another smile. "Even though Mr. Yates didn't do the right thing," he said, "it doesn't mean it didn't hurt him to lose you just as much as it hurt you to lose him." He was silent a long moment, letting her absorb those words. "You didn't stay to talk it out. You didn't compromise. You walked away. He made an offer you didn't like, but—correct me if I'm wrong—finding a middle ground wasn't even an option, was it?" He said it so softly she felt herself straining to listen.

She licked her lips. She swallowed. Then finally she shook her head. "No, it wasn't. When I didn't like what he said, I was outta there."

"You were out of there," he echoed. "And neither of you came up with a way to make it work. He didn't call you. But you didn't call him. Your feelings were hurt and you left. His ego was bruised, so he left too. But if I were he, it would have broken my heart to lose you. To watch you walk out of my life and never look back would have shattered me. If I were he."

A single tear fell from her eye at his heartfelt words.

"If you will humor an old man, I would like to tell you the story of when I fell in love many years ago."

Ava shared an astonished look with Gabby. Fernsby as a young man? Fernsby in *love*? It didn't seem possible. Both she and her sister nodded for him to go on. Ava was sure Gabby was dying to hear the tale as much as she was.

"I was so certain our love couldn't be real. I wondered how a woman like Mathilda could love me." He put a hand to his chest, as if even he couldn't believe he'd had the thought. Then he gave what sounded like a short bark of laughter, except that Fernsby didn't laugh. Ava wasn't sure he even knew how. She'd thought his laughter vocal cords had frozen long before he'd gone to work for Dane.

Still with his hand on his chest, he said, "Of course, I wasn't the man you see sitting before you today. I was flawed. And perhaps too arrogant for my own good."

Fernsby was still arrogant. But he was also wise. And Ava hung on his every word.

"I can say now that I couldn't see the forest for the trees. I was so convinced that Mathilda couldn't love me that eventually she became convinced of it as well. And *poof*." He waved his hands in the air like a magician. "She was gone forever. Out of my life. It was only in my later years that I realized the terrible mistake I'd made."

Fernsby never made mistakes. But here he was, admitting to a grave error.

He turned his severe countenance upon her. "Don't convince yourself that what you feel for Ransom and what he feels for you isn't real. From where I'm sitting, it looks as if it might very well be the real thing."

Ava's insides curdled. Had she made a mistake all those years ago? Was she making the same mistake all over again?

Fernsby wasn't about to let her off the hook. "You've got a second chance, my dear. Take it from me—those don't come around often." He wrapped his fingers around hers. Fernsby, the untouchable, was touching her for a rather prolonged period—three times in one sitting, in fact. His wise gray eyes bored into her, seeming to see all the way to her heart. "So don't cock it up this time."

Gabby's soft giggle filled the air. Because Fernsby never talked like this. *Cock it up?* Oh no, that wasn't Fernsby at all.

"Remember, love is a compromise because two hearts must meet in the middle to become one."

Oh God. Ava finally saw that she *was* cocking it up. She'd cocked it up back then, probably just as much as Ransom had. When she believed he didn't value her dreams, just like her parents had always ignored her achievements, she didn't stay to talk. She didn't try to compromise. She didn't even let him explain what he really wanted from her or what his offer meant to him.

Instead, she'd cut and run.

She'd been telling herself that it was all because *they* couldn't make love work, that there was something wrong with *them*. That if he'd truly loved her, he would never have *pretty-womaned* her. He would never have even come up with that terrible offer.

But the truth was that she had run because she was afraid he didn't value *her*. She'd been afraid he'd say he didn't love her, but that she'd make a damned good mistress.

Fernsby had opened her eyes. And Ransom had opened them for her, too, with all the caring, beautiful things he'd done over the last few days.

Her feelings were real. His feelings were real. Their *love* was real.

She'd cocked it up all those years ago because she couldn't stay and listen to him. Because she was afraid to compromise.

But she'd be damned if she'd cock it up again.

* * *

With Gabrielle at his side, Fernsby watched Ava drive away in her chauffeured car, like Cinderella rushing off to the ball.

"Wow," Gabrielle said, the thrill of wonder in her voice. "I can't believe you actually did that, Fernsby." And she held up her fist.

He eyed it, looking down his long nose, then splayed his fingers on his chest. "I am Fernsby, and I do not fist-bump."

Gabrielle laughed. She had a beautiful laugh. And she laughed a lot. Espccially at him. Just as his Mathilda had loved to laugh at him. He'd seen it as just another reason why she couldn't really love him. But with his great maturity—great in more ways than one—he saw now that it had been the laughter of love.

He stuffed the memories down deep once more, having trotted them out only for Ava's benefit. Because memories formed a rabbit hole, taking him down, down, down... to places he couldn't climb out of.

As they walked to the car where Lord Rexford awaited them,

Gabrielle skipped to keep up with his long strides. "But you did love my vegan wedding cake," she pressed.

"I give credit where credit is due," he drawled. Then he looked at her. "But please don't let it go to your pretty head."

She wagged a finger at him as he beeped the car lock. "Too late, Fernsby. It already has."

Now that his job was done concerning the erstwhile Miss Ava Harrington and her beau, Ransom Yates, he considered Gabrielle with determined eyes. When she finally fell, that girl would fall hard. And, as always, he would be there to offer sage advice and a helping hand to finding her way to true love.

And then there were Troy and Clay. These Harringtons needed his help. Desperately.

He would make it work out for all of them. Helping his charges along the path to love was his mission. He'd only ever failed once. With Mathilda. He wouldn't fail again.

After all, he was Fernsby.

Chapter Twenty-One

Ransom sat in his office, twiddling his thumbs and wasting away the early afternoon hours when there was so much to be done. His phone was ringing off the hook, but he'd ignored it. All he could think about were those scant minutes in Ava's office. Thirty minutes against fifteen years without her. Thirty minutes of the best sex of his life.

No, not sex. Lovemaking. He hadn't made love to a woman in fifteen years. He'd taken other women to his bed, but that had been sex. Right from the beginning, he and Ava had always made love. Then he'd lost her to one stupid mistake and a chick flick.

Why had he even made that offer, practically begging her to leave her life behind and come with him?

After his grandmother died, he'd realized he'd never get enough time with Ava, that he couldn't keep leaving her behind. Added to the mix, it rankled that his mother had never come out to see the old lady. Or him. He never saw his brother. They'd been estranged, though he hadn't wanted to use that word at the time.

With his grandmother's death, it seemed as though his last link to his family had been severed too. Ava had become the only link to his past. And he'd wanted her. Craved her every moment of every day when he was away. So he'd asked. He didn't think he'd demanded. He thought he'd merely suggested.

Even when she'd thrown that damned chick flick at him, he'd never watched it. Never tried to see the point she'd made.

He flipped on his computer, pulled up his streaming account, then he punched his intercom button.

When he heard the brief, "Yes, Ransom? What do you need?"

"Hold all my calls for two hours," he instructed. "I'm not available to anyone." Then he quickly added, "Except Ava Harrington."

He was very much afraid she wouldn't call. He was very much afraid it would be like the last time, where he waited for her to call… and waited… until he got on with his life and tried to put her behind him.

What a mistake that had been.

He should have called *her*. He should have flown right back from Paris and gone straight to her apartment. Though they'd always been at his place—it was almost as if she'd been living with him—she'd still had a life outside of his. Her apartment. Her job. Her classes.

Her dreams.

He searched for the movie, and when it came up, he was dumbstruck by how cheap it was. Something that cost so little to watch and yet had so devastated his life. He'd never thought about *Pretty Woman*. It was just a reference she'd thrown at him in a moment of high emotion.

But she'd said it again today. She'd never forgotten, not the way he had.

He didn't just rent it, he bought it, so it would always be there to remind him.

Closing the blinds against the sun streaming across the computer, he sat in his office chair, his big-screen monitor blazing with a chick flick.

It was a cute story. The characters were funny. Especially the hotel manager. The meet-cute was pretty dang risqué for the current times. Because Vivian was a lady of the night. And Edward, for lack of a better word, was her john. Yeah, it was daring. And sexy. Yet heartwarming.

When he got to the part where Edward snapped the jewel box closed before Vivian could take the necklace, Ransom laughed out loud. He thought about going online to see if that bit had been ad-libbed or was part of the script, but he didn't. It was charming to think it hadn't been planned.

He watched Vivian grow under the tutelage of the hotel manager. The guy was a fairy godmother figure. Ransom found himself enjoying the movie, laughing. And feeling his heart break as Vivian's did.

When Edward asked Vivian to be his kept woman, a lance pierced Ransom's heart.

Even as Edward said he wasn't treating her like a lady of the night, or even a mistress, the floodgates of understanding opened inside Ransom as Vivian told him he'd just treated her exactly like that.

Ransom saw it all. He'd been a clueless jerk. He'd been blinded by the exquisite lovemaking, by the joy he felt when they created a meal together, by the happiness that welled up from his soul when he was with Ava. Yet, all the time, he'd accommodated only himself, sweeping aside her dreams. For so long, he'd believed it was all about that—his subjugation of her dreams, his narcissistic belief that only his dreams mattered at the time, that she could always find hers later.

But holy hell, *this* was what she'd been talking about. He'd asked her to be his kept woman. He'd offered to create a job for her. Then he'd actually *blamed* her for walking out and never calling him back. For never wanting to discuss the issue. She'd deleted him from her life, and he'd wallowed in his hurt and anger, never seeking out the real reasons for it.

And all the while, the answer had been waiting for him in Vivian and Edward's story.

He was the one who'd broken them. He'd been so busy making his bid for fame, practically shouting at the world, *look at me, look at me*, that he'd stuck Ava in his suitcase and closed the lid on her. He'd asked her to be nothing more than a plaything he could pull out when he wanted amazing lovemaking, or even a hike along Italy's Blue Trail when they were traveling.

He'd pushed for a change that benefited only him. It didn't matter that he'd just lost his grandmother or that he was estranged from his family. It didn't matter that his success was supposed to be all about not being like his father.

He had become *exactly* like his father. Working all the time, missing out on his family, never seeing his mother for years until she was almost on her deathbed. And even now, when he went to see Adam and his family, he was always rushed, always thinking about the next big gig, always shortchanging the visits.

He didn't have kids he could force to work in his restaurant, true—and he was willing to try new things. But like his father, who put his work first, who spent time with his family only because he had them working in the restaurant, Ransom had put his career first over the love of his life.

So she'd left him.

And he was probably well on his way to giving himself the same heart attack that had killed his dad.

He watched the entire movie. He cheered for Vivian's triumph. He clapped when Edward finally acknowledged the hotel manager, when he finally paid attention to all the little people.

Even after the credits rolled, he sat in contemplation for fifteen long minutes, one for each of the years he'd wasted. He absorbed Ava's message to him through the movie. Everything he should have seen back then, everything that hammered at him now.

Ransom knew exactly what he had to do if he didn't want to lose her all over again.

Grabbing his cell phone, he walked to the window, already tapping her icon saved in his Favorites menu, and opened up the blinds to the glorious bay and the magnificent towers of the Golden Gate.

Though she would have seen his name on the screen, she didn't ignore him. And she didn't hang up on him when he said her name. "Ava." Just her name.

She said only, "Yes."

His throat clogged up. "Can—" Then he rushed it all. "Can you meet me at Alamo Square as soon as possible?"

* * *

It wasn't a demand. It was a question. And Ava heard the plea in it. "Is now soon enough?"

His soft chuckle rumbled over the airwaves. "Well, I'm not actually there yet."

She smiled as if he could see it. "Then soon." She was still in her chauffeured car, and she wouldn't be going back to the office.

He whispered, "Soon," before he added, "I need to tell you something."

"And I have something to tell you too."

They hung up with gentle good-byes, his words ringing in her ears.

She wouldn't walk away this time. Not after that conversation with Fernsby and Gabby—well, mostly Fernsby. He'd helped her realize she didn't have to be afraid of a second chance. She wouldn't cock it up. She wouldn't let Ransom cock it up either.

He was already in Alamo Square when her driver dropped her off.

The park wasn't overcrowded, but tourists sat on blankets on the grass or stood on the sidewalk snapping pictures of San Francisco's famous Victorian Painted Ladies across the street. The homes' pastel colors glowed gloriously in the late afternoon sun against the backdrop of high-rises and business buildings.

Ransom sat with all the other onlookers.

Her heart beat faster, her breath came quicker, and her skin heated with memories of their morning sojourn in her office. Crossing the grass on her toes so her heels didn't sink into the sod, she was only steps away when she realized what he'd done.

Sitting on a blanket he'd spread out, his shoes lay beside him, socks tucked inside, and a book of Shakespeare's sonnets next to him.

She stood over him and whispered, "Where are the snap dogs?" Just as Vivian had.

He pointed. A hot dog stand was busy serving customers on the corner.

Her heart wanted to burst right out of her chest. "You watched *Pretty Woman*."

Looking up at her, he smiled. "I did."

And she read the meaning in all the props. This wasn't a short-term gig where he'd satisfy both her catering and her physical needs, then fly off when his job was done.

He might even love her. Because really, what man would watch *Pretty Woman* all by himself if he wasn't in love?

Picking up the book of sonnets, he patted the blanket beside him. Ava sat, her legs curled beneath her, one hand supporting her as she gazed at him, a man more beautiful than any of the Painted Ladies.

"I *pretty-womaned* you." The mocha color of his eyes was softer, gentler, and maybe a little misty. "I'm so sorry, Ava. Everything you said this morning was right. I didn't mean to, but I ghosted you. And I understand now how you felt. Nobody ever wants to be erased or deleted by someone they love." He raised her hand to his lips, kissed her knuckles in the softest, most exquisite caress. "I always intended to come back to you, to talk it through. But when I got home to my apartment, all your things were gone."

"You could have come to *my* apartment."

He closed his eyes, almost as if he couldn't bear the pain. "I should have. But the longer it went on, the harder it was to come to you. I told myself this was the opportunity I needed to concentrate on my career." When she winced, he added quickly, "I know how wrong that was. But back then, I was trying so hard not to be like my father. To be a huge success. To never settle for *good enough*. I convinced myself that letting you go was for the best. Even while I wanted to call you, run to you, beg you to come back, I told myself that you could do your schooling and work on your dreams without me dragging you down or begging for your attention. The real truth was that I made success more important than love. More important than you." He held her hand over his heart. "But I forgot the most important lesson my father taught me—that loyalty and family and love trump some nebulous definition of success. I realize now that's why he didn't expand, why he didn't take chances, why he wouldn't even change the menus when I suggested it. It wasn't because he didn't value my suggestions. It was because he was afraid that by expanding, by changing, he would lose his family."

"And yet," she whispered, "he lost you anyway."

"No," he said on a harsh breath, his hold tightening as he pressed their linked hands to his chest. "*I* lost him. *I* lost my family. *I* lost their love." He gazed deeply into her eyes. "And through my ambition, I lost you, the best thing in my life."

Ava rarely allowed herself to cry. But just as with Gabby and Fernsby earlier, as she faced everything she'd done wrong, a tear slid from the corner of her eye.

Ransom reached up to catch it, bringing his finger to his lips as if he were kissing it away.

"I lost you too," she murmured. "You offered me that job, but I didn't hear you say you needed me."

"I'm not sure I said it out loud. But I did need you. More than anything."

She blinked away another tear. Kids were throwing Frisbees, dogs were chasing balls, young lovers were kissing all around them. But her world had shrunk down to Ransom alone.

"All I heard was that I wasn't good enough for anything more than tagging along after you, that the only thing I could do was hitch my wagon to your star."

He stroked her cheek, his eyes more sad than T. Rex's when Cammie and Dane left him behind. "I never meant it that way," he said so softly that she leaned closer, breathed him in along with his words. "I couldn't stand the long separations. I couldn't live without you. I just didn't say it that way. I wanted to be calm, cool, collected—lay out my plan, offer you a sweet package so you'd agree." He looked at her a long, long moment. "As though you were an employee. But now I realize I did that so I didn't have to lay my heart on the line."

"And maybe I walked out because I wanted to say yes so badly." And she had. She wanted her dreams, she wanted her degree, but oh, how she'd wanted him. "I ran out before I had to compromise with you, before I compromised my dreams." She stared at the Painted Ladies, not truly seeing them, but seeing into the past, into her heart. "I kept remembering all the times my parents ignored me and my siblings. How I overachieved just to make them *see* me—making the honor roll at school, being on the winning debate team, becoming class valedictorian. I wanted them to see me, to love me. I did it all to get their attention." She swallowed hard, bitter tears rising in her eyes. "But they didn't even come to my high school graduation. They left me behind. They left all of us behind for another ski trip that was just like all their other ski trips. Until it killed them."

He kissed away another tear that escaped.

"I wanted so badly for them to let me in. And I was so perfect. I did everything the right way. I never made a misstep." She paused, needing to breathe. "They died without ever seeing me. And the truth is, I don't think they ever would have. They didn't see any of us." Instead, they'd left behind a mountain of debt that she and Dane had to deal with while caring for their three younger siblings.

"That's why you had your dreams, isn't it?" Ransom asked in a gentle voice that seemed to stroke her nerve endings.

She nodded, sniffing back the tears. "Even after they were gone, I still needed to prove to them that I was good enough to love. Maybe that's why I couldn't just manage a nursing home, why I couldn't just make life better for the residents. I had to own all the facilities. I had to build an empire." She blinked, her vision cleared, and suddenly she saw everything. "That's why I walked out that night. Because after all the things I'd done to make your life perfect, you only wanted me as your mistress.

You didn't want *me*." She put her hand to her chest as if she had to hold her heart inside. "You only wanted how good we were in bed together."

He cupped her cheek, his thumb a soothing caress across her skin. "I did it all wrong. I should've told you why I needed you with me. I should've told you that I was a mess whenever I was away from you. *You* are my success. And loving you meant more to me than anything else."

"But that wasn't true then."

He shook his head. "It *was* true. I just didn't know it until after I'd let you go. I was a fool. I should've run after you, begged you to stay. Climbed a fire escape. Whatever I had to do to keep you in my life."

She rolled her lips together, pressing hard before she cried, and finally said, "I should have stayed and told you exactly how I felt. Instead, I just raged. Who can ever hear someone who rages at them?"

He smiled very softly then. "You should've sat me down and made me watch *Pretty Woman*."

She laughed, too, just as softly. "There were so many things we should've done."

"But we didn't." At his words, another tear rolled down, into his fingers gently cupping her face.

"We wasted fifteen years," she murmured. "Because of all the things we should have done but didn't. Because I couldn't compromise."

He didn't let her take all the blame. "Because I couldn't see that love was more important than anything. *You* were more important. Instead of being so different from my dad, I turned into him. A workaholic. And now I have nothing else in my life—no love, barely even family."

She leaned into the hand against her cheek. "A very wise man told me that love is a compromise because two hearts must meet in the middle to become one." She smiled. "He also told me not to cock it up this time."

Ransom laughed, loudly enough to stop a dog in its tracks, a ball in its mouth. "Fernsby."

She had to laugh too.

"I'm sure as hell not going to cock it up either. I love you, Ava Harrington. I love you with every cell in my body. And I would give up everything I have—my restaurants, my cookbooks, my TV show, and most especially all my success—if I could have you back in my life."

"I love you," she whispered. "You don't have to give up anything. And neither do I. We're going to compromise in any way required to make our love work."

He pulled her close, his lips almost touching hers. "I always knew you'd make your dreams come true. I always knew you were perfect for me."

When he kissed her, his lips on hers were heavenly.

She pulled back just to breathe again, to look into his eyes and see the love shining in them, to let him see that love reflected in hers.

Then, rolling to her feet, she grabbed his hand, pulled him up. "What we really need now is a snap dog to celebrate."

Hand in hand, they ran across the grass to the hot dog stand. When they finally had their dogs with all the good toppings and skins that snapped when they bit into them, she leaned in to kiss him with mustard all over her mouth.

Finally, she didn't have to be an overachiever. Because Ransom would love her no matter what.

Chapter Twenty-Two

"I need to make love to you again." Ransom's words were as beautiful as the love sonnets he'd been reading to her.

The fading sun still warmed her as she opened her eyes, but the flame in his gaze heated her all the way through.

"It was totally hot in my office earlier," she said, gazing up at his beautiful face. "But this time I want hours with you in a real bed."

Then it seemed like only moments before they were entering Ransom's Pacific Heights flat. Ava gasped. "How did you manage all this?"

The dining table was laid with a damask cloth, the champagne glasses were crystal, the silverware actual silver, the plates real porcelain, and a sideboard held silver warming trays. Beneath the damask, the intricately carved table legs added to the elegance, the chairs facing the lights of the harbor.

As dusk fell, the living and dining room lay in shadow. They were beautiful in their simplicity, a white leather sofa, a chrome-and-glass coffee table, matching end tables, a state-of-the-art sound system, and a flat-screen TV bigger than the span of her arms.

Through his floor-to-ceiling windows, the dark bay overlooked Sausalito, Tiburon, Alcatraz, and a brightly lit dinner cruise sailing through the dark waters.

"I have a restaurant in the city, remember?"

He'd made a phone call, but when? Then again, discovering the logistics might strip away the romance of it all.

Ava lifted the lid of the first warming dish and moaned as she breathed in the scent of the hearty goulash.

"Czech goulash, not Hungarian," he said.

"You know that's my favorite." Another foodie love letter. "Hungarian is good, but it's soupier. The Czech is thicker." Her mouth watered, not just for the goulash, but for Ransom. "I haven't had goulash in years."

She hadn't bothered because no one, except the Czechs themselves, could make it like Ransom.

He opened another warming tray to reveal the traditional white dumplings.

"You actually serve this at your restaurant?" she asked in awe.

He raised a brow. "Of course. It was one of your favorites. And Honorine approved of adding it to the menu."

Her heart beat like a drum in her chest. "You never stopped thinking about me?"

His beautiful gaze on her, he shook his head. "I told myself it was because you had such excellent taste. But everything I made was for you."

Ava threw herself at him, wrapping her arms around his neck, kissing every part of his face until he took her cheeks in his palms and held her still for the most delicious, ravishing kiss.

Then he whispered, "May I serve you?"

He created a perfect plate, the goulash with three perfectly round dumplings placed delicately around the edge soaking up the juices. He accompanied that with vegetables.

"For color," he told her. Bright green broccoli, carrots that popped orange, and white cauliflower, all heavily roasted with a hint of char.

"Please sit." He pulled out her chair, sneaking it back in to bring her close to the table.

He sat beside her, and for a moment, they simply enjoyed the view of stars and moon and the illuminated spires of the Golden Gate.

Then she dug in. "Every morsel is perfect," she said, gobbling it all down despite the snap dog they'd had in the park.

When they were done, the last of the dumplings wiping up the stew's remnants, he whisked away the plates, returning with two bowls and setting one in front of her.

"English trifle?" Her voice rose with wonder. "Is it as good as Fernsby's?" Fernsby's trifle was incomparable.

He raised an eyebrow. "Who do you think taught me how to make it?"

The combination of bananas, ladyfingers soaked in sherry, strawberry jam, and whipped cream melted on her tongue.

"And?"

She lowered her voice as though Fernsby lurked just around the corner. "Do not ever, *ever* let Fernsby know that I said your trifle is even better than his."

"It's our secret." Ransom zipped his lips, and she wanted to kiss him. Then, once again, Ransom stood. "What would you like? Coffee, latte, mocha?"

She tugged him down by his tie. "You," she whispered.

He pulled her up and into a kiss, going deep, teasing her with his tongue. Then, hauling her up in his arms, without even letting her catch her breath, he carried her into his bedroom.

The room was done in deep shades—a dark mahogany dresser and matching tallboy, a burgundy coverlet, navy pillows. The bed was big and masculine, just like him. He let her feet slide to the thick Persian carpet.

"What I like," he said, a flame in his eyes, "is that you're wearing a very feminine business suit—the consummate female executive, commanding yet sexy as hell. And now I get to strip you down to the naughty lady I know you are."

She raised a haughty brow. "Naughty? I've never been naughty in my life. I'm always perfectly circumspect."

The heat of his smile reached deep inside her. "Oh, I remember so many delicious times when you were naughty, even filthy."

She clapped a hand over his mouth. "Don't say another word about that. It's our secret."

Behind her cupped hand, he sweetly said, "Like our secret that you prefer my trifle recipe over Fernsby's?"

She eyed him. "Is this some sort of blackmail?"

He shook his head slowly. "I'm just letting you know I love your secret self." Then he lowered his mouth to hers and made the secret parts of her burn for him.

Instead of ripping their clothes off like this morning in her office—had it really only been this morning?—they made undressing a slow dance.

Ransom peeled her suit jacket down her arms. She pushed the jacket off his wide, muscled shoulders. He slipped the buttons loose on her blouse. She pulled his tie free and undid every shirt button, each one punctuated by a kiss.

Standing back, Ransom gazed at her in just her bra and skirt and heels. "My God, your breasts are beautiful."

Then he stepped in, cupping her, tweaking a tight bead through the lace.

Ava moaned. He'd always made her moan like that.

And he always would.

* * *

Ransom salivated for her, but before he let her skirt fall to the floor, he spoke the truth in his heart. "I love you so much. I should never have let you go. I should have followed you and gone down on my knees to beg you to take me any way you'd have me. I'm so sorry it's taken me fifteen years to admit that."

She placed her palm on his cheek. "Maybe we weren't ready," she whispered in the sweetest, most seductive voice. "Maybe we needed all that time to learn who we are on the inside." She put her fingertips to the swell of her breasts. "Maybe we simply had to become the man and woman we are now to really understand what our hearts had lost."

She was right. He understood his past so much better now, how the estrangement with his family had led him into not calling her. And how her past led her into walking out the door and never texting him again. They both had pasts they had to deal with. But deep in his gut and wrapped around his heart, he knew neither of them would let anything come between them again.

Pulling her close, he tugged on the zipper of her skirt. "Then let's not waste another moment. Ever."

He kissed her as her skirt fell to the floor, while she unbuckled his belt, unzipped him. He tasted her while he toed off his shoes and she kicked off her high heels.

Only then did he step back. "You have the most amazing taste in lingerie." She always had—scraps of silk and lace that made his heart beat faster and his boxer briefs grow tight around him.

"I do so love how tight these are." As she slipped her fingers under the waistband and bent to peel them away, he felt the rush of her breath on his erection.

"Ahh. Now I remember being naughty." Her lips engulfed him, shooting pleasure to his extremities and heat to his core.

"I always loved the perfection of your mouth on me." His words were guttural, almost dragged out of him. And he groaned.

Curling her fingers around him, she pumped in time with her lips on his crown.

Despite what they'd done this morning, despite those two magnificent releases, he was so ready, so close. He had to pull her up, and smiling, he wagged a finger at her. "Oh no. When I come, I want to be deep inside you."

"Do you have another condom?" she asked in the sweetest tone with the deepest caramel melting in her eyes.

"Oh yeah," he drawled.

"Well, I'm on the pill. And I've had very good doctor's reports." With her lips against his, she whispered, "So don't use it."

"My reports are all good too." The thought of being skin to skin made him rock hard.

When she added, "I want to feel all of you this time. Every single—" She wrapped her hand around him. "—beautiful inch of you."

The slow dance ended there—he damn near tore her sexy lingerie from her body. In another moment, he had her spread out on the bed like the most delicious feast ever laid before a starving man.

And feast he did. Touching and teasing, licking and sucking, until she cried out with the first of her pleasures. There were so many more to come.

Pulling on his hair, then grabbing his shoulders, she tugged him up. "Now, Ransom, now, please."

He reared up to fill her the way she begged him to, and her

body clamped down on him with the throes of her climax.

Every inch of her was sweet to him. He'd never forgotten a moment, a touch, a whisper, a taste.

He knew how to make it the best for her. Pumping slowly, her body spasming around him, he didn't let her come down. He stroked her with his erection, just on the inside, in short, lingering caresses. Until her fingernails dug into his arms and her lips dropped his name and her eyes squeezed shut as if she'd gone to another place where there was just him inside her, just pleasure shooting through her, just the aching need between her legs.

When her limbs trembled, it was time, and he touched her sweet pearl, sliding his fingers around it, faster, then harder. Even if she hadn't cried out, he would have felt her climax in the tight grip of her body around him, the squeeze and release. He slammed home deep inside her.

And Ava screamed.

He'd always loved that scream, loved how good he'd always made her feel. Taking her hard and high and fast, her pleasure went on endlessly until she dragged his climax from deep within him.

He shouted in hoarse sounds, unable even to say her name, unable to remember his own.

In those long, beautiful moments, the only thing he knew was how sweetly, how perfectly, how desperately he loved her… and always would.

⋆ ⋆ ⋆

Ava lay in Ransom's arms after the most incredible, out-of-this-world lovemaking she'd ever known. It was even better than fifteen years ago, as though in getting older and learning more about themselves, they'd somehow opened up to this greater joy.

"I'm not the same woman I was at twenty-one," she admitted, running her fingers gently over his chest. "Or maybe even thirty."

He stroked a hand through her hair. "I'm not the same man either. All I had going for me then was my desire for success. I didn't consider anything else. I knew you were good for me, that I wanted you with me, but even for you, I wasn't willing to lose my chance."

The words would have hurt only hours before, but they were real. And she could admit now that the same was true for her. "I wouldn't have given up my education or my dreams for you either. I just didn't understand that neither of us had to give up anything at all, if only we'd compromised. We both still had so much to learn that I'm not sure we could have made it work then. Not just because of the argument or because you asked me to go with you and I got offended. Eventually, something would've happened, something would have soured us, because even if people love each other, they can't work things out if they refuse to even consider the other person's side."

He kissed the top of her head. "Is that you trying to alleviate some of my blame over the way we broke up?"

She tipped her head back to look at him. "I'm just saying that we both made mistakes. You couldn't see beyond your dream for success, and I couldn't compromise. And we'll still have to compromise. You can't stop traveling to be with me, and I can't follow you around the world. So we'll have to figure it all out."

"We will," he said. "Because I'm never letting you go again, and I'll do whatever it takes."

She trailed her finger across his lips. "Maybe that's what love is about. Figuring out how to do whatever it takes to stay together. Even if it means compromise. Even if it means having to give up something."

"But you should never have to give up your dreams."

"And you should never have to give up yours. Between us, we'll find a way."

"What was it Fernsby said to you?"

"Love is a compromise because two hearts must meet in the middle to become one."

He pulled her in for a kiss to her forehead. "He's a wise man as well as an excellent baker. There has to be give-and-take in love. And that's what we'll do. Because our love is perfect."

She tipped her head to smile at him. "Nothing's ever perfect. I know. I tried to be perfect. And it never worked."

He kissed her like a vow. "Ava Harrington, you are the most perfect creature on God's green earth. And I love you with everything in me."

"Maybe we're perfect together in a way we couldn't be before. I will always love you, and I will never walk out the door without talking to you."

He laughed. "Okay, don't make promises you won't be able to keep. But after you walk out, just promise you'll come back and talk."

She giggled. "You know me too well. But I promise. We both promise."

"We'll always talk it through. And we'll always find a way to make it work."

"Because now that we've reunited, I am not un-reuniting."

He kissed her with abandon, his laughter seeping through. And when he said, "Reunited in love," she answered, "Forever."

Epilogue

One month later

They attended the christenings of five Maverick babies. Where once Ava would have shuddered at the thought, now she felt aglow with the festivities.

Paige and Evan's house was decorated to the nines, with Happy Christening banners and paper flowers and moons and stars and anything that might glitter to catch the babies' attention.

Evan had once owned a mansion in Atherton, but he'd left that to his ex-wife. The more modest Los Altos house was now a true home, with kids' toys strewn about and bouncy chairs for their twins, Savannah and Keegan. In the backyard, Evan had already set up a swing set, monkey bars, slide, and sandbox, even though the twins were only seven months old.

It was late October, but this was the Bay Area, and it didn't have the fall colors of the East Coast, except for the massive Liquid Amber tree shading the back garden whose leaves had begun turning a deep orangey red.

"You look happy." Dane sat beside Ava on the couch.

She let out a sigh of satisfaction. "I am happy. Very." They both looked across the wide expanse of the living room to Ransom, who was talking with Susan and Bob Spencer.

"Well, it certainly took you long enough to get back together."

She turned to Dane, her head reared back a little. "What are you talking about?"

Dane leaned back, crossing his arms thoughtfully, "I saw all those sparks between you two way back when you took care of his grandmother in the nursing home, and Ransom and I were working on the resort."

"There was a spark," she admitted, though that was such an oversimplification.

He snorted a laugh. "It was way more than a spark." Then he leaned close. "You crackled like fire, sister dear."

She felt herself blush. Dane had known all this time. "But you never said anything."

He shrugged in a typical brotherly gesture. "It was your business. I was hoping you'd talk to me about it when it was obvious things had gone wrong. But you never did."

And wasn't that the Harrington way—talk about anything else but love. It was why Ava had never said anything about Cammie. None of the family had, though they all knew how Dane felt, especially after the "incident" with Troy. And yet, at the family mastermind a week ago, Clay had apologized to her for his outburst at the wedding. He'd even told her she'd made the right choice with Ransom. And here she was talking about love with Dane. So maybe things were changing. At least a bit.

Dane held her hand, squeezed her fingers, smiled at her. "I'm happy for you. But hell." He puffed out an exasperated laugh. "You two took even longer than Cammie and I did to figure it out."

Cammie stood in the cluster of Maverick ladies, absorbed into the fold just as Ava had been, and Gabby, too, who was cooing at Ari's little girl, Penelope, now three months old. She was surprised Gabby wasn't in the kitchen fussing over the christening cake—two tiers, one vegan and one with so much butter it would slow your blood flow. But there was time enough for any fussing Gabby felt she needed to do.

In a few minutes, Ava would join the group of women and babies, talking with them, laughing with them. Because this bunch knew how to laugh. But for now, she enjoyed this quiet moment with her big brother Dane, while Troy had his head together with Matt Tremont, and Clay, without a flavor of the month in tow, was engrossed in conversation with Will Franconi.

"Well," she said softly, reflectively, "together we raised a couple of handsome Harrington boys."

"And a beautiful Harrington chef," Dane added.

But perhaps there were still some lessons to impart, especially about love. Their parents' legacy of love—or lack thereof—had an effect on them all, to the point where she'd kept her long-ago affair with Ransom a secret. And Dane had kept his feelings for Cammie locked down so tightly they were even a secret from himself. She wondered now if one of her other brothers, or even Gabby, was keeping their own secret about love.

"Raising them all," she mused, "I don't even remember now how hard it was, after Mom and Dad died."

Dane snorted. "It's like women forgetting how hard childbirth is. All you remember is the good stuff, like holding the baby in your arms for the first time."

She shot him a look. "Cammie's not…?"

He shook his head. "No. It hasn't happened yet. But it will when it's the right time."

Dane would be an amazing father. He'd been a good big brother to teenage boys, and they'd grown into intelligent, strong men. He'd doted on Gabby, and their sister had grown into a brilliant woman.

"So you're off to some big gig of Ransom's?" Dane asked, looking across the room as Ransom pecked Susan Spencer on the cheek and headed toward Paige and Evan, who were each holding a twin.

Her gaze on Ransom's beautiful face, her heart swelling as he let one of the babies take his pinkie in a chubby finger, she sighed with joy. "We haven't exactly worked out all the logistics yet."

She wasn't the least bit worried. Because they would never let anything come between them again. No matter the compromises they had to make. *Compromise* was no longer a four-letter word.

"We're going to Milwaukee to see his brother, Adam, and his family." She looked at Dane. "Did you know his brother has a chain of burger joints out there? They're all the rage."

Dane waggled one of his eyebrows, turning his handsome face comical. "Meeting the family, huh?"

Ava elbowed him teasingly in the ribs, but said nothing.

Then, being older than her and playing the devil's advocate, Dane echoed her earlier thoughts. "Why is talking about love so off-limits in our family?"

Ava snorted. "You really don't know?"

Dane's gaze found Cammie. "I didn't. Not for a long time." Then he turned to Ava again. "When we were kids, and I looked at Mom and Dad, it was like they were the only two in the world to each other. I thought that's what love was supposed to be like. To the exclusion of everything else."

"But they excluded us from that world too."

He nodded. "Then I started to realize they were bad examples of love. Two people truly in love have room for more love in their lives than just each other. They have room for kids and family and friends."

Ava breathed deeply, remembering all the times she'd wanted them to notice her, to *see* her. "Love is inclusive rather than exclusive." She laid her head on his shoulder a brief moment. "I wonder what would have happened if I'd said something to you about Cammie right after you went ballistic when Troy asked her out."

He mused with her. "I wonder what would have happened if I'd asked you what happened between you and Ransom instead of deciding it wasn't my business."

Ava shook her head. "We're talking about Harringtons here. People can't tell us anything. We have to figure it out on our own. Or wait until Fernsby has a talk with us."

This time, Dane reared back. "Fernsby talked to you?"

She nodded.

"Hell. He talked to me too."

They both looked at Fernsby as he stood over a bassinette, holding one of the newly christened babies, though Ava wasn't sure which one.

At that moment, the man looked up. And winked.

Dane whispered, "That's scary."

"Very scary," Ava agreed.

Except that the last scary look Fernsby had given her four months ago in Dane's home theater had heralded Ransom's coming back into her life.

Maybe that scary look was actually a good thing.

* * *

Ransom was aware of Ava every moment as he mingled his way through the reception. She'd been sitting with Dane for a while, then she'd joined the ladies. He loved standing back to watch her, so beautiful, so charming. And all his.

After making his way to Rosie, he hugged her. "Thank you so much for the painting. It's gorgeous. The view of the bay at sunrise is the exact view I see out of my office window every day. How could you know?"

Rosie just smiled. "The bay is one of my favorite subjects."

"Honestly, you guys didn't have to give me anything for helping out with the wedding. It was my pleasure, and I wanted you both to have the best." Ransom held out his hand to shake Gideon's.

Gideon slapped his two big hands around Ransom's and shook. "You bailed us out. We don't how to thank you."

Rosie, with the prettiest smile, said, "Gideon handcrafted the picture frame. He's got a whole setup for woodworking in the garage. People are asking for his frames as much as they're asking for my paintings," she added with a laugh.

They were such a special couple. They'd recently moved into a larger home to accommodate Jorge and baby Isabella. Ransom would have said he'd never seen a happier couple, but as he looked around the christening reception in Evan and Paige's living room, it was filled with loving couples.

His gaze once again alighted on Ava laughing with Cammie and Kelsey and several of the Maverick ladies. What a feeling to be half of one of these loving couples.

Rosie gave his shoulder a little push. "You better go to her. I could feel something brewing between the two of you even at the wedding."

Gideon chuckled. "Oh yeah, all those longing glances. Will just wouldn't stop talking about it. I swear he's the biggest gossip."

Rosie rose on her toes to kiss his cheek. "*I* swear, all of you Mavericks are the biggest gossips around." Then she whispered to Ransom, "Go to her."

He didn't need another push. All these Mavericks might think they'd cornered the market on love, but he truly had. He'd found Ava again, and she'd found him.

And a little while later, he was arm in arm with his beautiful Ava when Fernsby and Gabby rolled out another fabulous creation. One tier was Victoria sponge, Fernsby's winning cake from *Britain's Greatest Bakers*, and it was all vegan, if one could ever imagine a Victoria sponge as vegan. Gabby had done the honors on that, under Fernsby's tutelage. The other tier was a classic sponge, with nothing vegan about it.

No one knew which was which except the two bakers.

Gabby and Fernsby had worked on the cake the entire morning before the christening, in a collaboration. They'd piped all the babies' names on it in tiny perfect script. Instead of flowers, they'd added balloons in all the colors of the rainbow.

And, incredibly, both tiers were equally delicious.

As they stood with Gabby, Ava hugged her sister. "You've made another amazing cake."

Ransom added his two cents. "I can't believe one of these is vegan."

Gabby beamed. "That was all Fernsby's recipe. I'm selling the cake in my vegan bakery, but if you want to know the truth—" She cast a glance at Fernsby, who was fawning over Susan Spencer. "Don't tell Fernsby, but I couldn't have figured it out on my own. He's brilliant." She put a finger to her lips. "And don't tell him I said that either."

Ava laughed. "Didn't you tell me that day at the chophouse that he was the wisest man you knew?"

Gabby rolled her eyes. "I should never have said that. It totally went to his head."

They all laughed. Ransom would always love Ava's laugh.

"So," Ava said, squeezing his hand. She'd already talked with him about what she planned. "Here's what I would really love from the two fabulous cooks in my life."

Gabby frowned, as if she were afraid of what was coming.

Ava rushed on before her sister ran away. "Ransom is taking over the catering for all my US facilities." She put her hand on Gabby's arm, sliding all the way down to her wrist. "And I'd really, really, *really* like it if you and Ransom could work together on some vegan offerings. Right now, we've got salads, vegan soups, and vegetables." She shrugged. "But honestly, we need really fabulous vegan food. I know you two can do it."

She looked at her sister with hope. Ransom knew how badly Ava wanted this.

Many years ago, when he'd taken stock of the rising number of vegans and vegetarians around the country and the globe, he'd had one of his people approach Gabby. But she'd given his representative a blistering no. He'd understood it to be a result of what had happened between him and Ava. Gabby was the most loyal of sisters, and she wasn't going to forgive easily.

He hoped she could forgive him now. "I'd really like to work with you on this, Gabby. I can create menus, but figuring out how to make them vegan or vegetarian is beyond me."

He waited for her to smash him down while Ava squeezed his fingers. That's what they had—solidarity, togetherness. Even if Gabby slammed him, Ava's love would pick him up again.

But he wanted this to work.

For just a moment, fire blazed in Gabby's blue eyes, and narrowing them at him, she said, "Don't you dare hurt my big sister ever again." A smile lurked on her lips as if she were making a joke. But he knew she meant every word. And there would be consequences.

His arm around Ava's shoulders, he pulled her close. "I love your sister more than anything in the world. And I promise I'll never hurt her."

Ava sniffed as if she wanted to cry, and she kissed his cheek. They'd shared so many kisses and touches and lovemaking over the past month. But somehow that kiss, in front of her sister, was one of the most special he'd ever known. It held love and ownership and appreciation and total belief in him.

"I have to admit that marinated tofu you made at the wedding was yummy. But we can do so much more." A smile stretched across Gabby's pretty face. "So I'd love to work on the menus with you."

Ransom felt Gabby's forgiveness wrap around him at last, like a warm blanket.

Then Ava clutched his arm. "Oh, oh, I knew there was something I wanted to talk to you about."

Ransom had no idea what. If her sister hadn't been standing right there, he'd have wished for a litany of the sexy, seductive things she wanted to do with him tonight.

Instead, she shocked him. "You haven't billed me for all those renovations on the kitchens."

Ransom smiled because he had that answer all worked out. "Consider it a donation to your subsidy fund for all the people who can't afford a decent place to live when they're too old to live on their own."

The two of them stared at him. Then suddenly, both sisters engulfed him in hugs.

When they finally let him go, he said, "Really, ladies, it

wasn't that big a deal." He smiled at Ava. "All your kitchens were up to code, and I only had to do a few modifications to make the flow easier."

Ava whispered the only words he ever wanted to hear. "I love you."

Gazing into her eyes, he said, "I love you more than anything."

Gabby coughed loudly. "Oh my God, I need to get out of here. This is getting way too sappy for me."

Ava just smiled. "You said that about the final scene of *Pretty Woman* too."

Ransom reeled in his beloved. "She's young. She has so much to learn."

Thank God he had learned how to love Ava before it was too late.

⋆ ⋆ ⋆

Ahhh. Fernsby allowed himself a mental sigh.

Love was definitely in the air. Ava and Ransom gazed starry-eyed at each other. Cammie and Dane could be at the opposite ends of the room, but their sparks still flew and crashed into one another.

Two down, three to go. There was still work to be done. These Harringtons had so much to learn about love.

He thought of himself as the Love Guru. He wondered what Mathilda would think of his vocation. And why were all the memories of his lost love coming back now, when it was a lifetime too late?

He surveyed the room full of Mavericks and Harringtons, including Robert and Fernsby's personal favorite, Susan Spencer. It must be all the love in the air that made him nostalgic.

Now, who should be his next project?

He looked to Gabrielle Harrington—beautiful, blond, blue-eyed, just like her mother in all the pictures he'd seen of the family. But Gabrielle was so different from her parents. She was hardworking. Look at that cake as an example. One tier was vegan, made by Gabrielle with only a few comments from him, and one tier was made with butter and eggs, the two major food groups. And not one person in this room had been able to tell the difference.

Dane even had bets going on who had made which tier. Little did they know that Fernsby himself had put the betting idea into Dane's head.

Standing back, Fernsby tapped a long finger against his lips. So, who needed his help the most right now?

Eenie meenie miney mo, catch a Harrington by the toe...

* * *

Clay felt more animated than he had in months, almost back to the place he'd been when he'd first started his internet platform for artists.

He let it spill out all over Gideon Jones. "I'm telling you, that kid Dylan—" He punctuated his words with sharp slices of his hands through the air. "—he's a major talent."

Gideon clapped him on the shoulder. "Thanks for mentoring him. It means a lot to me."

"Thank *you* for sending him my way," Clay said. "In the world of street art, he could be the next Banksy." Then he added, "Or even the next San Holo."

Since meeting Dylan, Clay had studied street art more closely. It was no longer the graffiti of old—spray cans on bridges with gang symbols. It was big business, big art, both physically and metaphorically.

"He's got talent for sure," Gideon said. "He just needs a guiding hand."

"I like the kid a lot," Clay admitted. "He's good people."

"He'll be aging out of the foster care system soon." Gideon nodded gravely. "So I'm really glad he has someone like you as his mentor."

"Anything I can do. I love helping talent like his."

But Gideon was looking over Clay's shoulder. "I think Fernsby wants to speak with you." Then the man stepped away with a smile, heading back to his new wife and family.

Suddenly, Fernsby was right there, saying sternly, "Sir." His gaze turned first to Cammie and Dane on one side of the room, then to Ava and Ransom talking with Gabby on the opposite side.

Damn. A prickle in his gut told him what was coming. Clay held up both hands in the universal *stop* sign, just in case Fernsby didn't get the one-handed version.

Fernsby, however, did that expressive look again, from one couple to the other.

In the harshest voice he could muster, Clay said, "No way. You are not matchmaking for me, Fernsby. Absolutely not." Then he pointed to Troy. "Go pick on him. He's older."

But Fernsby, that most resolute of butlers, did not follow instructions and head over to Troy.

Instead, he smiled. For a man who smiled so rarely that it might be considered nonexistent, it was scary. More than scary.

It was terrifying.

⋆ ⋆ ⋆

ABOUT THE AUTHORS

Having sold more than 10 million books, Bella Andre's novels have been #1 bestsellers around the world and have appeared on the *New York Times* and *USA Today* bestseller lists 93 times. She has been the #1 Ranked Author on a top 10 list that included Nora Roberts, JK Rowling, James Patterson and Steven King.

Known for "sensual, empowered stories enveloped in heady romance" (Publishers Weekly), her books have been Cosmopolitan Magazine "Red Hot Reads" twice and have been translated into ten languages. She is a graduate of Stanford University and has won the Award of Excellence in romantic fiction. The Washington Post called her "One of the top writers in America" and she has been featured by Entertainment Weekly, NPR, USA Today, Forbes, The Wall Street Journal, and TIME Magazine.

Bella also writes the *New York Times* bestselling "Four Weddings and a Fiasco" series as Lucy Kevin. Her sweet contemporary romances also include the USA Today bestselling "Walker Island" and "Married in Malibu" series.

If not behind her computer, you can find her reading her favorite authors, hiking, swimming or laughing. Married with two children, Bella splits her time between the Northern California wine country, a log cabin in the Adirondack mountains of upstate New York, and a flat in London overlooking the Thames.

Sign up for Bella's New Release newsletter:
BellaAndre.com/Newsletter

Join Bella Andre on Facebook:
facebook.com/authorbellaandre

Join Bella Andre's reader group:
bellaandre.com/readergroup

Follow Bella Andre on Instagram:
instagram.com/bellaandrebooks

Follow Bella Andre on Twitter:
twitter.com/bellaandre

Visit Bella's website for her complete booklist:
www.BellaAndre.com

NY Times and *USA Today* bestselling author Jennifer Skully is a lover of contemporary romance, bringing you poignant tales peopled with characters that will make you laugh and make you cry. Look for *The Maverick Billionaires* written with Bella Andre, starting with *Breathless in Love*, along with Jennifer's new later-in-life holiday romance series, *Once Again*, where readers can travel to fabulous faraway locales. Up first is a trip to Provence in *Dreaming of Provence*. Writing as Jasmine Haynes, Jennifer authors classy, sensual romance tales about real issues such as growing older, facing divorce, starting over. Her books have passion and heart and humor and happy endings, even if they aren't always traditional. She also writes gritty, paranormal mysteries in the Max Starr series. Having penned stories since the moment she learned to write, Jennifer now lives in the Redwoods of Northern California with her husband and their adorable nuisance of a cat who totally runs the household.

Newsletter signup:

http://bit.ly/SkullyNews

Jennifer's Website:

www.JenniferSkully.com

Blog:

www.jasminehaynes.blogspot.com

Facebook:

facebook.com/jasminehaynesauthor

Twitter:

twitter.com/jasminehaynes1

Printed in Great Britain
by Amazon

bf2c7197-8501-4258-9a33-2f7cca2b731cR01